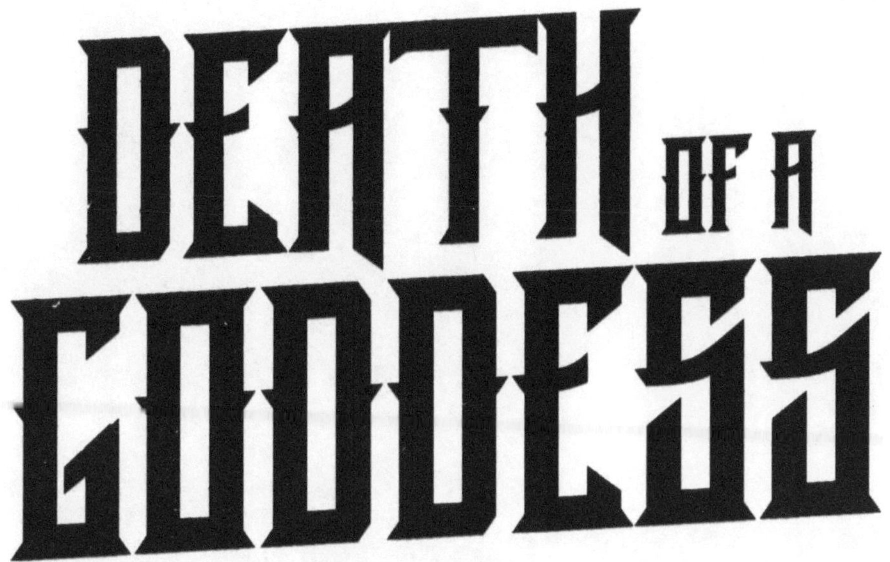

DEATH OF A GODDESS

WAR OF THE STAFFS: BOOK V

STEVE STEPHENSON
K.M. TEDRICK

Black Rose Writing | Texas

ISBN: 978-1-68513-402-0
PUBLISHED BY BLACK ROSE WRITING
www.blackrosewriting.com

Printed in the United States of America
Suggested Retail Price (SRP) $21.95

Death of a Goddess is printed in Book Antiqua

*As a planet-friendly publisher, Black Rose Writing does its best to eliminate unnecessary waste to reduce paper usage and energy costs, while never compromising the reading experience. As a result, the final word count vs. page count may not meet common expectations.

DEATH OF A GODDESS

PROLOGUE

Cyra the sorceress was a young woman aged beyond her years by dark magic. Once a beautiful woman, she now looked more like an old hag. Talchic, his real name, Melgor, hid his real identity to avoid being killed by his companion. He had upset his superior by causing quite a ruckus while trying to escape from her lair. The dwarvan stronghold of Zigar Shan which had fallen to an orc army a millennia ago. Then he had lost his right arm in a battle with four magic users and having never been actually seen by the sorceress, had gone to Cyra as an ally to further his plans to reach the city of Dormin. While still a powerful warlock, the loss of his dominant arm presented a challenge, especially when it came to physical combat.

His ultimate goal had been to kill the undead vampire warlock, Taza, wielder of the Staff of Adois – a staff of pure evil made under the direction of the vile goddess, Adois. She had it created to counter her brother's Staff of Adaman, which was created to restore the planet, Muiria, to a pure place of good, and rid the world of evil influence. Jealousy had been Adois' main driving force. But she also wanted to gain more power in the struggle of the gods. Never had a set of twins been such extreme opposites.

Cyra and Talchic had escaped Dragon Isle before the final battle ended when Cyra cast a powerful teleportation spell that took them to the mainland. It was here in the windswept northlands empty of all but the hardiest of creatures that they now stood. Both were breathing heavily from the confrontation on Dragon Isle and for the moment, at a loss for words.

Cyra straightened her back, her spine cracking. "It seems we need a new start, Talchic," she said with a sigh. "We will need to stay hidden from everyone, for I was marked by the entity that guards the Dragon's Tear in Edain, a death sentence should it ever find me again."

The Tear had been constructed by the original dragons that had migrated to Muiria through the Void to protect Edain, the wizard's homeland in the islands.

She continued, her voice shaky and her body trembling. "I fear the entity will come after me or send wizards. We must go into hiding until I am forgotten. We will take a sabbatical from magic for the time being to throw off the wizards."

Talchic nodded. He dared not disagree, or he would be left to die in this accursed wasteland. "Yes, my lady. We must start anew. But where? We will be hunted in both the East and the South."

She smiled. "You are correct. But there is a city I am familiar with to the west. I have friends I can call on for help, and I will be able to place myself in the upper echelons of the city's power structure. But for now, I'm afraid we must stay here before I dare use such a powerful teleportation spell without alerting the wizards of Dragon Isle."

Talchic was not happy with that decision. The last thing he wanted to do was to remain in these cursed lands. He had things he wanted to accomplish, but what choice did he have? For now, he was dependent upon her protection.

CHAPTER ONE

Prince Tarquin of Partha, as the prophecy had foretold, had been instrumental in the destruction of the Staffs of Adois and Adaman that were used by the vampire warlock, Taza, in an attempt to conquer the world. The Prince, along with his dwarvan friend, Botreg, also a veteran of the War of the Staffs, had decided to visit their companion Hority, a monk of the dwarvan god, Clor. An odd god, who was much avoided by the pantheon of dwarvan gods, because his monks collected garbage and waste to increase his power. Clor's closest ally was the god, Dolgar the healer, who had some influence upon the god of refuse. Clor's monks never bathed, except when caught out in an unholy downpour of pure rain. So, like their god, they, too, were ostracized by most people.

Tarquin decided to make one last trip to the valley of Clor, because his wife Ress was pregnant with their first child.

"Do you have to go now?" Ress asked. "I'm pretty far along, and it won't be long before the babe arrives."

"I know, dearest," Tarquin said. "Better to do it now, before the birth, so that I can be here afterward."

"You must promise to be back in time. I will be very unhappy if I have to do this alone. Birthing is not an easy job, Tarquin. Although I must do the physical work, it would be nice to have you here for moral support."

"I know, my love. I promise I will be back in plenty of time."

His wife reluctantly allowed him to visit their friend Hority. The prince had been going stir-crazy in Parthia, the capital of New Partha. Being the hero of the war was not what it was supposed to be. He was recognized wherever he went and cheered by crowds for no reason other than riding down the street. He had promised Ress that it would be a short trip to Clor's valley. Besides, no one could stand the smell of the monks for a very long time.

The ride from the dwarvan capital, Nars, where he met Botreg, was quick. They rode south on the north to south dwarvan road and then down well-marked trails to the Valley of Clor. The valley itself was long, narrow, devoid of trees. It was as miserable a place as Tarquin could have ever imagined. A perfect place as could be for a god that reveled in waste. It was the lone outpost for the worship of Clor that anyone knew of, including the monks of the valley.

Long before Tarquin and Botreg crested the hill that overlooked the valley. They spotted smoke rising into the morning air and by habit, he and Botreg drew their weapons. The wind pushed the smoke towards them, and they could smell the acrid odor of burned flesh. Before they reached the incline leading down into the valley, they came across over a hundred horses staked out and two guards in leather armor that swept upward at the shoulder and hem of their close-fitting armor. They knew at once that this was no chance gathering. It was an attack on the valley.

With his sword held high, Tarquin rode hard at the guards. The two guardsmen had their bows out and struck first, notching their arrows. They got off one volley that missed Tarquin and Botreg before the horsemen collided with them.

The Prince avoided a wild swing by the leather-clad soldier's bow, countering with a vicious downward stroke that cleaved the man's head in two. Botreg dueled the last man until the guard overswung with his blade, giving Botreg the opening he needed to skewer him in the back.

Tarquin hardly stopped his horse as he shouted, "This bodes ill for the Clorians!"

After cutting loose the horses and chasing them off, the prince and his companion spurred their horses down the incline that led to the head of the valley. As they went, they saw the signs of battle. The first Clorian they encountered was face down, an arrow sticking out of his back. As they advanced into the valley, more signs of fighting emerged. There were spots where the Clorians had stood their ground. Most had gotten off spells before they were killed. Tarquin looked down at the charred corpses of men in the strange armor. But there were areas of dead monks, too, where they had taken their last stand against the invaders. The two riders reached the main portion of the valley, where the monks lived. They saw nothing but death.

There were signs that the Clorians had been dragged from their caves and overhanging rocks and brutally murdered. When they reached the mound in the middle of the valley, they reined in their horses. This was where the abbot had walled himself off in a small cave for the past several hundred years. His wall had been broken open exposing the decapitated abbot lay dead amongst the detritus that had filled his hole. The anger rose in each warrior to a boiling point.

They then heard the clash of weapons in the distance and spurred their horses onward. The fighting became clearer as they neared the Clorian library, a cave to store the fruits of their years of wanderings. There, a group of interlopers had surrounded four dwarves. Tarquin waited not a second before charging into the fray, his horse pushing its way into the mass of enemies on foot. His sword, Dragon Bolt blazed with the fire of anger, swinging left and right bringing down enemies with each swing. He was followed by Botreg. The two attackers pushed into the ranks of enemies. Sword blades covered in blood leaving a trail of broken, dead bodies behind them.

Before long, the attackers became the defenders as the trapped dwarves surged out from their defensive position. Their blood lust high from the attack on the unarmed simple Clorians. Then a mournful horn blasted through the valley and the enemies withdrew. Tarquin turned his horse around, watching as the strange attackers scrambled over the western wall of the valley. Tarquin and Botreg were so incensed at what had taken place here in the sacred valley of Clor, they snatched up their bows, sending arrow after arrow into the fleeing men. They managed to kill several, who fell and rolled back to the valley floor.

Once the attackers had disappeared over the valley's edge, Tarquin dismounted. A familiar smiling filthy dwarf came up to him with tears running down his cheeks creating runnels in his dirt-encrusted face.

"Hority what has happened here?" Tarquin asked.

This particular dwarf had followed Tarquin to destroy the Staffs of Adaman and Adois and fought the vampire warlock on Dragon Isles as well as other adventures. He hugged Tarquin, causing the human to turn his head away because the Clorian smelled so bad. He waved a strange staff that was mostly a branch with a piece of pumice tied to its end. But that branch was more than just a stick. It was a powerful staff that brought death to all it attacked.

"A terrible act has occurred here. Me brothers lay broken, and the Abbott drug from his cave and treated most vile. If it had not been for the dwarvan brothers of Thierry, we would all be dead."

The warrior monks of Thierry had been tasked with cataloging the Clorian library and aiding in the protection of the valley. There were but three left. These were diligently going through the piles of dead men, dragging out the wounded.

"The enemy managed to break into the library, but we know not what they took," Hority continued.

Tarquin stood among the dead and noticed the brothers of the god, Thierry, had not been lazy in their endeavors. Their job had been to catalog the contents of the Clorian archives. The cave entrance had been widened and deepened to allow the dwarves access without having to crawl into the cave. The old librarian had died without the Clorians' knowledge, leaving piles of documents had accumulated inside the opening. Also, the library proper had not been accurately cataloged, just manuscripts on an assortment of parchment, rags, and whatever else the Clorians could get their hands on.

Tarquin looked at his friend and asked, "What happened here in the valley?"

Hority shook his head, dislodging a small cloud of dust in the air from his matted hair. "It was late last night that the brothers of Thierry and I saw flashes of light coming from the upper end of the valley. I knew at once it was spells being cast. As ye know, we are a peace-loving community, preferring to be left alone to contemplate the glory that is filth in this wasteful world. All praise to Clor."

Tarquin knowing that Hority could pontificate on his religion for hours interrupted, "Hority please tell us exactly what happened."

"I ran towards the light and encountered these foul men, Clor curse them. I used me, staff on them, but there were too many. Me brothers were being killed all over the valley. I ran to our most holy dwarf the abbot. But I was too late. In horror, I saw them drag him from his holy cave and cleave the head from his body. It was then that I gathered the remaining monks and retreated to the library. I knew safety for my brothers lay in the hands of the warriors of Thierry. We crested the path only to witness two of the brothers overwhelmed and killed. Three other brothers emerged out of the darkness and charged. I took me staff and joined in the fray. I saw several of the knaves leaving the library with pouches that must have held books or parchments, but I could not catch them. Afterward, it is as ye saw, we formed a circle and fought into the morning until ye showed up."

Botreg gave Hority a lite slap on the head causing a dust cloud. "Come, good friend, we must learn what these dogs know."

"But we must be off!" Hority fairly shouted. "There are foes on the loose, and I can feel the wrath of Clor surging through me veins."

During their journey to find and reunite the Staff of Adaman, one of Botreg's duties was keeping the small dwarf, Hority, from becoming overanxious. He grasped the thin dwarf, pulling him back into the group, before the monk could yell his battle cry, *Foes*, and dash off after the attackers

Botreg had been a trained assassin who had run afoul of the guild. The only way to escape their vengeance was to give up the life and become a Borderer in the dwarvan king's army, which was where he had met Tarquin. The Borderers were an elite division of the king's army. Tarquin had been the first human allowed to serve. The two outcasts had quickly become friends, in part to survive life in the dwarvan army.

Botreg, called the dark dwarf because he dressed all in black, went to one of the wounded that had been lined up along the trail, watching over by the Theirrian monks. He roughly grabbed one of the strangers with a deep cut to his head, asking in a gruff voice, "Who are ye? Where do ye come from?" When the man shook his head, Botreg motioned to Hority. "If ye please."

As the monk stalked up to the first man, his smell preceding him, his anger was palpable. He touched the enemy soldier with his magical staff. Hority believed the staff was a gift from Clor to help him protect the valley. The man died instantly, slumping to the ground to lay still in the rocky dirt. The dark dwarf went to the next soldier, and Hority was called forth again. It was not until the fifth man died that they got the information they needed.

A soldier cradling his wounded arm said, "I'll talk. Just don't let that staff get anywhere near me. We are Guras' men, and we come from Markdale across the great sea. We were hired by the warlock lord in Trudoc, in the west of this continent. We were to raid this library. A warlock that was with us was to cast a spell to find the treasure we sought. That was our mission. I swear."

Tarquin who had been listening in on the interrogation leaned in and asked, "What did you seek in this out-of-the-way place?"

The man next in line blurted out, "Treasure, milord. That is what was whispered about the campfires."

"What sort of treasure?" Tarquin asked.

"We weren't told. But the warlock was very keen to get here," the first man quickly answered.

After several hours of questioning, they learned that the Guras lived across the western ocean and were a great shipping nation. Apparently, their navy ruled the seas in that part of the world. These men were mercenaries, serving the warlocks in Trudoc.

Tarquin turned to Botreg. "I need to contact Celedant. He'll come with Azimuth. Then Eldahir and Morganna can be flown here. Ress is with child, but even with my parents to care for her, she will be distraught to be left behind. I myself have reservations about leaving her at this time, but I believe she will understand the importance of the mission. What has happened here in this peaceful valley needs to be rectified."

The Prince then called to Hority and arranged to have one of the Clorians take a message to Ress in New Partha.

Tarquin took out a small crystal given to him by Celedant that could be used only once and only in extreme circumstances. Holding it tightly in his right hand, he mentally called to Celedant, who was on Dragon Isle in the Master's Council Chamber. The Prince felt a connection to the wizard across all the miles that separated them. In his mind, Tarquin pictured the destruction of Clor's valley. And somewhere deep in his psyche, he knew that the wizard had heard his cry for help and would come as soon as possible.

Chapter Two

The city of Edain was the only wizard training ground on the planet Muiria, located far away in the northern sea on Dragon Isle. Celedant the wizard sat in the council room, surrounded by his fellow master wizards, who oversaw the island and steered the everyday workings of the wizard's training grounds. Celedant was a reluctant member. He was named a master after he had helped destroy the Staff of Adaman and Adois during the War of the Staffs. He was known to miss meetings to rendezvous with his bonded golden dragon, Azimuth, leader of all the dragons on Muiria. He was also known to disappear for weeks at a time, never informing the other masters about where he went.

Receiving the warning from Tarquin, he mentally connected with his bonded dragon and related what Celedant had garnered from the prince's mind.

Azimuth immediately replied. "I will be at the beach in a turn of the clock."

The wizard made his excuses to the other masters and hurried to the library, making a short stop at the kitchen pantry to grab some rations, which he tucked into a pouch. Leaving the kitchen, his boots stomped on the marble flooring and down a circular stair of wrought iron. Once in the library proper, he found his best friend on the island, Brill, a wizard who had decided he was not made for the outside world. He stayed with the island's collection of books and other magical manuscripts.

Celedant hastily grabbed Brill's shoulder, almost causing the librarian to drop the chin-high stack of dusty books he was carrying. "My old friend, I am in need of some information but have limited time."

Brill put aside the books he was carrying. "But of course. As always, I'm at your service. What is it you need?"

"I need a copy of a map of the west coast and possibly the lands over the western ocean," Celedant said.

Brill looked deep in thought before answering. "I think we have such maps, but they are little used. And I might have to spend some time searching for them. Come."

Brill led Celedant down the isles between hundreds of bookcases that held dusty tomes and scrolls. Celedant remembered that as a student, he enjoyed exploring the treasures that these tomes held.

Brill held up his hand and whispered more to himself than to Celedant. "This is the place to look for the unused maps – a likely resting place for what you are seeking."

Brill removed a stack of maps off a viewing table and smiled at Celedant. "I've been meaning to clear this away."

He and Celedant attacked the maps, quickly shuffling through them looking for their goal.

"Ah ha! Here is the map of the west coast," Brill finally said. "But it is old, before the time of the quakes. As you remember, although you were a young wizard, when an elvan prince and the evil ruler of a southern city of Zeiglon had fought with the staffs, causing utter destruction with floods of ocean water covering the grasslands of what is now called old Partha, salting the ground and causing the great desert to form as well as devastating earthquakes, bringing disasters throughout the northern hemisphere."

Celedant had never told Brill of his adventures in the South and that he had indeed been during the destruction of old Partha.They spread the map out on the table, and Brill turned his back to search further. Celedant was running out of time, so he whispered a spell that caused the librarian to fall asleep on his feet. Celedant caught his friend before he hit the stone floor and gently laid him on a nearby couch. Rolling up the map, Celedant placed it in a map case, which he had hidden under his cloak. Now to the beach and his rendezvous with Azimuth.

Sprinting up the stairs, his boots rang on the circular stairway, causing looks of consternation from the patrons. He emerged from the library right in front of Ilmaderd, one of the Masters of Edain. Celedant drew up just short of running her over.

He hurriedly excused himself, but she grabbed hold of his arm. "Where to traveler?"

Celedant disliked the high elf and curtly responded, "My business is my own. Please remove your hand from my arm."

He shrugged her off and strode towards the hall's front doors as she called after him, "This business better be important. A master can't just fly off for no good reason."

Celedant ignored her as he pushed open the huge doors and exited into the sunlight. It was a short distance to the beach where Azimuth waited for him in dragon form. It was little known that dragons could change forms into an elf or wolf. What the people of Muiria called dragons were actually firedrakes. While true dragons remained hidden in their aeries on the northernmost island of Dragon Isles.

Azimuth, well over one hundred and fifty paces long, mentally laughed. "So, your departure was not well taken I assume."

"No," the wizard responded. "I am somewhat of a nuisance to the council. They sit here and gather dust. But by the gods, I will not allow myself to become so complacent."

In mid-stride, he levitated to the saddle atop Azimuth. As he strapped himself in, he telepathically spoke to Azimuth. "Tarquin says that the Clorian Valley has been invaded and most if not all the clerics have been murdered."

The dragon made an angry rumbling sound deep in his throat. "It will take two days flying with no stops. Hold on."

Chapter Three

Azimuth flapped his wings twice launching himself into the air with the mighty muscles of his back legs. Celedant cast a warming spell to keep from freezing to death at the height the dragon would fly. He thought about the defenseless Valley of Clor, hoping beyond hope that most of the simple monks had survived the attack, even though the picture Tarquin had mental sent him did not bode well. The wizard had grown to like the odiferous character that was Hority and hoped the small smelly dwarf was still alive.

Two days went by quickly as the two friends discussed what was transpiring in Edain and the dragon aeries on the northernmost isle.

"My mate just laid a new clutch of eggs," Azimuth said proudly. "Twelve in all."

"Congratulations, my friend. They should hatch and be the right age for the next class of wizards and sorceresses in the Fall."

"Yes, we're pleased to have so many."

Celedant could hear and feel the pride in his bonded dragon's voice. "It's been a while since your last clutch."

"Yes, as you know, since we are immortal, the need to reproduce does not happen frequently. And only the queen can do so. Otherwise, we would be overrun with dragons."

They continued to talk. Then as the sunset over the Clorian Valley, Azimuth burst through the dark clouds. "This place reeks of death," he said, making a face.

"Land near the library. That's where the monks of Thierry would have fought and most likely withstood the assault. The giant golden dragon back winged, settling on a ledge well above the library in a hidden spot. Celedant cast a levitation spell to dismount from Azimuth and almost immediately, the dragon transformed into a wood elf, plainly dressed in sturdy clothes for traveling over rough terrain.

The wind whipped Celedant's cloak as he stepped onto the edge and called down to Tarquin. He and the dwarves raised their heads to look up and waved them down. Making their way along the trail to the library's wide ledge, the two friends observed the pained, tired expressions on all those present.

Tarquin approached and hugged Celedant. "Well met, my friend. The valley and Clorians have been much abused."

Celedant glanced around at the blood-covered granite, his expression grim. "Please fill me in on what occurred here."

Tarquin quickly told the wizard of the events before his arrival. "Something important has been taken from the library. We understand from their wounded that they were looking for treasure, or maybe a treasure map might be more apt. Apparently, their warlock found what he was looking for. It must be important because the soldiers were mercenaries from across the sea from a city called Markdale. The Guras, as they called themselves, serve a warlock guild in Trudoc. They went west once they had finished their evil deed here. The Abbott is dead, but many Clorians remained hidden from the attackers in their caves and mud-walled cavities."

"What has occurred since?" the Wizard asked.

Tarquin motioned down to the valley. "The prisoners are burying the dead. Meanwhile, Hority is getting a grasp on who survived. As you might have guessed, Hority is up in arms ready to follow the attackers."

Celedant turned to Azimuth. "It seems we have to follow these knaves; we'll need Eldahir and Morganna. Hopefully, they can accompany us."

Azimuth nodded. "I will excuse myself and contact them."

The dragons still thought it best to hide the fact that they could take mortal form from everyone, except the elves, wizards, and sorceresses. He disappeared over the edge of the cliff and transformed to use telepathy to mentally call the two elves.

In the meantime, Hority and Botreg came up the path towards Celedant. Both had relieved smiles on their faces as soon as they recognized him. Hority ran to him, arms flung wide, and hugged him. Celedant was well used to the smell of the dwarf. He remembered with a smile when they'd had to forcefully bathe him during their travels in search of the Staffs, so as not to give their presence away or offend others.

He was locked in a bear hug and lifted off his feet by the dwarf, who held his breath to keep the odor at bay. Finally, the Clorian put Celedant down and began to spew forth fast-paced words.

"I couldna save me, brothers. There were too many of them." Tears ran down his grief-stricken face. "Everywhere I turned, I ran into a bunch of them. While I could ply me staff with the best of them, all I heard were the cries of me brothers and sisters. I have failed Clor." He hung his head sadly.

Celedant placed a hand on the shoulder of the dirty frock in an attempt to reassure him. "Clor understands what has occurred here and certainly does not blame you. Besides Hority, we know where they are going, and we'll exact revenge for your fallen comrades." That seemed to appease the dwarf, but he went and sat down, hanging his feet off the ledge and sobbing over what had been perpetrated in the valley.

After greeting Botreg and Hority outside the library. Celedant spent most of the time with the head of the Therian librarians, using the list of contents to determine what was missing. The problem was that the dwarves had only gone through half the documents. The task had been slow and onerous, because the Clorians had written on anything they could find, from scraps of paper to badly cured animal skins.

Their search was a long and tedious one. But it could not be rushed, even though their enemies were getting further away. Celedant read from the manifest, while the librarians searched for and located the document. It was well into the night when the wizard and the librarians came across the missing item. It should have been sandwiched between a paper on cockroaches and their importance in healing spells, and where it was best to find rats. In between those two, the inventory showed that there should have been a "Map of the West."

Celedant perused the inventory for any other mention of the West. But they found none. While he did that, Eldahir and Morganna arrived, and Azimuth brought them to the cave, where they had to stoop to get through the door. They called to Celedant and hugged each other. The two wood elves had also been vital in the War of the Staffs. Then the wizard got right to business.

"Eldahir, do you know of any documents concerning the West?" Celedant asked.

The elvan warrior shook his head. "I apologize for not spending more time in study, but my duty called me into battle."

The two wood elves had fought beside Tarquin in the war and were married the following year in a double ceremony with Tarquin and Ress. It was supposed to have been a joyous occasion attended by their family and friends. But Morgana's father and mother, both undead Illanni or vampire dark elves, had shown up unexpectedly, and the ensuing small battle had sparked an elvan war. Morganna, born an Illanni, had always looked more like a Wood Elf than an Illanni, much to her parents' disgust, had been transformed into a full Wood Elf by the dwarvan God, Dolgar.

What had happened here in this peaceful valley could not be forgiven. Revenge was on both their minds. A day later, they heard someone shouting Eldahir and Morganna's names' over and over. The odor preceded him as Hority burst into the library and ran up to the pair, grasping them each in a bear hug. Eldahir held a cloth over his nose. Celedant could not be happier to see the excitable dwarf in a better mood, despite his horrific smell. The wizard wished that for the good of these monks, Clor would one day change his heavenly tenants and make them take baths. But he doubted that would ever occur. Dolgar had managed to persuade Clor to change his tenant, concerning the searching of sewage, because of the health concerns of his monks. There were too few Clorians to risk them getting diseases from sewer waste.

The wood elves thanked him for the hug, and Celedant cast a spell counteracting the hideous smell that followed Hority everywhere he went.

"What has happened here, my dear friend?" Eldahir asked.

Shaking his head sadly, Hority said, "I have thought long and hard on the subject, and I believe a god of cleanliness must have sent these heretics to ruin Clor's recent rise in power. The ways of the gods confound me."

Celedant was about to dispute that claim but stopped when he realized that there was one who would dare. Only one goddess would be so vicious, Adois. With the downfall of her minion, Taza, he would not put anything past her. She would not allow Taza's defeat to stop her plans from going forward. She had punished him severely for all eternity. But the wizard was willing to bet that she quickly found someone just as evil to take up her cause.

The Wizard placed his hand on the dwarf's boney shoulder and led him outside as the sun slipped over the western portion of the valley. But Celedant let go of the distraught dwarf, concerned that he might get lice from his friend. There were a few campfires in the valley, obviously where the monks had gathered after a long day of burying the raider's bodies and taking their own dead to a large cavern that would serve as their tomb.

"Do not despair my friend," Celedant assured him. "We have uncovered what the warlock was after and can leave at first light in pursuit." That cheered up the distraught dwarf who wanted to run off and follow the mercenaries, were it not for a strong grasp from Celedant.

"Easy, my friend," the Wizard said. "We'll catch up to them fast because we'll be mounted on horses, and they'll be on foot. Rest tonight and wait until tomorrow. You must be exhausted from your long night of battle."

"Aye, I am. As long as ye promise…."

"I promise. We will catch these marauders and make them pay," Celedant assured him.

Chapter Four

During the previous year, the witch and warlock remained hidden from all outsiders until Cyra came to Talchic saying, "It is time to go. Gather whatever you want to carry." When he had placed what he needed in a small satchel, which he slung over his shoulder, the sorceress faced him and held out her hands. "Take my hands. We'll be in Trudoc in seconds."

He had only heard stories of the city, so he held her hands. The scene before him shimmered and within seconds, they stood before a great city built of stone on rolling hills with the vivid blue of the western ocean at its back.

Cyra was suddenly in a hurry. "Come, the warlocks of the city will pinpoint the power of the spell and send us a not too friendly welcoming committee. They will not know if we be friend or foe."

She ran south and shouted back over her shoulder. "I dare not use the spell again. I fear popping up out of thin air where we are going would be far too dangerous."

A befuddled Talchic asked, "But you teleported from the Isle to the northern coast."

She laughed. "I took a chance. We could have ended up in the sea or entrapped in a stone outcropping."

The warlock gulped and fought back his anger. Had he known that beforehand, he never would have attempted it with this witch. He could have been killed. Talchic had too many things he still wanted to accomplish to allow his life to be cut short.

They ran for several miles. But Talchic was breathing heavily and falling behind. She drew up and waited for him to catch up, pointing to a trail that seven soldiers had ridden on earlier.

Hardly having difficulty breathing after the run, she said, "Look. A patrol and most importantly, horses. Come, I will hazard a simple spell."

The riders had stopped at a nearby stream to water their horses and refresh themselves. When the witch and warlock caught up to them, they had just remounted and were ready to continue their journey. With a mere word, the soldiers slumped over their horse's necks or slid off them altogether. Smiling, she waved him forward. The first soldier was on the ground as the horses milled about grazing on the plush grass. She quickly bent down with her dagger in hand and slit the man's throat. She motioned to the warlock to do the same until all lay dead. He gulped down the bile that rose in his gullet. Not daring to upset his mistress, he began his grisly task. Although a warlock of evil repute, the slaying of the sleeping men was morally against his standards. Yet he knew that if he did not follow her orders, he would be dead on the ground along with the soldiers.

Afterward, they mounted two horses and galloped south, trailing the other horses behind them. Cyra had yet to tell Talchic their destination, but he knew that to question her would be futile. She was quick to anger and even quicker with a devastating spell. After several days of hard riding, switching out the horses as they went, his mistress pulled up on her reins and pointed towards the distant hills.

She circled her horse and pointed. "There in those hills, our allies await us. It is the ancestral home of the white orcs."

The warlock grimaced. He well remembered the tall white orc-guard at the former dwarvan stronghold, Zigar Shan, now under orc control. Huge, it had stood nearly nine feet in height, broad of shoulder, and rippling with muscle. It had blocked his way in and out when Talchic or rather Melgor had liberated his hidden gold from the former dwarvan city. He hated the very sight of them but hid his distaste less his mistress realize his disgust.

As the sun crested in the eastern sky, Hority, Botreg, and Tarquin showed the destruction to Eldahir and Morganna, who had been flown in by Azimuth the night before. After the tour of the battlefield, the elves were more than eager to follow the raiders.

"What was done here is abominable and not to be tolerated," Eldahir said.

"I agree," Morganna said. "It cannot be tolerated. If I did not know better, I would think that this is something Taza would do. But I'm sure he is residing in the lowest level of the seven hells."

"What's frightening is that whoever ordered this devastation, must be as bad or worse than Taza," Eldahir added.

"And that, my friends, is what has me so worried. It seems like as soon as we eliminate one great evil, only to have it replaced by another," Celedant said worriedly. "I fear that Adois is behind this."

His words brought startled looks from all within hearing distance.

"Surely, she wouldna…," Botreg began.

"Ah but I believe she would. She has merely chosen a new champion to spread her evil ways," the Wizard said.

"In that case, the sooner we put this new threat down, the better," Eldahir said.

Everyone agreed.

The next morning, Eldahir, with his hundreds of years in the elvan cavalry, acquired the sturdiest Guras' horses for himself and the others who would be making the journey with him.

They ate a hearty meal of venison, thanks to Hority's hunting skills. Though none of them had known that he had any particular skill in hunting in the first place. During their previous travels, he had never once offered to go hunting for fresh meat. Afterwards, they mounted their steeds and rode on a narrow track along the western side of the valley until they spotted where the Guras had made their escape. The edge of the valley showed the passage of their enemies, as the grass was crushed down. Morganna jumped from her horse and surveyed the area.

"Fifty to sixty made it out of the valley," she informed them. "We should have no problem following their trail. Apparently, they have no fear of reprisals as they do nothing to hide their tracks." She mounted her horse and the small group galloped after the men.

They ate their mid-day meal in the saddle.

"Azimuth can't ye just fly up and finish them off?" Botreg asked. He was one of the few dwarves to know that Azimuth was really a dragon.

Without turning in his saddle, Celedant answered for his friend. "We follow because I am curious about what was so valuable in the library. Why send so many soldiers and a warlock for a simple document, when they could simply have asked the monks for a copy. As I mentioned previously, I fear that dark evil was behind this raid."

"Azimuth can always scout ahead if their trail runs dry," Tarquin added.

They continued following the trail going slowly. They did not want to overtake their enemies and alert them to their presence. The track wound westward toward the unknown. After a week in the saddle, the great desert began to encroach on the southern foothills that joined the Mordwelian Mountains to the Sargorian range.

Botreg pointed to the deep sands of the desert. "They canna survive long in armor this side of the hills. We trained here while with the Borderers, and it's hot enough to fry yer brain. That is if ye aren't captured by the nomads that roam the wasteland. Then I'm afraid yer death would be much worse than a fried brain."

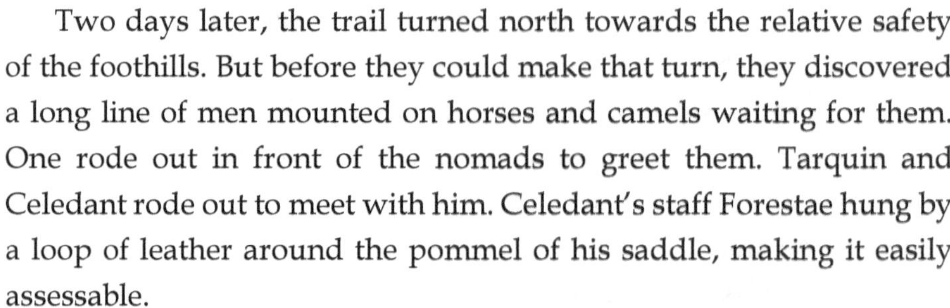

Two days later, the trail turned north towards the relative safety of the foothills. But before they could make that turn, they discovered a long line of men mounted on horses and camels waiting for them. One rode out in front of the nomads to greet them. Tarquin and Celedant rode out to meet with him. Celedant's staff Forestae hung by a loop of leather around the pommel of his saddle, making it easily assessable.

They neared the nomad, who looked the way Tarquin expected of a desert-dwelling people. A loose fabric normally covered his face, and his skin was weather-beaten and brown from constant exposure to the harsh conditions of the great wasteland. As they drew closer, Celedant and Tarquin spotted the long lance resting on the stirrup and sticking high in the air. The Nomad also sported a sword in a bejeweled scabbard.

Tarquin reined up before the man with Celedant on his right. "May we be of service to you?" The man smiled, showing that he had several teeth missing. The rest of his teeth were pearly white, but the smile could not hide the evil intent behind it.

"We wish your horses. And while we're at it, we will take you for slaves," the Nomad stated authoritatively.

Tarquin appeared to be thinking before he asked, "Just where will you sell us? Come to think of it, I would not mind having your scabbard."

The man ignored Tarquin and laughed. "In Trudoc on the western ocean. You will make excellent galley slaves."

The young man looked towards Celedant before turning back to the nomad and saying, "I don't think so."

Tarquin's sword was out of its sheath instantly, but the nomad had anticipated the move and already had his sword pointed toward Tarquin as he spurred his horse forward. Tarquin swung his sword to the left of the horse, catching the oncoming sword and deflecting it away. The other rider managed a backhand swing that Tarquin barely ducked in time as he fell forward against his mount. Only the horse's head and neck prevented him from falling off.

The line of nomads spurred their horses forward, coming directly at Tarquin's friends. Celedant grabbed Forestae and cast a fireball that rolled across the seared landscape. It brought down a goodly number of their enemies. The rest of their party had just about reached the wizard and Tarquin, when Hority called upon his god's wrath and great columns of fire fell among the raiders.

Tarquin's ongoing battle continued with the nomad leader, who was a skilled fighter and horseman. The prince thought he was better with a sword, but the advantage was lost when mounted. The two turned their horses, sand flying in the air, each searching for an opening in the other's defense. The leader of the nomads swung, and Tarquin pulled away almost in time. The sword hit the prince on the side but slid off his chainmail. It would leave a painful bruise. The two riders slashed and parried blows for some time, until Tarquin had an opening and stabbed across his horse, catching his adversary in the chest. The sword went in several inches, causing the other horseman to go berserk, his sword swinging right, left, and overhand at Tarquin.

The others of their party caught up to Celedant, who continued sending green balls of fire at the attackers, who either fell dead, or their horses reared up and took off running, turning away from the battle. Eldahir and Morganna had taken out their bows, sending arrow after arrow into the nomads. The nomads closed to a short distance of their commander, before sending a shower of arrows and spears at Celedant and the others. But both Celedant and Eldahir had cast protective spells over the group that deflected the projectiles and made them disintegrate on impact. Seeing the magic users and the power they yielded, the remaining nomads spurred their horses and camels into the desert. But Tarquin and their leader fought on. A blood lust had taken hold of the nomad chieftain, who refused to back down to what he considered a young upstart.

Their swords clashed with sparks flying as Dragon Bolt struck out again and again, offensively and then defensively. The nomad tried to beat Tarquin down using overhead swings. The tactic worked, as the prince had to keep backing up his horse. Then the attacker missed and chopped down into the saddle. Tarquin stood up in the stirrups and swung Dragon Bolt at his opponent's head. The tip of his blade cut across the nomad's face. He wheeled back and when he came forward, Tarquin struck at his neck severing it halfway through. A look of shock was the nomad leader's last expression as he fell backward, looking at Tarquin in disbelief as blood welled out of his neck and mouth. He toppled over the back of his horse, one foot still in a stirrup, startling the horse. It took off running, dragging the dead body of the nomad that bounced across the sandy desert land.

Celedant called out. "See what they have in the way of gold. We may need all we can muster when we reach Trudoc."

They gathered a goodly amount of loot from the fallen nomads, while Eldahir and Morganna recovered what arrows they could from the battle.

"Take their water and horses," Tarquin ordered Botreg. "We may yet have need for them. Leave the camels. They will not fare well where we are going." Turning to address Morganna, he asked, "Can you and Eldahir lead us back to the trail of the Guras?"

"We can," she replied.

Chapter Five

The tracks led at an angle into the foothills of the Sargorian Mountains with the southern side made up of arid canyons with high crag-like hills. Further north into the foothills, the terrain changed into forested lands and if one ventured farther north, it eventually reached the great swamp – a place where Tarquin and those who had ridden with him remembered none too fondly.

Morganna stopped her horse and spoke to Eldahir. "They went up this canyon. Either they have used it before, or they are using magic to navigate."

"These canyons all look the same," her husband replied. "Either of your thoughts could be right."

Seeing the married couple discuss the trail made Tarquin think of his wife and the time this was taking away from their being together, especially with her being pregnant. He hoped he wasn't going to miss the birth of his child by going on this adventure. Ress would never let him live it down. She might even attempt to kill him, if he was lucky.

Then the wood elves rode back to the others to report their findings.

When they finished reporting, Tarquin shook his head. "This is the perfect place for an ambush. We must stay alert."

The group had been riding several hours to the northwest when they found a dead body. The Guras soldier, who had been wounded during the attack on the valley, had finally succumbed to blood loss. They had only gone a few yards when wild cries echoed from the canyon walls. Orcs ran down the path towards them, while others that had taken up position in the rocks on the sides of the valley, started firing arrows at them.

Morganna used the sorcery she had learned as an Illanni or dark elf. She cast a spell, sending a lightning bolt toward the on-rushing orcs. Eldahir, Tarquin, Botreg, and Azimuth charged forward.

Hority gave his battle cry, "Foes!" But his horse reared, and he fell, hitting his head on a rock where he lay as if in a deep sleep. Meanwhile, Celedant erected a dome of protection around him and his horse to deflect the arrows being sent his way. The wizard sent balls of blue flame after the archers. Every time one hit its target, the archer was killed or severely wounded. Morganna drew her bow and fired arrows unerringly at the orcs hiding in the rocks. Elvan magic kept the arrows straight and true, hitting their targets unerringly.

Using their horses as battering rams, Eldahir, Tarquin, Botreg, and Azimuth crashed heavily into the charging orcs, plowing into them as the warriors swung their swords left and right, dispatching the enemy as they went. Feeling a deep pain in his shoulder, Tarquin was nearly pitched from his mount. He took a quick look and saw the feathered end of an arrow sticking out.

The orcs before them broke. They'd had enough of the magical lightning bolt impacting them, and the bloody swarth the horsemen had created. They ran back up the valley. But those on the steep sides had not seen the main group break contact. They continued shooting arrows at Tarquin and the others. Morganna and Celedant dealt with them easily, until Morganna felt a pain in her leg. An arrow had struck her in the thigh, pinning her to the saddle. By that time, Eldahir had returned and added his bow to the fight. Then several huge ogres appeared, throwing large boulders down the cliff. Eldahir stopped his horse and aimed unerringly at an ogre striking it in the eye. It pitched forward to bounce off the sides of the cliff until settling with a thump on the trail.

That was the final blow of the battle. The archers slowly retreated. The ogres as well. Tarquin leaned over in his saddle, the arrow sticking straight through his shoulder. Morganna held the shaft of her own arrow wound, each movement of the horse causing her a great deal of pain.

Hority awoke and seeing that the battle was over, whined, "Ye could've waited for me to awake before ye started the battle." He then sprinkled a hand full of dust, thankfully praying that everyone had survived.

Seeing Hority in front of a giant boulder with a dour look on his face and gaining his wits about him, Botreg called to him. "Hority yer needed. We've wounded."

Meanwhile. Eldahir and Celedant helped the wounded down off their horses. Eldahir carefully broke the arrow shaft between his wife and the saddle before lifting Morganna off her horse. He would remove the remaining part of the arrow from the saddle later, as it had not gone deep enough to pierce the horse beneath it. Hority ran over to where Tarquin and Morganna were gently laid on the grass. His dirt encrusted legs showed below his equally stained habit. He looked at both and whispered a prayer to Clor, scattering dirt over his head and holding his hands above their wounds. A dark brown mist appeared and settled on the arrow strikes.

He looked at both and said, "Me sacrifice to me illustrious Clor is working. That will numb the pain somewhat as we remove the arrows."

He broke the fletching of the arrows near their skin. Then with a quick movement, he jerked each arrow through. Both of the wounded felt the shafts pulled through their bodies, but there was little pain.

Then with a smile he said, "Tarquin, this is the best part. I will wash out the wounds to clean out the arrows filthy path through yer body. I like to see what flows out first so I can offer it to me god, Clor."

Botreg reached down and patted the dirty dwarf on the shoulder. "Now's the time for healing not talking."

"But of course," Hority said in a whispered reply as if he was a scolded child. Then he readied a water pouch. He stuck the end into one opening of the wound and squeezed hard. After a few hard tries dirty blood began leaking from the wound. Using a cloth, he caught the blood, before bloodied water issued out of the exit wound. He took the dirty blood and wiped it on his forehead while he muttered a prayer to Clor. All those present knew that the dwarf was offering the befouled blood to his god.

He performed the same procedure on Morganna and gently collected the dirty blood. Again, he smeared the blood on his forehead. He looked up. "Does anyone have a healing potion? I used all of mine in the valley of Clor."

Celedant handed him two vials, which Morganna and Tarquin each drained in one gulp. They instantly felt warmth spread throughout their bodies. Their wounds were then washed on the outside and bound tightly with clean linen to keep them from becoming infected. Hority picked up the two bloodied cloths and stuck them in his satchel that served as his backpack.

Botreg had promised his onetime companion, Baldo, the new abbot of Thierry's monastery to take care of the dirty little dwarf. "What are ye going to do with those?" he asked dubiously.

The dwarf looked up at him. "I'll study what came out with the blood, and the blood itself. Then I'll record it me book."

Botreg smiled. "I didna know ye could write."

Hority looked horrified. "The great Lord, Clor, came to me in a dream and spoke to me. Instead of carrying around all me findings of waste, which can become quite burdensome, I can now examine it and record me findings for prosperity."

"If it keeps ye cleaner, I'm all for it," the former Assassin said with a wry smile.

Celedant with a grin on his face mounted his horse and called to the others. "Gather whatever money they have."

Eldahir scavenged for arrows that were still usable.

Tarquin came up to the wizard with a large pouch. "It looks like our prey bribed these orcs to attack. Look at these strange gold pieces."

"It seems that our quarry is aware of our pursuit," Celedant mused. "We must be extra cautious from this point on."

Chapter Six

Celedant and his little band journeyed up the canyon to its head to a winding path that led up and over into a hardwood forest, a place where many diverse monsters dwelt. It was reminiscent of their previous jaunt through the great swamp, and the terrors they had encountered in its dark environment during their other adventures. In crossing over the top of the foothills, they lost track of their quarry on the large granite areas that led down to the first of the trees. Even Eldahir was unable find any signs of passage by such a large number of men. Celedant hazarded a guess that the warlock could be the reason.

Heading west, they rode through the upper portion of the forest where the trees were few and smaller than the ones further down the slope. Before long, they came across two orc enclosures. The orcs had shut their gates and barred them. They watched the riders approach with fearful eyes. At both places, Celedant cast a protection spell on himself and rode up to the gates of the small villages.

Flipping a gold coin over the wall at each village, he asked, "Have you noticed a large body of men passing near here?"

In both cases, he was told that the men were going west.

Then one day when they had reached a clearing, Tarquin spotted something and pointed toward it. "See the smoke? It's not a campfire. That's something big."

Botreg motioned to the smoke and said what everyone was thinking, "We might have caught them at last."

"Yes, but is it too late for the folks they attacked?" Celedant asked.

They rode slowly toward the smoke until they were close enough for Eldahir to slip off his horse and jog into the woods. He returned a full quarter-turn of the clock later. "There is a village ahead that was attacked and burned. We can search the debris and see if we can find any evidence that the ones we follow were responsible. If that's the case, we must be very close behind them."

The town had been razed to the ground. Fires still burned within the palisade, which in places had been torn down. They dismounted several hundred yards away and carefully approached the ruined town. As they drew closer, they kept alert, always scanning the area. Then at the main gate that had been pushed inward, they discovered a dead ogre and several dead Guras.

"It was an ogre town. Be wary," Tarquin quietly warned.

They had just entered the front gate when a swirling mist formed in front of them. Then a grotesque figure stepped from the mist, a huge reptilian-like being that looked like it had been skinned. There was no skin on its body, exposing the creature's muscles, sinew, and bones. Springing into motion, Eldahir and Morganna sought a spot where they could fire their arrows into the creature, while the others advanced. Celedant immediately cast a lightning bolt at the creature, which struck it on the left side, flinging it into a burning house. As Tarquin, Azimuth, Hority, and Botreg neared, the creature stepped out from the burning house. There was a deep blackened hole in its side where the lightning bolt struck, but that did not slow it down. It reached out, grasping Azimuth by the neck.

Azimuth was about to morph into dragon form, but before he could, Tarquin was there swinging Dragon Bolt with all his might. There was little resistance as he severed the arm holding his friend.

Botreg ducked and rolled through the monster's legs, neatly standing back up and running his sword through its back. Hority was about to use his staff on the creature, but it backhanded him with its remaining arm. Arrows pierced the creature as it kept up its own attack.

Tarquin and Botreg were too close for Celedant to use any more spells. The prince ran at the creature, but it grabbed Tarquin's sword. Dragon Bolt turned a fiery red and slid through its fingers, penetrating deep into its chest.

"What's keeping this thing alive?" Tarquin shouted as the creature picked up a flaming piece of wood and attacked.

"It's a demon," Celedant called out in response.

"I hate demons," Tarquin called back with a sigh.

It easily turned away the swords and stuck back, sending Azimuth flying. He landed on his back; the breath knocked from his lungs. Finally, Dragon Bolt caught the flaming wood squarely and cut through it. Standing within an arm's length of the creature, Botreg plied his sword masterfully and cut the demon down. It screamed an unearthly utterance and fell to the ground, slowly turning to ash that a black haze blew away in the mountain air.

Celedant scuffed the pile of ash with his boot. "Must have been a trap left by the warlock. If he hadn't before, he definitely will know we are on his trail after this battle. The death of the demon he summoned will alert him to that fact."

Advancing into the village, they discovered dead ogres everywhere, killed by crossbow bolts or hacked down singularly. But there were men strewn about the enclosure, too. In places, they found dead Guras, many of whom were sprawled on the ground with grain, and haunches of deer or beef.

"They seem to have attacked the city for food. But why kill them all," Tarquin asked Celedant.

"They are an evil lot and probably have exhausted their food supplies," Celedant replied. "I guess they're city born and can't live off the land. Gather what coins you can. Also, gather a haunch of venison. I wouldn't mind a hot meal."

Hority spoke up. "Is it right for us to defile the dead by taking their coins? Clor might disapprove because they are shiny and clean."

"If you were hungry and stumbled upon this place. Would you not search for food and aid from anyone inside?" Tarquin asked him. "This is the same situation. We will aid who we can and gather coins from the Guras for the difficulties ahead."

Celedant smiled serenely. "Even the mighty Clor must, at times, take clean objects to properly immerse in filth at a later period."

"Clor will instruct me later," Hority said, giving in. "I must gather some debris to sacrifice to Clor this evening."

While the other members sought out coins and food, Hority searched for wounded ogres. Treating them and bandaging their wounds turned out to be difficult until Botreg came to translate. Most had escaped the attack with small injuries and had hidden from the marauding men. At times, Hority was seen to lean down and pick up an odd bit of detritus as he traveled about the city. When he returned to the group, his satchel was bulging and clanking with each step.

"Come Hority," Celedant said. "We must ride hard and find a suitable campsite before dark."

Smiling the dwarf said, "I wanted to take embers to light me holy fire, but they burned holes in me satchel. Perhaps I can use our fire?"

"As long as ye do yer experiments away from the camp and promise not to burn down the forest," Botreg answered.

Hority's expression became serious. "I'll have no part in a cleansing fire. Think what would be destroyed. Beetles, bird nests, bird eggs...."

Seeing the seething look on Botreg's face, Tarquin commanded, "Come Hority. We need to ride."

That quieted the dirty monk, and their little group once more followed the trail westward. They rode slowly for the rest of the day not wanting to overtake the men they followed. That night, they dined on a haunch of roast venison and had a delightful meal. Hority went ten paces away from the others and built a small fire with a burning log from the camp's fire. Picking up the log, the fire began burning his hands. He ran to his fire and tossed the lighted log on it. Then sitting on his cloak, he removed fruit, grains, and bits of the Guras clothes he had taken from his pack, placing them before the campfire.

Hority began chanting. "Clor is great. Clor is great."

He continued as he slowly picked up each piece of his sacrifice and waved it through the smoke before placing it in the burning fire. He then waved the smoke over himself and rubbed it into his clothes and skin. He did this for each item and when he was finished, he put out the fire and fell fast asleep with a contented smile upon his face.

CHAPTER SEVEN

They picked up the tracks again the next day, but they were close, and it was hard to keep hidden behind their enemy without being discovered. Eldahir ranged out in front of the others, keeping watch on the Guras soldiers and making sure his friends did not run into them. A couple of days later, the column stopped. Only Eldahir's keen elvan eyesight picked out the captain studying a piece of parchment. The warlock stood close beside him. When he folded up the map, the captain motioned the column south.

They're heading back over the top of the hills, Eldahir thought. *They're making a break for the desert.*

He was about to report back to Celedant when a human voice stopped him. "Hold it right there, elf. Move and you'll have a crossbow bolt in the heart. Now slowly climb down from your horse."

Eldahir wondered how on Muiria the Guras had snuck up on him as he started to dismount. The elvan warrior landed on the ground before the Guras.

"Go ahead and disarm yourself, elvan scum," the man in charge said. He stood to the side of two men.

Eldahir motioned he would and started removing his bow. Once it cleared his shoulder, the elf whirled the bow at the two crossbowmen, catching them by surprise as they had let their guard down while the elf was disarming. The flying bow caught both in the face.

The elf queen's general drew his sword and struck down the leader with a thrust through the chest. He then whirled away from the dying man to stand between the crossbowmen, who were desperately trying to draw their swords. One soldier used his crossbow to block the elf's blade and chunks of wood flew in the air as the sword work continued. The men could not draw their swords, so they tried to bludgeon him to death with their crossbows. Eventually, Eldahir struck both down with the efficient handling of his weapon that he had learned while defending the elvan forest from the creatures of the great swamp.

As they fell dead at his feet, three more attacked. One man ran away, having seen enough of the elf's sword work. While the braver ones stepped forward with overhanded blows. The elf easily deflected them downward. Then with lightning speed, he crushed the first attacker's nose by smashing the hilt of his sword into the man's face. Then with a twirl of his sword, the elf neatly decapitated the Guras soldier. The second man tried to lunge at Eldahir's chest. Eldahir knocked the blade away with a backhand slash.

The Guras recovered and tried another overhead blow. But the elvan warrior caught the downward stroke and headbutted the man in the face. Blood flowed from his enemy's nose, while tears momentarily blinded him. That's when Eldahir struck. His blade drove deep into the man's chest. He did not wait long. Letting go of his sword, he grabbed his bow from the ground, and ran after the man who had darted away, making crashing noises as the Guras tried to get through a briar patch. It was a definite sign that these were indeed city dwellers. Eldahir took out his dagger and threw it at the man, striking him in the shoulder.

The man fell forward, but he was held up by the dense briars.

His bow drawn, Eldahir called out to him. "Turn around and come to me, or I'll shoot you where you stand."

The Guras soldier fought his way back through the briars until he reached, Eldahir who disarmed him and tied him to a tree.

"How did you know I was following you," the elf asked. "Lie and I will cut your throat."

The soldier with a full blond beard and multiple scratches from the brambles answered, "Our warlock knew you were trailing us. He cast a spell that silenced any sound we might make."

"Why did you attack that particular valley?" Eldahir asked.

"We were ordered to follow the warlock. He had a map of the area," the bound man answered.

Eldahir was glad that the man was a talker, he would have hated to have to torture him. Wanting to know who they were following, he asked, "Did this warlock have a name?"

The man sighed. "His name is Tyrus. As evil a man as I've met. If he learns what I have told you. I'm a dead man."

Eldahir stooped pulling his dagger from the man's shoulder, while the man squirmed against his restraints and kept repeating, "Please do not kill me. I told you all you wanted."

The Elvan General looked upon the man with pity and pointed to the south. He threw the man's sword into the briar patch. "There's your chance to escape." Removing the man from the tree, he tied his hands and feet together.

Even as Eldahir turned back to mount his horse, the man began wriggling toward the briars and his sword. As soon as he freed himself, he took off. Eldahir knew the Guras would not return to the others and risk death. No doubt, the warlock would use a dark spell on him to see why he had survived when the others had not.

Chapter Eight

Eldahir repeated his findings to the others when he joined up with them.

"At least we don't need to go near Zigar-Shan," Tarquin said quietly.

All agreed with that sentiment. That dwarvan city now was home to the orcs and their ilk.

"Come along then," Celedant said. "We can't sit here postulating. We need to move."

Following the Guras down into the canyon, they exited the foothills to a scene of flowing grasslands across the western horizon. The desert ended in high dunes several miles away to the east. Tarquin motioned them forward into the deep grass. The terrain was made up of rolling hills several hundred paces high. The path of the Guras was plain for all to see as they had trampled down grass extending into the hills. Instead of following directly behind, they moved parallel to the tracks, in hopes of missing any more traps like the one Eldahir had fallen into. Morganna, Eldahir's wife kidded him mercilessly about being caught by the enemy, much to the delight of the others. The stoic wood elf, a general in the elvan cavalry, was normally regal and unperturbed, but was now riding with a scowl on his face.

Hority rode quickly up to the wizard from the back of the column. "Clor has warned me that strange beasts are about to attack!"

Celedant called to the others. "Take tight hold of your horses. I'm going to flatten the vegetation around us."

The wizard stood up in his stirrups and waved his staff about his head, causing the wind to pick up. His friends griped their reins hard, keeping their horses as calm as possible as the wind continued gaining speed. Suddenly, the grass around them was pulled up by the roots. The horses nervously danced around as the wind spread out, placing them all in the center of the spell as the wall of wind expanded. Then as suddenly as it had begun, the wind ceased, and the silence of the plains returned. The companions stared at the destruction of the plants out to at least a hundred paces. Then dismounting, they staked out their horses and settled in to wait for the attack.

"My good dwarf, mind the spells you cast, especially those that might set the grass ablaze," Celedant called to Hority. "I would hate to be caught in the middle of a plains fire."

"Ye are the wisest of the wise," the odiferous dwarf replied. "I shall not forget."

Azimuth spoke up. "I can smell them. They're close."

Their wait lasted a mere quarter-turn of the clock before they heard blood-curdling war cries issued from the distance as middling-sized beasts charged from the tall grass. The attackers reminded Tarquin of the giant white orcs but with four arms, each carrying a weapon. He quickly grabbed his bow and began shooting arrows into the oncoming creatures. A second later, the others followed suit, their arrows slamming into the front rank. The volley felled multiple creatures, but the mass continued coming.

Hority rushed into the horde swinging his branch and yelling, "Foes!".

Tarquin and Botreg ran after the dwarf and slammed into two of the attackers. It was like running into a wall. They both fell backward, and their enemies slowly advanced. Both were on their feet instantly as the enemy attacked. Their attackers' favorite weapon was a sword that looked as if it had a sharpened star shape on the end of the blade. Tarquin avoided the first attack then rammed his sword under the helmet, through the creature's chin, and up into the brain. Botreg rolled under the swing of his opponent's blade. Jumping up, he cut one of its legs off as it fell. The assassin avoided the four arms and jabbed a dagger between the joint of the back plate and neck guard. Then Morganna and Eldahir were amongst the attackers.

Hority rushed in and out of the creatures, swinging his branch and bringing enemies down with each swing. Morganna used the swift moves of her sword, a trait passed on to her from her elven heritage and years of serving in the Illanni or dark elvan army. Eldahir preferred a more bullish way, running into the midst of the creatures. Celedant rode into the melee with both sword and staff raining down upon his enemies. Not to be outdone, Azimuth changed back into a dragon and took off, sweeping over the rear ranks of the vast horde and incinerating them with magical fire that burned the enemy, but not the grasslands nearby.

Soon thereafter, the attackers turned into defenders. Too many had fallen, and they began to back away from the fight. Tarquin and his friends began butchering the warriors from the nine hells, slowly forming a circle around those remaining that got smaller and smaller by the minute. Eldahir and Morganna picked off the creatures with their arrows, forcing them into one last charge, when Tarquin was attacked by an unusually tall adversary. He swung first at the thing's face, causing it to flinch as his first sword stroke went wide. Then the Prince neatly turned his sword, bringing Dragon Bolt down on the creature's arm. The magical blade cut completely through one of its wrists. When the monster grasped his severed wrist with one hand, Tarquin drove his sword into its face.

Tarquin looked around for others to fight, but the battle was over. Everyone stood gasping for breath in the middle of the killing field, except Azimuth. He had enjoyed being back in his natural form and had yet to return to his elvan shape. After the fight was over, each of the enemies dissolved into dust and was blown into the air by the plain's breeze.

Interrupting the tense situation Hority called out, "Tarquin, can we collect a full suit of armor? It would greatly benefit me order. Besides, there is a particular smell to it that I have never experienced before."

Botreg strode over to him and picked up a helmet. He tossed it to Hority. "This will have to do," he said sternly.

The dirty cleric nodded gleefully. "All praise to Clor, a glorious battle and a helmet to study." He then started back to the horses with a serene look on his face.

Unbeknownst to Hority and surprised by all, no one had suffered a wound of any kind.

Celedant joined Azimuth. "Just couldn't resist. Could you?" he teased.

Harrumph! I'm tired of walking around on two legs and getting smacked around by lesser beings.

"I understand, my friend. You don't really have to travel as an elf, except when we're near a settlement. We wouldn't want to scare the citizens half to death," Celedant said.

It's not like we have to hide the existence of dragons any longer – not after the Battle of Southgard and the Battle for Dragon Isle. Even for those who weren't there to see us, word has spread like wildfire throughout the territories.

"Even so, for those who have never seen a dragon, you're a fiercesome sight. No sense in creating panic among the innocent." Celedant paused before continuing. "So why did we hide you from the monks?"

Force of habit I think, Azimuth replied. *But as I said, I'm tired of using a two-legged form. And there is no reason not to create a lot of fear for our enemies.*

Joining the others, Celedant told them, "Azimuth has decided to remain in his dragon form, except when we're near a village or city."

"Good, maybe he'll scare off some of the ones who want to attack us," Botreg said.

The rest of the way turned out to be quite a joy. The animals they came across skittered away, hidden in the tall grass. The wind blew gently in their faces, and the swaying of the tall grass almost put them to sleep in the saddle. With Azimuth flying overhead, they did not need to worry about sneak attacks. It reminded Tarquin of the sea voyage from Bau's Port to the escarpment, during the time of the War of the Staffs. With his mind free to wander, Tarquin thought of his beloved Ress and how far each step took him further away from her and their unborn child.

The most dangerous part of the pursuit was when Eldahir rode off looking for their enemies. Azimuth could easily have done it, but there was too great a chance of him being spotted, which would give their presence away. At some point during the battle and this part of the ride, the little group had gotten off course and were now five miles away from their quarry. But they were still behind them and hopefully hidden from sight.

Chapter Nine

The dwarf's leather armor was sweat stained. He had been running for hours through the high grass, pondering his past life. His name was Zeffan, an insult to a dwarf that meant human spawn, but he had been sired by a human mother and a dwarvan father. They had loved each other dearly and to keep from being ridiculed, they had gone deep into the hills to have their son.

Zeffan was a foot taller than most dwarves and had taken the name as a young dwarf in honor of his mother, who had grown old and died before he reached adulthood. His father taught him everything he needed to know to survive in the wilderness. But he still missed his wife, even though their partnership had been destined to destroy them both because of the short life span of a human and the long life of a dwarf. Zeffan knew his father grieved and spent much of the day beside his wife's grave. Then one day he left with a curt nod to his son. Zeffan never saw his father again.

Zeffan eventually tired of the hills and the home that had been such a wonderful place for him. He set off for the city. There he spent many years as an expert in the outside world, which soon banished the stigmatism of being called Zeffan. He was accepted by the folk of the surrounding territories. His reputation grew, and he learned of the wide world. He ventured into cities filled with a myriad of people, combined with creatures he would normally have fought in the wild. But the ever-inquisitive dwarf learned their ways and soon understood the cities with their diverse and large populations.

The reason he sprinted through the countryside, following a trail he could easily pick out by the bent grasses, was because he was after prey. The caravan he led had been attacked and destroyed to the last dwarf. He had been scouting ahead and never heard the attack until he smelled smoke coming from the direction of the camp.

He had been too late. The attackers had hit the camp shortly after midnight and were gone before Zeffan returned. The camp had been stripped of everything, the wagons burned, and even the horses were taken, no doubt to carry the stolen goods. Taking a quick look for any survivors and finding none, he took off following the broad swarth of crumpled grass.

He was enraged by the wanton death and destruction, and he followed the trail at a steady mile-eating pace. He would not allow their killers to go unpunished. Zeffan caught sight of the marauders that afternoon, three days from the destroyed camp. They were great white orcs from the hills near Trudoc. But there were too many to take on alone, at least until nightfall.

The sun was low in the sky when the grass disappeared. That night, Tarquin's party found a small ravine with a stream running through it. Botreg banked the fire with rocks from the stream so as not to alert the Guras soldiers they were following. The next day, Eldahir and Azimuth in wolf form went on foot toward where they thought their enemies were or had camped. Wolf and elf easily kept pace with each other, noting that as they got further away from the rest of their group, trees appeared to the west. With his elvan eyesight, Eldahir saw a great forest rising out of the morning mist. Several miles onward, Azimuth and the wood elf found the burned-out fire pits the soldiers had left.

Eldahir knelt and felt the ashes. *The ashes are still warm,* he told Azimuth telepathically.

Yes, I can smell that they are, Azimuth replied. They spoke this way for two reasons. As a wolf or dragon, Azimuth did not have the power of verbal speech. He would have to take his elvan form to do so, but they also did not want to risk alerting the enemy to their presence by speaking.

Looking toward the woods, Azimuth growled, alerting the elf, who followed his gaze and saw a group of ten soldiers running their way. Eldahir sighted his bow and fired. The foremost man fell, and the wood elf took off running back the way he had come.

Come, Azimuth! There is no room for you to change back into a dragon. There are too many for you to take on in your present form.

Knowing he was right, Azimuth raced after him. *I wish I could breathe fire in this form. I'd show them who's boss!*

Eldahir laughed mentally, the smile on his face the only sign of his mirth. *Indeed, my friend. And what a sight that would be.*

The race was one-sided, and the pair had to slow down at times to keep the soldiers in sight. They were leading the enemy back to Tarquin and the others. Whenever a guras appeared confused, Eldahir would fire an arrow and down one of the soldiers, while Azimuth raced ahead, changed into elvan form, and told his friends what was happening.

"Let them come," Celedant exclaimed. "We shall catch some flies."

They spread out in a funnel shape with Eldahir positioning himself at the end of the trap. The elf had slung his bow across his back and waited with his sword drawn.

He called out to the Guras. "I tire of running. Come get me."

The Guras drew their swords and with a war cry, ran toward the elf.

As they neared, Tarquin and his friends stood up, weapons drawn.

The Guras stopped once they knew they had run into a trap and slowly dropped their weapons. Celedant came forward with Azimuth a step behind him.

Celedant asked the group of Guras, "Is your troop still going to Trudoc?"

A man who looked to be a sergeant cleared his throat, recognizing that he was dealing with a wizard or maybe even a warlock. He had heard rumors that those who possessed magic had ways to make a person talk. He wanted nothing to do with that, especially if that meant torture. "Yes, milord, that is our destination."

Celedant nodded and quick as a rabbit, cast a spell over the Guras. One by one they dropped to the ground with serene smiles on their faces. Hority, who had snuck up to stand too close behind the wizard fell in a heap. There were groans throughout their group as Celedant gravely said, "His curiosity will get him killed one day. Take my word for it. Botreg, take care of your charge."

Celedant walked to the middle of the group and cast another spell, effectively erasing the soldier's minds of the past half day. When they awoke, they would be confused as to what had happened, but the spell would prevent them from ever knowing. They would continue on their way with a vow not to tell anyone.

Botreg took one last deep breath of clean air as he approached the rancid-smelling dwarf. He picked him up and carried him back to camp like a child in his arms muttering, "Come along, Hority. Too bad there isn't a stream nearby. I could give ye a bath. When ye woke up, ye would most likely rub dirt over yerself, but at least ye would smell better."

CHAPTER TEN

Zeffan, a dwarf of the West, watched as his quarry drew to a stop and dismounted. Something was wrong. He sped up to a full run, cutting to the side of the pack of orcs ahead of him. They handed the reins of their stolen horses to several orcs that had stayed behind and began snaking through the grass.

The dwarf ran ahead of them between the tall grass until he saw a group of travelers that had surrounded some soldiers laying prone on the ground. One dwarf dressed in dark black was carrying a seemingly dead dwarf away from the others. He barely had time to access the situation and draw an arrow from his quiver, when the troop of white orcs broke from the tall grass.

He let fly his arrow, taking out the first orc. "Ware! Behind ye!"

Several arrows immediately flew out from the travelers, taking down the front row of attackers. They then broke apart as Tarquin, Eldahir, Azimuth, and Morganna ran at the attacking orcs. Zeffan still fired one arrow after another and watched as the battle developed. Tarquin slid to a stop in front of the largest of the orcs and blocked a mighty swing of the creature's sword. The human barely recoiled from the power of the attack. Instead, he countered with a thrust that penetrated the orcs guard going deep into its belly. The others engaged the troop of orcs, during which Zeffan kept up a steady stream of arrows that peppered the white orcs, bringing some down and wounding a great many more.

Seeing the battle well in hand, Zeffan dropped his bow and charged into the fray swinging his axe. He slid neatly through the legs of one of the white orcs and chopped upward. Then as the creature fell, he reversed his stroke and brought the axe down, splitting the back of its head. By this time, the ground was covered with orcan dead. The few remaining orcs retreated from whence they had come.

The foreign dwarf turned in the tall grass and sprinted after the retreating orcs. He caught the first and brought it down with a swift swing of his axe. Then an orc running before him dropped to the ground with an arrow in the back. He, the man, and the elves killed the remaining orcs before they could reach their tethered horses.

The two orc guards abandoned the horses and ran at Zeffan, who deftly avoided their blows, turning one with his axe. Redirecting his weapon, he struck one in the leg and as it fell, took off its head. The second one struck, hitting the dwarf in the shoulder. But that seemed to make Zeffan madder. He turned in a circle, gaining speed and power and sliced through the orc's torso, which sprayed blood into the air as it fell to the ground.

Standing behind him were Eldahir, Morganna, Azimuth, and Tarquin, their weapons still drawn, unsure they could trust the dwarf before them. Zeffan turned and stared at the newcomers, breathing heavily from his ordeal of running behind the mounted orcs. Hesitantly, he raised a hand in welcome. He knew that if he ran for cover, the elves could easily put three arrows in his back before he was more than a few feet away.

A youngish human wiped his blade on a hand full of grass, sheathed his sword, and advanced. Zeffan grounded his axe cautiously waiting. He had seen the man in action and knew he was a superior swordsman whom he believed had lived an extremely hard life. The dwarf hoped he was friendly. The man with shaggy brown hair called out. "Friend, my name is Tarquin. Be at ease. It seems we both wanted these foul beasts dead. I, myself, have been attacked by similar orcs in the forest of the elves in the East."

Zeffan stepped cautiously forward. He had seen such rogues wander the land before and was warry. He would later be astounded when he discovered that this so-called rogue was a prince of Partha. These had taken prisoners, however, and had them bound and laying on the ground being watched over by the remainder of the group.

Pointing in the direction of the prisoners, Zeffan said, "Those are Guras mercenaries and serve the warlock guild in Trudoc. Ye will never find something as vile as that ilk."

Tarquin pointed at the prisoners. "We follow a large band of these men, who defiled this monk's valley."

Hority, who had miraculously awoken from the spell, was up and on the move.

Tarquin called out harshly, "Stop this minute, Hority."

Zeffan turned to find the smallish dwarf sneaking up behind him. The dwarf in the tattered frock halted, suddenly seeing something of interest on a dead orc. "Look, Tarquin, an animal's skull! Can I keep it for further study?"

The strange dwarf watched what was transpiring with fascination.

The human turned to a darkly dressed dwarf who had just reached them and asked, "What do you think, Botreg? Shall he keep it? Hority is your charge."

The dark dwarf apologized. "He woke early from the spell, and I could barely catch up to him." Then he nodded adding to Hority. "Whatever ye think is interesting, ye can take to examine. Mind ye put the findings in yer book not yer satchel. Then see to this dwarf's shoulder."

Hority approached the newcomer, his smell preceding him. Zeffan looked askance.

"This is Hority, a Clorian monk and a great healer, despite his smell," Botreg explained.

Zeffan knew these were eastern folk by their accents and that they traveled with elves. The only elves he had ever come across had been traders from the East.

"Sorry, Master Dwarf, as I was saying these men attacked a monastery to which yon monk served as protector," Tarquin explained. "That is why we are here. What of you?"

"I am called Zeffan, and I roam the woodlands working for whomever will have me," the Traveler explained.

The other dwarfs looked at one another. Even Hority muttered a questionable, "Human? Yer short for one of them and look an awful lot like a dwarf."

Tarquin pointed to the other dwarves. "Don't be alarmed by their responses. I, too, was tagged as a Zeffan when I served in the dwarvan army."

Zeffan laughed for the first time. "I bet ye was."

CHAPTER ELEVEN

T he group mounted their steeds and rode towards the woods with Zeffan mounted on one of the orcan horses and guiding the other horses with the stolen goods from the wagon train behind him. After several days journey through the dense forest, they emerged onto a gradual sloping plain that led to the sea.

Zeffan pointed to the city. "Trudoc lies before ye. It is one of the greatest merchant towns on the west coast. See yon tallest tower sticking up in the middle of the city? That is the warlock guild's seat of power."

They sat in peace for a while, watching as a flotilla of white sails headed out with the morning tide.

Celedant motioned to the city. "It seems we have reached our destination. Yet there is no sign of the Guras."

"If it's the Guras ye seek," Zeffan said. "They will be at the tower."

"There was a warlock with the men we followed," Tarquin began. "Would he be there as well?"

"Most certainly," the Dwarf replied. "He was no doubt sent out by the warlock leader in charge of that place."

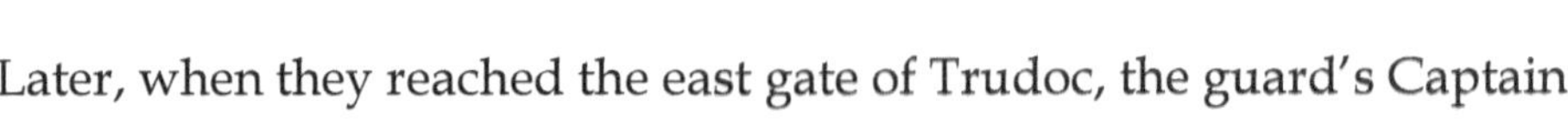

Later, when they reached the east gate of Trudoc, the guard's Captain called out. "Hoy, Zeffan, what brings you here?"

The Dwarf smiled. "I'm in search of employment."

The Guard smiled. "Well then, I'm sure you'll find something to your liking here."

It took only a little while to get information at the main gate. Overseeing the gate, the captain of the guard knew Zeffan and readily took Celedant and Tarquin along with the trusted dwarf to a back room, locking the door behind him. He greedily took the five gold pieces offered by Celedant in exchange for information.

Somehow, Hority had given Botreg the slip and followed the others with the guardsman. The unkempt dwarf immediately filled the room with his powerful odor. But he ignored the others, elated at the mess in the room and thinking immediately that this was a holy place of Clor. He at once began searching through the trash spread across the floor.

Tarquin immediately assuaged the Captain's concern. "Don't let him bother you. He is completely unconcerned with what we say. He is at home amongst the garbage, lost in a world of his own making."

The guard's captain eyed the smelly little dwarf and shrugged. "He smells like he belongs in a sewer." Shrugging, he got back to business. "Its best that no one knows I told you this. But the man you are following is the grand warlock of the guild Tyras. One cannot be too careful when dealing with them. An evil lot they be. Their mercenary soldiers are also fanatics."

"Where might they be found?" Celedant asked.

The Captain leaned out his window and pointed west. "It the largest building in the city."

"One more question," Celedant said. "Where might we find a ship's captain?"

"Go to the docks and see the dock master," the man explained. "He knows where every ship that sets sail is going. And if it's passage, you're looking for, he can tell you about that as well."

The Captain looked at them as if no more information were forthcoming and stated, "If that's all. I've a tour of the gatehouse to do."

The others quietly filed out of the small room and gathered just to the side of the gate. Botreg literally had to pull the dirty dwarf after them. Hority had found a bag of rotten food and was quietly spreading it out on the ground. Before he left, the dwarf had grabbed a mealy apple half-eaten and happily bit into it, offering Botreg the rest. Tarquin's best friend shook his head, pulling even harder on the dwarf, while muttering something indecipherable under his breath.

Once everyone was gathered outside, Tarquin asked, "You inquired about a ship. Will we be taking a trip on the ocean?"

"The Guras are from Markdale on the other side of the ocean," Celedant replied. "I'm just gathering information for any path we may need to take in this adventure." He looked around and rubbed his hands. "Now to find lodgings."

Botreg leaned in with a smile on his face. "We go to the city center and take the choicest one there. Right?"

Celedant shook his head. "I'm afraid not, my friend. We cannot stay in an expensive hotel. Our funds are limited, and we may need a ship. Come. We'll find a decent, cheap hotel along the way. Besides, I would like one that oversees this warlock's guild."

"We will have no trouble with gold, once I sell these horses and trade goods," Zeffan chimed in. "Besides, I know just the right place for us to stay."

"I thought you might be leaving us once we got to the city," Tarquin said.

The Dwarf shrugged. "I'm currently free of any obligations, and ye have piqued me curiosity. Besides, this looks to be quite some adventure, and I would like to tag along if ye have no objection."

"By all means," Tarquin said after getting a nod from Celedant. "Having another good fighter on our side could prove to be quite helpful."

CHAPTER TWELVE

As Cyra and Talchic rode the trail to the south, the sorceress filled him in. "We're going to the white orc city ruled by their leader, Bloody Claw. They once gave me sanctuary in exchange for the use of my powers. I will stay in the orcan city. I am afraid the warlocks that rule Trudoc would perceive my powers and imprison me. Talchic, you will take up residence in the city to keep watch on the warlock's enclave," she commanded. "My ultimate plan is to take over the warlock guild and rule Trudoc. In the meantime, I want to know everything you can find out about the guild and their headquarters."

The rest of their journey continued mostly in silence, until they approached the orcan city on their horses, which was fine with Talchic. He and Cyra did not have casual conversations. He thought she might be incapable of such a thing, unless it had to do with their current situation. He wished that he could go off on his own, but without her protection, he could end up in a situation where he could not protect himself. Losing an arm was quite inconvenient.

"It has been some time since I was last here," she called over to Talchic. "Let's hope the same chieftain is still in power. He will remember me and my abilities. Otherwise, I might have to impress a new one with my spells."

Talchic nodded. That meant death to the white orcs. But could she fend off the town's entire military force? He knew she was very powerful, but he wasn't sure if even she could accomplish such a feat. He hoped for both their sakes that she could if it proved necessary.

They drew up their mounts as they came to a small river crossing issuing forth from a deep valley. Twelve white orcs stepped onto the trail.

Talchic readied a spell in case things did not go as Cyra planned.

Cyra called out to the orcs, "Does Bloody Claw still rule here?"

The lead soldier nodded. "He still rules us, and his claws stay wet with the blood of our enemies. I remember you, witch. Though the years have not been exceedingly kind to you. I will fetch the horse guards to guide you to the city."

Cyra and Talchic waited some thirty clicks of the clock until ten white orcs finally rode up. The Captain, in full plate mail, called to Cyra, "Bloody Claw will see you, witch."

They were escorted into town. Talchic noted small towers of stone built along the road, flying flags painted with a bloody claw on them. Orcs manned the tops of the small fortresses. He was amazed as they crested a small hill and the city opened up before them. It was built entirely of stone and well-built at that with fitted stone, not like the shoddy construction of the eastern orcs that he was used to seeing.

The gatehouse was a full three stories high and well patrolled. As they rode through the gate, Talchic noticed two gates and a portcullis guarding the interior. Their escorts proceeded up a long road lined with stone houses. There were homes interspersed with businesses. Never had Talchic seen such an orcan city.

Cyra laughed. "Quit gawking. What you are seeing is real. This city rivals Trudoc. In fact, they could probably take that city over if it weren't needed for trade."

They drew up in front of a multileveled castle. "The one-armed man can wait here," the orcan Captain said. "He is under the claws' protection and will not be bothered."

Cyra looked to Talchic. "This may take a bit. The Claw likes his negotiations."

Celedant and his friends rode their horses through a section of the city, keeping their eyes on the great tower that stood higher than any other in Trudoc. They came to a crossroad, and before them lay the warlock's compound that consisted of a huge manor house. At its center was a tall lone tower that reached into the sky. Celedant led his little troop around the warlock's guild. There were three main gates well-guarded by Guras, two in front and one at the back of the mansion. At this early hour, they watched as servants came and went under the watchful gaze of the guards.

Celedant turned in his saddle and spoke quietly. "I feel a great dark power emanating from this compound. It is warded against magic on the outside, but I think I have a spell that will help in finding what was stolen from the Clorian library."

"Clor help us. But look they are carting out their garbage," Hority said, aghast. "Heretics they be. Their waste should be accounted for and stored on the property. This reeks of cleanliness and is the worst of all sins."

Tarquin, who had been riding behind the dwarf in the wake of Hority's odor said, "Steady, my stout monk. We cannot do anything about this unholy place yet. Come nightfall in the next few days, we will strike at the heathens."

The others smiled at what Tarquin had said to soothe the monk, fearing Hority would charge the gate and give them away. When

Hority was incensed, he did not stop to think, but would charge into the middle of a fray unconcerned for his own safety.

Spotting an inn across from the side of the mansion, they took rooms there. Hority was naturally given a space in the stables, as no innkeeper would allow the monk inside to foul his establishment. Unfortunately, only one of the rooms looked out at the warlock's mansion. Celedant opened the window and regarded the structure, recalling the ride around the mansion. The entranceways were guarded, but not heavily.

The friends ate a warm, hearty meal first. Botreg had taken Hority's out to the stable to him. It was a welcome repast. On the road, they often had to make do with hardtack and dried meat and the occasional fruit, when they passed some. Once they set their plan into motion, they would have to make a hasty retreat, and it could be a while before they savored another hot meal.

"There are too many men posted at the gates on all sides but the rear entrance," Celedant said after returning to his room, and sneaking Hority inside. "The only ones I saw were up by the back door, where the wagons pull up for the garbage. That will be our entrance."

"Heretics," Hority muttered under his breath.

"We will deal with the heretics in due time and quietly at night," Celedant assured him.

They stayed at the inn for several days, watching and waiting. Noting that the guards changed exactly at noon and midnight, everyone agreed that they would strike at midnight.

That night, they waited until a cloud covered the moon. Celedant called his little group into his room and briefed them. "Not all of us will go. The fewer we send in, the less chance we have of being spotted. Tarquin, Botreg, Morganna, Azimuth, and I will go."

Hority was about to express his complaint but Botreg interrupted. "They will know yer coming from a mile away. Ye have not bathed in weeks and stink to high heaven."

The monk knew that what Botreg said was true, but he did not have to like it. He moved to the corner of the room to mope and rifle through his satchel. The sad monk sat down. He knew of another way into the manor, but he decided not to share it with the raiding party.

Unbeknownst to the others, Botreg had treated him harshly when he returned with rotten fruit or some other odiferous debris. So, Hority kept silent, waiting for the right time to tell them of the secret way he had discovered during his hunt for holy garbage.

"We'll take out the guards right before their shift ends," Celedant continued. "Then their replacements. I imagine the map is valuable to them. So, I'm guessing it will be kept in the tower. Just in case I don't make it to the tower, but you do, don't take the map. Draw a copy or memorize it. We want them to think we never made it to the top or if we did, that we didn't have enough time to search for it."

"I will be in the open while I pick the gate's lock," Botreg said. "Also, there are sure to be people in the street even at that hour. I'm quick, but it'll be risky."

"I may be able to aid in our endeavor," Celedant said. "I will cast a spell to cover our advance. Once inside, kill with extreme care. We can't leave bodies strewn about everywhere."

The others nodded their consent and left for their rooms to get prepared. They donned dark clothes and rubbed ashes on their faces and any exposed skin to make them invisible in the dark of night.

Later that night, the friends met again in the wizard's room. The four who were going, were nervous and ready to get on with the night proceedings.

"We'll leave from one of the inn's back windows and should be able to make it to the manor's wall with a little caution," Celedant informed them.

The members about to leave said their goodbyes. Eldahir hugged his wife, Morganna, tightly. An open display of love not often seen in elves by outsiders.

"Take care, dearest heart," Eldahir told her. "The place is filled with evil warlocks, and the danger will be great."

Morganna smiled, her eyes filled with her love for him. "Don't worry. I, too, have magic and can give as good as I get."

Chapter Thirteen

The witch was led through the castle to the main hall where Bloody Claw waited, sitting at the far end in a huge leather chair with one leg thrown over the arm rest. The claw was wearing fine silk robes, obviously traded for in Trudoc because nothing so finely made could be found in this part of the world. He motioned her forward to a chair that faced his. A small table with wine and fruit from all over the West, stood beside her chair, and an orcan servant poured her a small amount of drink before retreating a short distance. Cyra knew that the claw liked to hear himself talk. She would be in for a long ordeal.

Once seated and refreshed with wine, the orc chieftain asked, "How is my witch? Was the East good to you?"

"No and yes," she answered. "I have garnered a new disgust for the undead and their untrustworthy ways."

The orc nodded. "I never found them useful, and I'm glad there are few in my territory. We hunt them down whenever they appear in our lands." He cocked his head to study her closer. "You look different from the young woman who had gone east these years ago. What has happened?"

"Tis the sacrifice one has to make to become a more powerful sorceress," Cyra answered. She had undergone a serious change when serving the vampire warlock, Taza. Gone was her beautiful appearance. Now she bore an aged and haggard look – a side effect of Taza's infusion of magical power from the Staff of Adois.

They talked about what had happened since she had been gone, and she was surprised to learn that the orc had spread his kingdom to the south some fifty miles.

"I have a thousand more soldiers to command, and generals to lead the armies. My city grows under my rule, and I have a son ready to take over when I die."

Cyra could see the hunger in his eyes for more land and diplomatically said, "Sometimes a kingdom can bite off more than it can chew. Also, an ambitious son might act and bring change according to his own plans not yours. You must be worried about that." She could see the beginning of anger rising in his eyes, but she continued anyway. "Be that as it may, what would you say if you had an ally ruling Trudoc, instead of just a trading partner?"

The Claw arched an eyebrow. "Just what are you proposing, my witch?"

"That city is ruled by the upper class, but propped up by the warlocks and sorceresses," she began. "It is my plan to take over leadership of the tower, and all the magic users that will join me. Then I will rule the city as well, and you will have a partner."

The orc chief laughed. "You alone have that kind of power?"

"Yes," Cyra replied, raising her head haughtily. "I could blow the tower apart with a thought if I wanted to." To embellish her power she added, "The one-armed warlock I travel with is also powerful. Together, we make a formidable team."

"I already have favorable treaties with Trudoc," the Claw stated. He shrugged, appearing nonchalant about what she proposed. "They don't bother me, and I have fair trading agreements for the goods that come into the harbor."

She smiled. "How about a permanent fortress in the city with enough soldiers to seize Trudoc if need be. You could also control the docks from afar. It would be best to allow the humans to run them and to keep their guards upon the walls, so that the populous doesn't suspect anything is afoul."

"What would you need from me, Cyra?" he asked his anger gone, replaced by curiosity and a power-hungry bearing that spiked his interest in what the witch had to offer.

With all the charm she could express she said, "All I need to start are two hundred of your finest soldiers."

The orc liked the idea. She could tell. "Such a change has come over the little girl that I took in all those years ago. In the short term, what do I get from this endeavor?"

She had him. He was talking gold and the bigger picture of this enterprise that could mean more territory and more riches. She cocked her head and said, "Two gold pieces per orc to you for the use of the soldiers and fifty gold pieces for the soldiers a month until my business is finalized. Then you can move in and with the help of my guild, and we can silently take over the city."

The bloody claw slapped his hand on the chair arm and demanded, "Five hundred gold for the use of my orcs. That is what it will take for our partnership."

She shook her head. "Four hundred gold. I can go no higher."

The white orc stared deeply in her eyes, and she saw fear. He had gotten his teeth into this venture and did not want to lose out on it. Had he been any good at math, he would have realized that she was offering no more than before. She had just put in another way. Finally, he relented. "Done. My friend, this endeavor will be fun."

The Chief gave a hearty laugh that exposed his filed teeth, and he spit in his palm before offering it to Cyra. She approached the throne and in turn, spit in her own palm before grasping the chieftain's hand. The deal was sealed. She handed over a pouch that was weighty and jingled much to the chieftain's liking.

He clapped his big hands and ordered more wine to be brought forward, which Cyra readily accepted. She could tell it was not poisoned so she took a deep swallow. After all, why kill her. The Claw now had too much to gain.

The orc smacked his lips. "I will give you two hundred of my finest warriors because I want nothing to befall my favorite witch, especially when she is about to enhance my fortunes."

She smiled and nodded her head at the kind gesture. "I will protect them to the best of my abilities."

Cyra then stood up, and waving goodbye to the chief, exited the hall. She was pleased the negotiations had gone so well. This was a crucial step in her plan. Without the white orcs as her army, taking over the tower and city would have been difficult, if not impossible. When she reached the front door, where Talchic waited, she smiled broadly.

"Everything is in place. We'll have two hundred orcan warriors to aid us in taking over Trudoc. I can smell the sweet scent of victory."

I hope you're right, Talchic thought. *Or this might mean the death of both of us.*

Chapter Fourteen

C eledant and the ones that was going on the mission went to one of the back rooms they shared. Opening the window, they went through it one by one and climbed down a knotted rope. The dark clad group stopped at the end of the alleyway to get a good look at the road ahead. The traffic was light at midnight, but there were still some revelers out and about. The Wizard waited for the right time and cast a spell that obscured them from the eyes of anyone looking their way. They then started across the street moving silently. Anyone looking at them saw nothing more than a darkened fog floating across the street. Celedant hoped that no one would realize that there was actually no fog on this night. As time passed, the fog dissipated as the spell wore off.

As they neared the corner of the wall surrounding the mansion, they turned the corner and after a hundred paces, they were at the gate where the garbage was hauled out. As they moved slowly through the darkness cast by the wall, Botreg ran ahead. He poured oil on the hinges and got to work. People passing in the night paid them little mind. He quickly had the lock open and thanks to the oil the dark dwarf had coated the hinges with, the gate opened with only the slightest squeak.

They slipped through the gate, hugging the manor's hedges as they neared their goal. Once they were near the loading dock, Botreg and Morganna went ahead and in a moment, they heard the dwarf quietly call for them. The remaining three hurried to the double doors, hugging the wall while waiting for the relief guards.

"Where are the bodies?" Tarquin whispered to Botreg.

The dwarf pointed at the hedges. "Behind them bushes."

Celedant shushed them, and they continued to wait.

Finally, the double doors were pushed open, and two guards stood for a second looking for their fellows. That was all it took for the assassin and the former illanni. They slipped behind the two guards, and neatly covered their mouths, before slitting their throats. When they were sure the guards were dead, the dwarf and elf dragged the bodies and deposited them behind the hedges with their fallen comrades.

The party of adventures entered the manor and found themselves in the kitchen. Celedant quickly led them up a narrow stairway that ended in the main hall. He stopped them on the stairs as he scanned the room. The only light came from several flickering torches. He then motioned for the rest to come forward.

"I'm going to try a small bit of magic to locate the tower," Celedant whispered. "In a manor filled with warlocks, I don't think they'll notice such a simple spell."

Celedant stepped into the hallway, chanting a few words. He stared off in the distance. When he came out of the trance, he said, "Come. It is but a short distance from here."

The wizard quickly walked to the right, across the main hall to another doorway. He cracked it open and peered down another corridor. He saw no movement, so he motioned the others to follow him. Two turns to make, and they would reach the tower.

They had gone halfway to the first turn of the corridor when a door opened opposite them. As the party was about to spring into action, time seemed to slow down. Celedant lowered his staff, Forestae, and the other's weapons were ready. They were about to charge the two men, who had opened their mouths to call out. No sound, however, escaped. The men suddenly dropped to the floor. Hovering over them was the smiling face of Hority.

"Well done, but we commanded you to stay at the inn," Tarquin whispered.

The smell was even more drastic than before. "I found us a quick way out, where ye'll not need to cross the street," Hority said.

Celedant stepped forward. "Put those two bodies in the room and let's go," he said sternly.

They moved down two more hallways before Celedant motioned for Botreg to come forward. "The door should be around the corner."

The dwarf motioned to Morganna. "I'll look and see what awaits us. If its but a single guard, ye can take the shot. If there are two, I'll slide down the wall and kill the first one while ye put an arrow in the other."

The elf signaled that she was ready. The assassin moved his head ever so slowly as he peeked down the corridor in the darkness, which he could do without alerting the guards. There were indeed two guards, and he held up two fingers. Morganna got two arrows out, ready to shoot both guards if needed.

Botreg inched forward, his body pressed up against the shadowy wall. The only light came from a flickering torch by the doorway. He was within several feet of the first guard, who seemed to be staring at the opposite wall.

He's sleeping on his feet, the dwarf thought.

Then with a speed that only a trained assassin could obtain, Botreg sprang. He felt Morganna's arrow shoot through his hair as he leapt onto the first guard, his dagger out and slicing through the man's throat. He rolled off the dying guard and saw the second guard slumped against the wall Morganna's arrow transfixed in the man's neck. He was still moving a little bit and blood bubbled out of his mouth as Botreg slid over to him. In one quick thrust, he jabbed his dagger into the man's heart, assuring he would make no more sound.

As the others came forward, Botreg chided the elf. "Missed the kill shot."

Morganna smiled. "Your wild spring onto the man's back got in the way of my shot. There for a second, I thought I had shot you in the head."

"Enough," Celedant ordered. "Hide the bodies and head up the stairs."

Azimuth, using his draconic strength, grabbed both men by their collars and dragged them up the stairs, depositing them around the first turn so that anyone at the bottom of the steps would not see them.

Celedant cast a spell on his staff, Forestae, to give out light for the ascent. The stairs wound round and round. Any moment, they expected someone to come barreling into them, and a bloody fight to ensue. Then, the stairs made a turn right into a massive wooden door, wrapped with several bars of iron.

The wizard turned and said, "Botreg, your expertise I believe."

The dark dwarf edged by everyone to examine the door and the steps leading to it. He pointed. "There are scrape marks on that second stair. It's a trap."

Botreg carefully stepped over the trap and examined the door cautiously. He went through several tests, running a thin wire around the door and carefully scanning the door latch.

Finally, he shrugged and turned to Celedant whispering, "Can ye put a protection spell around all of us. I don't want there to be a hidden trap like the one we faced, when the zombies had us cornered in Dormin during the war."

"Quite right," Celedant responded in a whisper.

Once the spell was cast, Botreg got to work on the door's lock. He had his lock picks out in his hands, working as silently as he could. Finally, there was an audible click, and Botreg opened the door.

Hority made to go up the stairs and through the door, but Tarquin put a firm hand on his chest. "Not quite yet, my smelly friend."

Botreg led them into a round room, followed by Celedant and the rest of the party. The room was neat, too neat for Celedant's liking.

Hority gave a disparaging look of disgust. The wizard then turned and cast a simple spell that issued from the head of his staff toward the door. A shimmering light glowed in the doorway. The others did not question what Celedant had done. In fact, the wizard had cast a silence spell on the doorway to keep others from hearing what was occurring within.

Then they heard a creak and rumble, as a great stone figure detached itself from the wall and took a stiff step toward them. Azimuth and Celedant immediately called, "Stone golem!"

They had faced such creatures before, on their quest to assemble the staff of Adaman.

Tarquin stepped forward, swinging Dragon Bolt. The sword blazed red, but hardly injured the golem. With one hand, the golem slapped Tarquin away, and the prince's body slammed into the tower wall. Celedant started a spell, chanting out loud, causing the legs of the golem to turn into mud, upsetting its balance, and causing the creature to flail its arms to keep upright.

Hority vaulted through the air, his feet landing squarely on the golem's chest. It legs now a mass of mud, unbalanced the creature, and it toppled over onto its back. Touching it with his branch the creature ceased to move and lay still, before slowly crumbling into rocky debris.

Then from the steps that led upward, they heard an incantation. Celedant dove, landing beside the crumbled mass of the golem before getting off a quick spell. Small darts of green energy shot forth, striking the attacking warlock before he could finish his spell. Celedant assumed it was Tyras, the leader of the band of men that had attacked the Clorian valley. Leaning against the wall, Tarquin was wide open for an attack. Knowing better than to get in the middle of dueling magic users, he dropped to the ground and crawled away as quickly as possible. The group heard curses before the newly arrived warlock sent off magical balls of energy that struck Celedant, even as he rolled away, setting his shirt ablaze. Hority appeared in front of the warlock.

Using his staff, Tyras swept Hority's legs out from under him and in the same motion, knocked the monk's branch across the room.

Then the warlock cast a lightning bolt spell, aimed where Celedant was temporarily blocked from view. The bolt missed Celedant, and ricocheted around the room, sending the rest of his companions scrambling for cover. The lightning bolt bounced off the walls of the circular room before it died out. Morganna had a clear shot at the warlock, and she let loose an arrow. The arrow bounced off a protection spell, the warlock had just cast and shot upward to splinter against the ceiling. Then Botreg appeared behind their opponent stabbing with his dagger. But that, too, could not penetrate the wall of protection. The warlock used his staff to strike Botreg in the pit of the stomach, quickly bringing it upward, he caught the assassin under the chin, lifting up the dwarf and flinging him back down the stairs.

With the flames on his shirt put out, Celedant was up and running toward the warlock. Calling a single word, he thrust his staff into the protection spell erected around his opponent. The spell blazed a dark green color and was gone. Celedant thrust his staff Forestae into the warlock's midsection and then brought it down on the back of his head. It drove the warlock to his knees. Then he brought the full weight of his sword on the warlock's skull. The magic user dropped to the floor and lay still, blood pooling under his head.

"Search for a map," he ordered the others.

There were three rooms above the first, and they split up to search them all.

Tarquin turned to Hority. Pointing to the main door, he commanded, "Sit by that door and use your branch if need be."

In the third room at the top of the tower, Morganna found a long thin container. She opened it and called to the others. "I think this might be it."

Celedant quickly ran to her side. She held in her hands a map of the western ocean and coast. He carefully scanned the parchment.

Beside him, Tarquin warned, "We don't have much time."

The wizard held up his hand. 'Silence. I'm memorizing the map, and it takes a little time. Finishing, he handed it back to Morganna. "Put this back exactly where you found it. Now all of you, grab a handful of papers or scrolls. We must make it look like we robbed the place. We don't want them to know that we are heading west, too."

Celedant put all the looted paperwork into a large bag that no one had noticed he was carrying at the start of the mission. They exited the tower room, with Botreg relocking the door. Then it was around and around the stairs back down the way they had come. At the bottom, they stopped for a moment to make sure the corridor was empty of guards, and then poured out into the hallway. At that time, a patrol turned the corner, and all hell broke loose.

Chapter Fifteen

Morganna fired an arrow that took down the leader of the patrol.

Celedant called to the smelly dwarf over the shouts of the guards. "Hority, it seems your way out of here is the best chance we have. Lead on."

"Oh, it's a wonderful sewer not cleaned in decades," the monk said, causing expressions of distaste from his companions.

Botreg gave him a shove in the back toward the way they had come.

Hority pushed himself up to the front of the others, while the guards clashed with Tarquin, Azimuth, and Botreg. The three held off five guards as the six members of the company retraced their steps to the place where they had found Hority. For once, they were happy to have the smell of the dwarf drifting back into their faces. It would be hard to lose him as long as they could smell him.

Morganna picked off the guards with her arrows, while Tarquin, Azimuth, and Botreg fought using their superior swordsmanship to cut down the two guards they faced. Before they could engage the last one, Morganna's arrow took the man in the throat.

She shouted, "Retreat!"

They pivoted and ran. Morganna shot one last arrow at the guards now pouring around the corner, drawn by the commotion of the fight.

Catching up with the others, Tarquin called out what was happening.

"We're here," Hority shouted back.

Morganna shut and locked the door. She knelt down using her elvan heritage to listen to what was occurring outside the room in the hallway. All she heard was a mass of boots pounding down the corridor away from them.

The monk led them to a well with the rope that had been pulled all the way up. The bucket sat beside the opening. "There is a ladder that leads down to the dry bed of an aquifer," he explained. "Go down one at a time."

One by one, the group descended the ladder and were soon standing on a sandy floor. It was pitch black, but everyone could see in the dark. Even Tarquin, thanks to his training with the dwarvan King's Borderers.

Before long, Celedant called for them to stop. "I think I need a little light to see where we are."

The light from Forestae showed an aquifer covered in sand and debris that delighted the Clorian monk. His eyes went wide at the treasure spread across the floor before him in the form of debris left by flooding water. On the way to the manor, he had rushed by such treasures to meet Tarquin.

Celedant handed the dwarf a pile of filth that soon disappeared into his satchel. "Come my odiferous friend, back to the inn."

He flashed a smile and silently praised Clor for sending him such close friends. The dwarf led the way. "There is the crack in the wall of the aquifer. It leads to the sewers."

Hority passed through the crack, at home in the filthy, nauseating tunnels. The rest of the group made quick time at a fast walk down the metal pathway along the side of the wall, where the sewer ran. They made pretty good time, until everyone felt a horrific, shrill screaming in their heads. Nearly everyone dropped to their knees, their hands pressed to their ears. Celedant, protected by a warding spell was unaffected, and he began channeling a spell.

Hority screamed, "Foes!" And he darted down the tunnel.

Celedant cast his spell, sending a bright fiery light shooting down the sewer, careful to avoid his friends. The light showed three figures ahead of them. The spell caused them to shriek louder and turn their backs to the group. The figures were free floating hags, their faces green with clinging flesh hanging from their bony heads, all with their mouths open and emitting a brain numbing screech. Celedant's spell hit the first monster, and it fell into the ooze that flowed through the tunnel. The creature lay in the sewer, its face looking up as it slowly sank beneath the foul water. Hority recovered faster than the others and began battling another one of the monsters, striking out with his pumas topped branch, he aimed at the creature's head. Finally, his staff caught the creature in the face. Its head turned to ash, and the creature fell dead before him. He used his foot to shove the body into the sewage.

While Hority was locked in battle with the first creature, the wizard got off another spell. A flash of light sped past him and engulfed the third monster where it floated. It was in pain and opened its mouth even wider, screeching and causing those near Celedant to writhe in pain. Blood welled from their ears, nose, and eyes. Finally, Morganna on all fours pulled an arrow from her quiver and got a shot away. The arrow struck true in the middle of the last creature's forehead.

Still reeling, Tarquin and the others staggered to their feet, their hearing greatly decreased. Celedant motioned them forward. "Hority! Get us out of this accursed place."

The dwarf took the lead through the vile sewer until they reached a ladder that led upward to a round medal grate. Hority pushed upward and peered around the sewer entrance. No one was in the stable yard. Up and out, he went, followed by the rest of the dazed group. They went to the horse watering trough and washed the blood and ashes from their faces, as well as the grunge from their hands and boots. Then they entered the inn. Without stopping, they quickly headed up the stairs to their rooms.

When they were halfway down the hallway, Celedant called out, "Meet in my room as soon as possible."

After cleaning up and changing into fresh clothing, the group assembled in the wizard's room, all but Hority. When the dwarf entered the room, the others made a pathway for him to stand by Botreg.

"I do not know what those creatures were, but they nearly killed us," Celedant began. "We were saved only by the bravery of Hority. Do any of you know what they were. I have not run across any such creatures in my travels, nor read about them in Edain's library."

Everyone shook their heads in a mutual no.

"It could have been by chance and our bad luck that they were there in the sewers. Or perhaps they were guards to the tower. Who knows for sure where our enemies lie?" Tarquin said.

The wizard spoke sternly to all. "We will move to an inn by the docks in the morning, and I will visit the harbor master. I have memorized the map but will not put pen to parchment until we are at sea. I would hate for our mission to end by some overzealous guardsman stopping us to examine what we are carrying."

Celedant had just finished explaining his plan to the group when the top of the tower blew up, shaking the floor beneath them. They rushed to the window to stare at the fire coming out of the tower like a giant chimney. The fiery debris rained down to the streets below, sending late night revelers running and screaming.

Celedant looked somewhat surprised. "Change of plans. We leave now and head to the docks. The taverns will still be open. We can find cheap rooms there."

Melgor or Talchic, as he was now known, had been sent by Cyra to observe the warlock Tower. He happened to be watching it from the street, when he saw the flashes of light from its top floor. He was not aware that Celedant was responsible for the lights in the tower, but he could feel the magic being wielded there and knew that a battle was underway.

Cyra needed to be alerted to this. A powerplay had occurred, and she just might be able to swoop in and take control. He quickly knelt and began a summoning spell. Cyra soon stood before him.

She looked quite displeased, and Talchic, knowing of her powerful magic, suddenly feared for his life.

"Why have you bothered me?"

Talchic told her about what had just occurred, and she quickly cast a spell to see into the recent past and what had happened in the tower room. She saw Celedant and Tarquin searching for a scroll in the room and interestingly enough leave it behind.

Grabbing the warlock's hand, she teleported them both directly into the room. The protection to magic spells that had surrounded the enclave was easily brushed aside, allowing her to enter the tower. They could hear the sound of a warning bell going off in the distance. She scanned the room, noticing the destroyed golem and dead warlock. There also was banging on the door. Someone was using a battering ram to enter. Dust flew from the stout oak door with each strike.

"Talchic, watch the door and kill whoever enters," she commanded. "I will find the document Celedant wanted, if it is still here."

At the sound of his rival's name, Talchic instantly became alert. Celedant was an old foe back before the warlocks and sorceresses of the evil city of Dormin had taken his right arm in an epic magical battle. He positioned himself so he could watch both the door and Cyra. She disappeared up a set of stairs into another room. The battering continued. The hinges were weakening, about to give way, when the door collapsed. Talchic hurriedly cast a spell, and a bright flame shot forth from his hand. He moved it up and down and sideways incinerating whoever stood in the stairway.

Then he heard Cyra call out to him. "I have it. Hurry to me!"

The warlock turned and ran. He heard the voices of his foes advancing up the stairway. Reaching the top of the steps, he shot into the other room, and his arm was quickly grasped by Cyra. He immediately felt a protection spell form around them just before there was a tremendous explosion. The top of the tower exploded, throwing debris in all directions. But the two magic users were long gone, reappearing in Cyra's room in the white orc's compound. She knew where Celedant and his pets were going and better yet, she had the map. She reasoned that it must have been left behind so that the warlocks would not miss it.

What Celedant had been so eager hide, she had just taken the more direct route, destroying any evidence of its existence.

Celedant and the company quietly left the inn in the middle of the night, while pieces of the tower burned in the streets, drawing a crowd of onlookers. They hurried to the docks, which were still crowded with sailors, drunk on the cheap grog that the bars and inns served.

"I know of a halfway decent inn just ahead," Zeffan called to the others. "At least we can trust them not to steal the horses."

The dwarf led them to a run-down building, dismounted, and entered through a thick wooden door bound by wrought iron. There were also fortress-like doors leading to the stables.

He returned a quarter-turn of the clock later. "I have two rooms, the last in the inn. We'll have to sleep rough. Dismount and follow me."

He led them to the stable door and pounded on it. The doors were opened by three well-armed men. The area within was lit by a lantern. After a quick word with Zeffan, the men took the horses into the stables. Celedant and the others entered the inn through a side door.

Zeffan paused at the door. "May I welcome you to the Hammerhead Inn. It's the best around."

The common room was crowded with well to do patrons, consisting of ship captains and traders from all parts of the west. Zeffan led them up the stairs, and they settled into their rooms. They were small but both had clean painted walls and the floors were well swept. Celedant spent some time staring out at the docks. There, ships were lit and docked well out into the harbor. Since there weren't enough beds, most of the group slept on pallets on the floor, provided by the Innkeeper.

The next day, Zeffan conferred with Celedant. "We can go to the harbor master after we eat. They have a tower that overlooks the harbor. We will find him there, and he'll know the comings and goings of all the ships. I suggest that ye and Tarquin accompany me. I am known, and we'll be less likely to be charged too much for the information." Sitting down at two of the tables, the group broke their fast with fresh eggs and thick sliced bacon for a hefty price. Botreg took Hority outside to eat, because his smell was turning heads and stomachs in the dining room.

After eating, Zeffan, Celedant, and Tarquin left the inn to find the streets teeming with sailors and traders. The warehouses were being filled with goods from distant ports. Wagon trains were being loaded, too. Zeffan took them on a circuitous route, not wanting to draw attention to Celedant. He knew that their escapade in the warlock's tower would expedite the guild's actions. The explosion had made it more difficult to hide a wizard in the crowds of nosey people. Although he was dressed like a normal traveler, Celedant struck everyone as a warlock or wizard. There was profit to be made in information amongst the citizens of the city, and the travelers wanted to stay secreted away for as long as possible.

The harbor tower was squat and built to overlook every approach to the city. Zeffan led them up to the gate and had a few words with the guards. One was dispatched to the interior of the fortification. While they waited, men in blue coats exited and entered the building.

Zeffan pointed them out. "Harbor men. They take in docking fees and record the ships names, goods, and routes. I have sent word to the master that the traveler is at his doorstep. I have found him to be a genial man. We should not have to wait long.

In no time at all, the guard returned and asked them to follow him. They wound their way up a spiral stairway, through a door to a waiting room. Once there, the guard knocked on an inner door. It was immediately opened.

A callow man greeted Zeffan. "Ah, what brings the famous traveler to my office at this early hour."

The dwarf introduced his companions. "It is good to see ye again, Hamish. It has been a while since I have done business with ye."

The man bade them to sit and poured four cups of tea in immaculately decorated porcelain cups and saucers. He held his up. "Cheers, my friend. What can I do for you?"

"We need a ship to Markdale that can take eight passengers, eight horses, and two mules," Zeffan told him.

Hamish sighed. "That is quit the load, but I can make it happen. There will be a charge of course, five gold per person and two per animal."

The traveler laughed. "Come now. Ye seek to rob us. Two and one.

"Nay not rob. Just provide a service," the harbor master said. "Three and two."

The dwarf smiled. "Two and one for old friends. It's not just me. I bring ye eight passengers and livestock."

The man looked hard at the dwarf and finally smiled. "Done. But only because you are an old friend."

Celedant was glad Zeffan had sold the orc horses, or they would have been short of gold to pay for the voyage and buy the two mules they needed.

"It may take a little persuasion to arrange passage," the harbor master added. "I can't negotiate with the captain. That will be your doing. Where are you staying? I'll send one of my men around, once I have a ship ready for you."

Zeffan having struck a good bargain smiled slightly. "I'll see ye again old friend, and the tea was excellent."

It took several days for harbor master to secure a captain, who was sailing to Markdale. The ship, the Fan Tail, had been carrying crates filled with furs, the sailors said. Having dropped off its cargo, it was sailing back to the western port to resupply and fill its holds with grain.

Everyone was chomping at the bit to depart, and Celedant and the captain arrived at a sum of fifty gold pieces for the passage. It was a large sum, but they were in a hurry to leave before the warlocks sniffed them out. The amount also sped up the departure of the ship.

When it was time to go, each member of the group took a separate route to the ship. Their horses were loaded on board as quickly as possible, using the ships crane and thick straps. The ship's crew had built makeshift stalls for the horses and mules. Botreg trailed them all, having to chivvy Hority forward. Any time the monk of Clor saw a pile of discarded material, he would kick his horse away from his minder, and race to the garbage. Botreg was happy that Clor had ordered no more searching the sewage.

Dolgar, the dwarvan god of healing, had met with Clor and advised him of the danger to his faithful, should they mess about in the sewage. Agreeing with him, Clor had appeared before the abbot and changed his mind about the sacredness of sewage.

At one pile of detritus, Hority actually jumped off his horse and grabbed a piece of rope. Botreg was beside him in an instant as the monk placed the rope in his bag.

The ragged monk called to Botreg. "I have a piece of rope. Surely it will be of use onboard a ship."

Botreg sighed. "I'm sure it will. But we need to get to the ship as soon as possible."

People were actually crossing the street to avoid the odiferous dwarf, which allowed them make better time through the noonday crowds. Besides that, Botreg now held the reins of Hority's horse, to keep him from rushing off in search of more treasure. Soon all the horses were loaded, and Tarquin and the others walked the decks, trying not to get in the sailor's way. While Celedant talked to the captain, Hority searched the deck for any trash that might be lying about. The problem was that the deck was clean and to Hority, it was plainly unholy. Then he found a bucket of black tar that the sailors had been using earlier. It was still partially liquid, and the dwarf was drawn to it.

"Ah, Clor has placed an offering in this bucket for me to find," he said aloud. "Another test from his high dirtiness."

He then took out his rope and slathered tar on it. Soon the rope was pitch black and the dwarf ran to Celedant calling, "I have found a holy substance, though I know not what it is."

Seeing Hority, Celedant turned to the captain and explained. "He is of an order that relishes garbage to pray to his deity. That is why he smells so bad."

The captain turned away from the smell as Celedant turned to the dwarf. "Hority, that's tar for the rigging. Not for worshiping. Now look, you've got tar all over yourself."

Hority's habit was covered in tar as well as his hands. The wizard cast a quick spell, and all the tar slid from the skinny dwarf's body.

The captain holding a scented cloth to his face said, "Young Dwarf, you may sling your hammock in the bilge deck at the bottom of the ship. There you find feted water and rats a plenty."

Hority was so happy, he jumped up and down, causing the tarred rope to become entangled in his beard and hair. Celedant cast another spell and again all the tar slid from his body. Then with a flick of his hand, he sent it back to the bucket it had come from. The other travelers hung their hammocks with the crew. Celedant got the only other berth besides the Captain's.

They sailed at high tide moving quickly with the wind behind them.

The crossing was relatively free from any storms, unlike the sea around Dragon Isle and the wizarding school at Edain. Those currents were only sailed by the Northmen out of Trondheim. The western ocean seemed serene to the passengers and aside from a few rain clouds, the trip was safe. They made harbor at Markdale and the group was glad to be off the rocking ship. Botreg had to go down into the bilge deck to fetch Hority, where he found the dwarf with a small lantern, lighting only a few feet in front of him. The smell of the dwarf was horrendous as he sat dangling his feet in fetid water.

"This is a most holy place," Hority said. "I have prayed to Clor for a safe journey, and he listened to me."

Disgusted, the assassin grabbed the monk by his filthy frock and dragged him away, before Hority began praising Clor any longer. Botreg knew that if left alone, the daft dwarf would have carried on for many turns of the clock.

Botreg led Hority up on deck, where the crew gave way to putrid dwarf, giving him a wide passage to the ramp leading to the docks. Botreg deftly grabbed Hority's satchel. Then when he was halfway down gangway, he waved to Tarquin, pointing at Hority and the water. The dark dwarf took a big jump onto the dock. Hority tried to keep his balance, but he was caught by surprise and tumbled into the water. He came up sputtering, his arms flapping around to keep him afloat.

Tarquin had climbed down a slippery ladder that led into the water. He yelled over the splashing, "Hority, over here."

The dwarf slowly made his way over to Tarquin, who helped him up out of the water.

Once on the dock, Hority, despite his bath, still stunk to high heaven. It would take several washings with strong soap to rid him of that. Tarquin approached the wet dwarf and demanded, "What have you got in that bag of yours."

Hority looked shocked. His sack was missing, until Botreg brought it to them. It held holy items of Clor. Should he let just anyone peer into it?

A debate was about to begin, but Tarquin snatched the bag from Botreg's hand, which could have proven to be momentous. He took a look inside and with a shocked face he lifted out a dead rat that was well decomposed. He tossed it into a nearby waste bin. Hority looked grief-stricken. Then out came rotten fruit covered in mold. It followed the rat. Lastly, Tarquin pulled out the monk's journal, carefully covered in a waterproof wrapping.

Finally, Tarquin spoke. "Hority why in the world did you carry that rotten filth with you?"

The dwarf began openly crying, creating runnels of mixed dirt and tears. Holding back more tears the monk said, "They were to be an offering to Clor for a safe passage."

Tarquin took on a stern voice. "From here on out. No decomposing animals or rotten fruit. Your reek is bad enough to clear the docks. We can't continue onward with you smelling so bad. It could draw attention to us from our enemies."

The monk shuffled away from the group with Botreg on his tail to steer him back in the right direction.

Celedant watched as their horses were lowered down to the docks from the ship's hold.

Once they were mounted, he told them. "We must keep to ourselves. I don't want a warlock's ship to come in unannounced and catch us off guard. Come. Let's look for an inn."

Chapter Sixteen

It took several days for the harbor master to secure a captain who was sailing to Markdale. The ship, the Fan Tail, had been carrying crates filled with furs, the sailors said. Having dropped off its cargo, it was sailing back to the western port to resupply and fill its holds with grain.

Everyone wanted to quickly depart, and Celedant and the Captain arrived at a sum of fifty gold pieces for the passage. It was a large sum, but they were in a hurry to leave before the warlocks sniffed them out. The amount also sped up the departure of the ship.

When it was time to go, each member of the group took a separate route to the ship. Their horses were loaded on board as quickly as possible, using the ships crane and thick straps. The ship's crew had built makeshift stalls for the horses and mules. Botreg trailed them all, having to chivvy Hority forward. Any time the monk of Clor saw a pile of discarded material, he would kick his horse away from his minder, and race to the garbage. Botreg was happy that Clor had ordered no more searching the sewage.

Dolgar, the dwarvan god of healing, had met with Clor and advised him of the danger to his faithful, should they mess about in the sewage. Agreeing with him, Clor had appeared before the abbot and changed his mind about the sacredness of sewage.

At one pile of detritus, Hority actually jumped off his horse and grabbed a piece of rope. Botreg was beside him in an instant as the monk placed the rope in his bag.

The ragged monk called to Botreg. "I have a piece of rope. Surely it will be of use onboard a ship."

Botreg sighed. "I'm sure it will. But we need to get to the ship as soon as possible."

People were actually crossing the street to avoid the odiferous dwarf, which allowed them make better time through the noonday crowds. Besides that, Botreg now held the reins of Hority's horse, to keep him from rushing off in search of more treasure. Soon all the horses were loaded, and Tarquin and the others walked the decks, trying not to get in the sailor's way. While Celedant talked to the captain, Hority searched the deck for any trash that might be lying about. The problem was that the deck was clean and to Hority, it was clearly unholy. Then he found a bucket of black tar that the sailors had been using earlier. It was still partially liquid, and the dwarf was drawn to it.

"Ah, Clor has placed an offering in this bucket for me to find," he said aloud. "Another test from his high dirtiness."

He then took out his rope and slathered tar on it. Soon the rope was pitch black and the dwarf ran to Celedant calling, "I have found a holy substance, though I know not what it is."

Seeing Hority, Celedant turned to the captain and explained. "He is of an order that relishes garbage to pray to his deity. That is why he smells so bad."

The Captain turned away from the smell as Celedant turned to the dwarf. "Hority, that's tar for the rigging. Not for worshiping. Now look, you've got tar all over yourself."

Hority's habit was covered in tar as well as his hands. The wizard cast a quick spell, and all the tar slid from the skinny dwarf's body.

The Captain held a scented cloth to his face and said, "Young Dwarf, you may sling your hammock in the bilge deck at the bottom of the ship. There you find feted water and rats a plenty."

Hority was so happy, he jumped up and down, causing the tarred rope to become entangled in his beard and hair. Celedant cast another spell and again all the tar slid from his body. Then with a flick of his hand, he sent it back to the bucket it had come from. The other travelers hung their hammocks with the crew. Celedant was given the only berth besides the Captain's.

They sailed at high tide moving quickly with the wind behind them, and the passengers heaved a sigh of relief that they has escaped before the warlocks had found them.

The crossing was relatively free from any storms, unlike the sea around Dragon Isle and the wizarding school at Edain. Those currents were only sailed by the Northmen out of Trondheim. The western ocean seemed serene to the passengers and aside from a few rain clouds, the trip was safe. They made harbor at Markdale and the group was glad to be off the rocking ship. Botreg had to go down into the bilge deck to fetch Hority, where he found the dwarf with a small lantern, lighting only a few feet in front of him. The smell of the dwarf was horrendous as he sat dangling his feet in fetid water.

"This is a most holy place," Hority said. "I have prayed to Clor for a safe journey, and he listened to me."

Disgusted, the assassin grabbed the monk by his filthy frock and dragged him away, before Hority began praising Clor any longer. Botreg knew that if left alone, the daft dwarf would have carried on for half a day.

Botreg led Hority up on deck, where the crew gave way to the putrid dwarf, giving him a wide passage to the ramp leading to the docks. Botreg deftly grabbed Hority's satchel. Then when he was halfway down gangway, he waved to Tarquin, pointing at Hority and the water. The dark dwarf took a big jump onto the dock. Hority tried to keep his balance, but he was caught by surprise and tumbled into the water. He came up sputtering, his arms flapping around to keep him afloat.

Tarquin climbed down a slippery ladder that led into the water. He yelled over the splashing. "Hority, over here."

The dwarf slowly made his way over to Tarquin, who helped him up out of the water.

Once on the dock, Hority, despite his bath, still stunk to high heaven. It would take several washings with strong soap to rid him of that. Tarquin approached the wet dwarf and demanded, "What have you got in that bag of yours."

Hority looked shocked. His sack was missing, until Botreg brought it to them. It held holy items of Clor. Should he let just anyone peer into it?

A debate was about to begin, but Tarquin snatched the bag from Botreg's hand, which could have proven to be momentous. He took a look inside and with a shocked face he lifted out a dead rat that was well decomposed. He tossed it into a nearby waste bin. Hority look grief stricken. Then out came rotten fruit covered in mold. It followed the rat. Lastly Tarquin pulled out the monk's journal, carefully covered in a waterproof wrapping.

Finally, Tarquin spoke. "Hority why in the world did you carry that rotten filth with you?"

The dwarf began openly crying, creating runnels of mixed dirt and tears. Holding back more tears the monk said, "They were to be an offering to Clor for a safe passage."

Tarquin took on a stern voice. "From here on out. No decomposing animals or rotten fruit. Your reek is bad enough to clear the docks. We can't continue onward with you smelling so bad. It could draw attention to us from our enemies. If you don't do as you're told, we'll have to forcibly bathe you with strong soap."

The monk shuffled away from the group with Botreg on his tail to steer him back in the right direction.

Celedant watched as their horses were lowered down to the docks from the ship's hold.

Once they were mounted, he told them, "We must keep to ourselves. I don't want a warlock's ship to come in unannounced and catch us off guard. Come. Let's look for an inn."

Chapter Seventeen

After their foray into the tower of the warlocks, Cyra and Talchic teleported back to her room in the orc capital. As she paced the floor in deep concentration, the warlock knew better than to disturb her.

She finally stopped pacing and taking out the map said, "Talchic take pen and ink and make an exact copy of this map. You will take twenty orcs and follow Celedant across the sea and kill them all. Then see where this map leads to." Cyra handed him the map.

"How do we get to the harbor with twenty orcs?" Talchic asked. "By the time we reach Markdale, Celedant will be long gone."

The sorceress stared at the warlock like he was an idiot. "I can teleport twenty orcs and you. That's about the maximum I can do. You will appear at the docks. Once there, you can get information from one of the harbor master's men. Pay what you must for transport. You will not be far behind Celedant. You should be able to sense the wizard's magic."

"Yes, of course. I will do your bidding," he replied.

The next morning, Talchic gathered with twenty of the huge orcs.

"Grasp hands," Cyra ordered. "You must be connected, or you all will die."

There were murmurings among the orcs, but Talchic shouted, "You will do as the mistress wants! Now grasp hands."

Cyra cast the teleportation spell, which made Talchic feel dizzy. When his vision cleared, he was in a dank alley along with the twenty white orcs. They exited the alley into a busy street located well away from the docks district. Talchic could ill afford a chance encounter with Celedant, especially in present company.

"Come," he commanded the orcs.

They headed to the first rundown inn they could find. The innkeeper allowed Talchic a room but insisted the orcs sleep outside in the stables. The warlock told the orcs that he would have food sent out to them and headed to his room.

He did not sleep well, thinking about what he had to do in the morning. After breaking his fast, Talchic went to the orcs. "Sergeant, I need you and one other to accompany me to the docks. The rest of you stay here and do not cause trouble. If you do, I'll kill you the second I get back."

Following the fish smell to the harbor, he was amazed at how busy it truly was. It dwarfed the small ports of the eastern city states. Soon enough, he found one of the blue jacketed harbor master's functionaries.

He asked the man to stop, but the man keep going until Talchic grabbed his arm and spun him around. His eyes widened when he saw the orcs and he apologetically said, "I'm sorry, my lord. But my mind must have been wandering."

Talchic answered the man back politely. "We all have moments like that. Now I have a question for you. Are there any ships leaving for Markdale anytime soon?"

The harbor man smiled and wiped the sweat from his brow. "It just so happens that the warship, Alagor, is to set sail tomorrow. They are almost finished loading goods on board. I would not hesitate to introduce the captain to you. He was very polite in our meeting this morning."

The harbor man took the warlock down the docks to a three-decker warship, where they saw the captain standing on the dock watching the cargo being loaded. Talchic was introduced to the captain, and the harbor master's man hurried away.

The Captain was busy and got right to the point. "How many berths do you need, and are they all for these big fellows with you?"

Talchic responded, "I have twenty orcs and myself."

The Captain blew out a breath. "I hate orcs. Foul, messy sorts they are."

"These are a different sort, more civilized so to speak," the Warlock stated.

"I dislike warlocks about as much," the Captain continued. "But this offers me a simple way to get gold for my ship. Two hundred-fifty gold to put up with the orcs on my ship. No negotiations."

Talchic took one pouch out and discreetly handed it over to the captain saying, "Here's 100 gold. I'll count out the remaining 150 and have it ready for you once we're on board."

The next day, Melgor boarded the huge, three-masted ship in Trudoc Bay followed by his twenty white orcs. The crew avoided the hulking orcs that lounged around in groups in various places on deck. This could be a boon for Melgor, if the orc groups did not like each other. They might fight and kill off a few of themselves. Melgor did not trust them as well as Cyra did, but she was a more powerful sorceress than he was a warlock.

After paying the captain the balance of the fare, he remained beside him.

The smooth-shaved Captain was dressed in neatly pressed clothes and his skin was tanned like leather after so many years spent at sea. "Don't let your orcs cause any trouble on my ship," he stated in a hardened voice. "Once your off at Markdale, I don't care what happens."

Melgor brushed back a lock of hair that had fallen over one eye. "They are my problem. If they get out of hand let me know. I have no qualms about throwing them overboard."

The crossing did not go as Melgor would have liked. A week into the voyage, a storm blew in from the south. The waves rose to break over the bow of the ship and man lines or ropes were tied along both port and starboard sides to offer the sailors hand holds as they went about their business. The passengers were ordered below deck where the motion of the ship quickly had most of them throwing up and huddled in miserable groups. Melgor confined himself to his hammock that swayed back and forth roughly. He downed a quick potion that kept him from getting sick. He would not offer any to the orcs. *I don't care how sick they get. I'm not wasting any potions on them. Besides, I only have a few.*

The sailors sent to pass out hardtack and water were rebuked by the orcs for the most part. The ones that could eat, found the biscuit-like concoction stale and tasteless. When they came to the warlock's bunk, they found him whistling a merry tune as his hammock swayed with the ship. He readily accepted the food and water and sat down at the built-in desk to eat. Three days passed before the storm blew itself out and the passengers were allowed on deck. The ship looked the worse for wear. In some places, the rigging hung down to the deck, and several of the sails were in tatters.

The orcs saw to the horses below deck. Many had bloody flanks from being tossed about in their narrow stalls. They were as anxious as the orcs to set foot on land. Melgor waited a goodly amount of time before approaching the captain, who had manned the wheel the entire three nights. He was dead tired with heavy bags under his eyes.

But as the warlock approached, he smiled and laughed. "T'was a huge storm that. Not one I have encountered in years. I know why you have come to see me. We are off a ways but not by much. I have recalculated our course to get us to Markdale. I would say we have a week more at sea."

Melgor opened up to the Captain. "Well, we won't be that far behind those we seek."

The other man said slyly, "So you chase another. I would hide if I knew that those giant orcs rode after me."

The warlock smiled slyly. "The man I seek will welcome battle with us and will probably kill us all, but I have my orders."

The captain laughed. "Then you are a fool. I would hide from whoever gave you the orders."

The warlock sighed. "Unfortunately, that is impossible. There is no place I could go that she would not find me."

CHAPTER EIGHTEEN

Debarking from the Fan Tail, Celedant and his party found an inexpensive inn on the main thoroughfare and settled into their rooms.

When Hority entered the inn, however, the owner called out, "You there. I'll not have you stinking up my inn. Out to the stables with you!"

The Clorian seemed happy enough and told Botreg, "This inn is too clean. The barn will be a much better place for me."

They settled in and had a hearty meal. Botreg took food out to Hority and found him dead asleep on a pile of dirty straw.

Once Botreg nudged him awake, Hority eagerly accepted his meal. "Come sit with me. I can tell you the wonderful things I have found and thick dust that covers most everything."

"Not tonight my friend. I need a good night's sleep," the former Assassin said.

Botreg then retired to the room he shared with Tarquin and settled into the comfortable bed, which was a far cry better than the rope hammock that had swayed unnervingly throughout their nights aboard the ship.

As Botreg drifted off to sleep, Celedant took out a large parchment and began drawing the map he had seen in the warlock's tower from memory. In the morning, he had an exact copy of the map.

The wizard called everyone into his room before breakfast. He had a serious look on his face when he said, "I want each of you to memorize this, in case I fall into the wrong hands. I can withstand interrogation to a point. But the right warlock can break a man eventually."

Tarquin looked at the map and saw the distance to where they had to go. He wondered how some long-forgotten disciple of Clor had traveled here and mapped the area drawn on the parchment. He also worried about his wife and how long it would take him to get back to her. He wanted so much to be there when the baby came.

Celedant pointed to an area at what looked like a great crater and their destination at the north side of the map. "That is our goal."

Also surrounding the hole was a short sentence printed in ancient Dwarvan.

"What are the runes for?" Tarquin asked. "Botreg, can you read them?"

The dwarf bent down to take a look. "Hmm, this is the ancient language, the secret that we tell to know one. But yer lucky. I'm not a typical dwarf and will translate." He stopped speaking and looked around. "Where is Hority?"

Tarquin laughed. "Probably out looking for foul things to store up for future study."

Botreg continued. "This says to beware the watchers. It goes no further about the watchers but warns others that it is an unholy place very clean. Typical Clorian monk."

Celedant tapped the map saying, "This is our destination. I fear that the warlocks are looking for magical items to shift the eternal war over this planet from good to evil."

After breakfast, the members of the group went their separate ways to purchase the goods they would need for the journey.

As Tarquin looked in on the horses, he caught a whiff of something awful, and he called out, "Hority is that you?"

A small head with a huge smile on its face peeked from around one of the stall doors and waved. "Tarquin, I found such things of which I have never dreamed."

Tarquin went over to the stall and look at what the monk had uncovered. He found Hority staring at his findings with religious fervor in his eyes.

His human friend saw several bird's eggs, feathers, a board with a rusty nail sticking out, several broken clay pipes, and a pile of rotten fruit. Tarquin laughed out loud. For a moment, poor Hority thought his friend was making fun of Clor.

Tarquin saw the dwarf begin to redden and quickly said, "We have been here less than a day, and you have collected such glorious things for Clor. It is miraculous."

Hority calmed down and Tarquin added, "This is a good city to collect offerings to your god."

The dwarf wagged his head up and down gathering up his offerings and stuffing them in his satchel.

Tarquin came out to the stableman and warned him about what was going on and not to let the dwarf set the barn on fire. The stableman blinked at him and went immediately to keep watch on the monk.

Later that day, the group gathered in the common room of the inn to enjoy their favorite drinks.

Tarquin looked to Botreg. "I found our wayward monk in the barn. He is just about to sacrifice several things to Clor. You might want to supervise."

Botreg knocked over his chair as he hurried from the room, murmuring under his breath. "Canna even enjoy a drink without havin' to keep that...."

The rest of his words were lost as he walked out the door.

CHAPTER NINETEEN

The moon was full and the wind still as Cyra and her orcs approached the city. She was mounted on a slender black horse, while the orcs marched behind her. It was time to strike. She needed to secure power before a new warlock or sorceress could consolidate theirs. Wouldn't it be odd if a sorceress had taken the tower? But she would not mind killing a woman. It could be done as easily as a man. They had been marching for days at a fast pace, but that did not seem to bother the great white orcs. Despite the late hour, the smoke of uncountable homes gave the city a perpetual gloom.

The gloom will be good for tonight's bloody work, she thought.

The gate guards gathered their arms and shut the gate as her column approached. As she rode out of the fog, the guards could see exactly what they were up against.

A sergeant called out, "What business do you have in Trudoc?"

Their eyes were on the endless column of orcs stretched out behind her. She could actually feel the heartbeats of the frightened men.

"I have no ill will towards you. My goal is the warlock's tower," Cyra answered.

Not wanting a full-blown battle, the sergeant called down to the soldiers behind the wall. "Unlatch the gate."

He waved the witch inside, and she led her orcs into the city.

The column quickly traversed the streets and before long, turned the corner of the city block that the enclave was situated on. A shadow detached from the shadows of a side street and a hooded orc joined her.

"The warlocks have set a strong guard at the front and rear entrances of the building," he reported. "It will be a fight to enter, and all the warlocks will be awakened."

She smiled. "Do not worry, my friend. I have a simple plan."

At a signal from their mistress, the white orcs broke from their column, running to the wrought iron wall of the complex, hidden by an age-old hedge that grew behind the wall. Inching towards the entrance, they found five guards standing half asleep on this smoky night. In complete silence, the orcs overpowered the guards, clamping their oversized hands over the mouths of the men and then giving a quick twist, snapping the soldier's necks with a gruesome sound.

Meanwhile, Cyra turn her horse off the street onto the paved road that led up to the warlock's manor. The guards at the doors to the house, along with two accompanying warlocks, made ready for a confrontation. They realized that a lone witch riding past the gate guards without a warning was not just a coincidence. In the darkness, the great white orcs entered the compound, spreading out with bow strings taunt to their faces and finely sharpened arrows at the ready.

Cyra lifted her staff, sending two of the guards hurling backward through the manor's door. That was the signal for the orcs to let fly their arrows. The guards lay crumpled on the stone porch, pierced by many arrows. She boldly rode her horse up the steps and into the giant main hall past the two dead guards. The orcs entered the building and spread out along the walls. Cyra rode her horse straight down the middle of the enormous, vaulted room.

From somewhere in the building, the loud clanging of a bell sent out a warning, bringing soldiers and warlocks spilling into the room. Many were cut down by arrows as they passed through the doorways into the hall, causing a pile-up of corpses in the entryways. Warlocks and soldiers dove through the openings rolling to upright positions. The men lacking bows rushed the orcs and were brought down by a hail of arrows.

The warlocks and witches that made it into the hall saw a woman mounted on a horse and concentrated their spells on her. Soon an eruption of magical energy spread throughout the chamber. Cyra cast spells continuously. Every offensive spell she could call forth was cast. A giant fireball rolled up the aisle to the back of the building, killing all that were in the way. She sent smaller balls of power at any magic user who showed themselves, decimating their ranks while she remained safe on her horse. A magical protection spell covering both her and the horse easily deflected any spells cast against her. She advanced into the hall still on horseback, magically commanding the mount's every move with her mind. And before long, her orcs had rounded up the remaining soldiers and magic users in the hall and had them tied up and gaged.

The witch dismounted and ordered her orcs to root out anyone left in the building. "Report back when you encounter resistance, and I will come and lend aid. Cyra went to one of the warlocks and pulled off his gag. "Where is the master of this manor?"

The warlock motioned with his chin, "That's the new master's body over there in the blue robe. The manor is yours. To spare blood, you should shout that he is dead. Most will surrender immediately."

She ordered her orcs to spread the word that the master was dead, and the new mistress was waiting for all in the great hall.

A flow of magic users came into the hall under guard. The warlocks and sorceresses' hands were tied tightly behind their backs. The orcs were sent throughout the building, calling out that the master was dead to those still offering battle. Soon, weapons and staves were thrown into the passageways as the residents began surrendering.

They came across a few pockets of resistance where warlocks or witches stood their ground. The magic users leaned out of their rooms and cast spells at the orcs, which moved from room to room until they were next to the ones occupied by the warlocks and sorceresses. Then the white orcs would storm the next room, killing all inside. While effective, several orcs were left wounded or dead from the magic yielded by the defenders.

The human guards, mercenary Guras, were herded to the front lawn and forced face down on the ground, watched over by the white orcs.

Cyra studied the assembled magic users, and she had to laugh. The defense of the enclave had been inept. Only thirty of her orcs had died from a mansion filled with magic users so far. Others were wounded but none seriously. As the orcs continued rooting out pockets of resistance, she remained mounted on her horse. She turned it to face the assembled crowd, which stood amid their slaughtered brothers and sisters.

"I am Cyra," she announced, "the new mistress here. I have swept you aside and now command you. I intend to make us a power to be reckoned with. This city will be ours. We will rule, or there will be bodies littering the streets. People will fear the new Sorceress's Tower."

The assembled throng could feel the powerful evil radiating from their new leader, and many smiled at the ambitious plans of the witch. Finally, a leader that would make the humans and other species of this city bow down to their power.

CHAPTER TWENTY

Celedant and the others left Markdale early the following day. Their horses were eager to get on the road after being confined in the ship for so long. The mules carried small casks filled with water for crossing the desert, as well as other supplies the group would need along the way.

"What can we expect on the western road to the desert?" Zeffan questioned the innkeeper.

The innkeeper had little information that proved of any use. He told him, "The west road is a dangerous trail. It's a place of highwaymen and monsters of differing types. The desert, however, is devoid of life, and there is no water until you reach the mountains on the other side."

The road was clogged with traffic, farmers bringing in produce and caravans going both ways. As the road cleared, they were able to set a steady pace. The sun kept it hot and humid, the trees held the heat in, making it feel like they were in an oven. The sun rose and fell as they journeyed through the thick jungle before making camp well off the road and hidden from view. A fire was banked with stones and a pot of beef stew soon bubbled merrily. Everyone was miserable, though, as the bugs were out, continuously biting them.

His smell preceding him, Hority came to stand next to Celedant. "I am worried. This forest is too clean for me taste. It looks like Clor has been forgotten in this far land. I feel uneasy."

The wizard knocked the ashes from his pipe saying, "Clor follows in your footsteps and is forever with you. He has not forgotten this land. Remember the waste that you found in the city?"

The monk in the befouled and ratty frock cried loud enough for the entire camp to hear. "I have betrayed me faith in Clor." He threw himself on the ground, grasping handfuls of dirt and rubbing it into his grimy face, hair, and throwing it on his robe.

Botreg, whose job it was to keep the monk safe and most importantly, keep his friends safe from Hority's somewhat questionable activities, ran up. Grabbing the dwarf by the collar, he hauled Hority to his feet saying, "Easy, me friend. There is time for chastising yerself, but this is not one of those times. We need to be quiet so as not to attract unwanted attention."

Both eyes wet from the thought that he had displeased his god, Hority stood up and nodded his head. "Praise Clor. I must be patient in our endeavors."

Talchic was nervous. His orcs were tired of being confined to the ship and their tempers flared. After being blown off course by the storm, another five days of travel passed before the city of Markdale came into view. It was even larger than Trudoc with a multitude of docks and ships anchored far into the harbor. The ship was soon docked alongside a wharf, and the sailors ran about rolling up the topsails and tying the ship to the dock.

The Warlock shook the Captain's hand. "Thank you for allowing us passage on your fine ship. I must say we were in capable hands during the storm. I felt safe under your command. I hope the orcs did not pose any problems on the voyage."

The Captain shook his head. "No trouble at all. But I must say I was apprehensive about having them on board."

"You needn't have worried. As I told you at the beginning of the voyage, had there been trouble, I would have dealt with them myself." Talchic bid the Captain farewell and walked down the gang plank

He got a room at an inn. The orcs again had to stay in the stables. This was fine with him. He remained on edge, because he did not trust them.

Once in his room, the warlock took out the map and studied it. The parchment marked a westward road that they were to follow. It was humid in the city, and he worried about how hot the jungle would be.

Keeping the horses going could prove to be a problem, especially when they while crossing a dessert.

The next morning in the humid weather, Celedant took out the map that had been studied by his cohorts and gathered them around him.

He pointed to a spot on the western road. "We are near this point. We'll follow this road towards the west until we come upon a crossroad that appears on the map as a dubious route. It seems the west road turns into a trail, and we'll have to be most cautious, for it will be a perfect place for an ambush. We'll cross this desert in the direction of these mountains. Once clear of the desert, we'll have to be on the lookout for the path north alongside these mountains. We must keep a sharp lookout for this other path that leads into the mountains towards our goal. These paths could be overgrown, and we might have to follow the game trails to our destination. Wherever that may be."

Celedant continued. "Remember, we are in a foreign land. There is no telling what new creatures we may face. We must be on constant vigilance, and that especially goes for you Hority. No running off alone. Always take Botreg with you."

There was a moan from the ex-assassin, bringing a smile to everyone's face. They were glad they did not have to babysit the Clorian monk. Although, no one would ever say that aloud to Botreg.

Hority looked back at his friend. "I will welcome Botreg in me endeavors. Just think of the wonders that await us in this strange land, and what I can record in me book."

They quickly broke camp and soon were back on the road setting a brisk pace. Eldahir and Zeffan rode ahead as scouts. Tarquin was glad to have the eagle-eyed elf and the experienced dwarf along on this venture.

Chapter Twenty-One

The further they advanced through the jungle, the hotter it got. Before long, sweat soaked their clothes, and those that wore armor found it hot to the touch.

Azimuth called telepathically to his lifelong friend Celedant. "Dragons like to lay in the sun, but I find this stifling. I long to fly above these trees and feel the cooler air."

"I'm afraid these trees are too intertwined for you to silently break through," Celedant answered. "Remember Zeffan has no knowledge of your abilities. Maybe we'll show him, once we reach the desert."

When they finished speaking, a clear call echoed through the forest, and their scouts returned at the gallop. Eldahir reigned in his horse and spoke quickly. "That's a horn call, or I'm an orc."

Tarquin issued orders like he was still in the dwarvan king's Borderers. "Form a circle, quickly, and be prepared. We're about to be attacked!"

A moment later from the woods, they heard huge bodies moving fast through the brush. Hority slipped off his horse and sprinted into the underbrush shouting his war cry, "Foes!"

Then from out of the woods, a dozen huge humanoid shapes charged, each carrying equally large weapons and wearing an assortment of armor. Celedant recognized them at once from their horned heads and shouted, "Minotaurs!"

The monsters charged into the group of circled horses. One fell forward dead. Behind it was the smiling face of Hority, waving his magical branch. The elves Eldahir and Morganna each got off two arrows that struck their targets true. However, the minotaur's thick hide appeared to take the impetus from the arrows, and they stuck out of the creatures likes pins. On the second volley, an arrow struck one of the advancing monsters in the eye, penetrating the brain. The creature fell dead.

Tarquin put heels to his horse and charged one of the behemoths. A giant rusted scimitar scythed over his head, and he struck out with his sword, Dragon Bolt. It sliced neatly through the tough skin and chainmail, causing thick red blood to spurt from the wound to its side. The minotaur went down on one knee, holding its midsection as blood poured through its fingers. Tarquin turned his horse around in a tight half circle and charged back at the monster. This time, he struck the back of the neck and severed through it. The horned head flopped to the side as the minotaur fell forward.

Wanting to even the odds, Celedant quickly cast a spell as the enemies charged. Green flame erupted from his staff, engulfing two of the creatures and sending them flailing around as they tried to put out the unquenchable magical fire. The wizard turned his horse and saw all the others engaged in battle. He watched Azimuth's horse take a massive blow to the head that spit it open, causing its rider to fall to the ground. A minotaur was about to chop downward at his oldest friend. He knew the axe would harm even a transformed dragon, so he used his staff to shoot a bright blue ray of energy at the creature. It struck mid chest burning through the breast plate and continuing through the body. It fell dead onto Azimuth, who used his draconic strength to easily push it off himself.

Meanwhile, Zeffan battled a minotaur yielding a long spear. The dwarf easily deflected the weapon, but he could not get to within striking distance. Frustrated, he charged his horse straight into the monster. It bounced off, throwing Zeffan to the ground. The minotaur raised his spear for a downward stroke when suddenly its eyes widened, and the body fell sideways to the ground. The dwarf looked up and there was the smiling monk, Hority, who nodded and charged off continuing to yell his war cry.

Morganna and Eldahir, husband and wife, dismounted and fought back-to-back using their superior elvan movements to dodge and roll out of the way of the two minotaurs' weapons. Eldahir rolled under the creature he was fighting, slicing the hamstrings. As it crumbled to the ground, the elf finished it off by stabbing it through the heart. Morganna's minotaur stopped as its friend was killed by Eldahir. Using that pause, Morganna rammed her long sword deep into its stomach. The minotaur gripped the wound and ran off into the bushes, but not before launching a last attack at her. It bore a huge club, and with a desperate swing, despite its wound, the monster struck Morganna a heavy blow to her side, flinging her several yards away.

The remaining minotaurs retreated into the brush, and that was when Botreg attacked. He spurred his horse forward, standing on the saddle. As he neared one of the last of the creatures, he vaulted, using his assassin honed skills to land on its shoulder. He quickly swung both legs around the creature's neck and with incredible force drove his sword into its skull. As it fell, he jumped to the ground to land right in front of Tarquin's horse. If it had not been for his friend's superior horsemanship, Botreg would have been crushed by the horse's flailing fore limbs.

The group stood or reined in their horses when they heard whistling. Out of the brush came a smiling Hority. His hair and robe were tangled with twigs, and he reverently held the horn of one of the minotaurs. "Look, Tarquin, a new monster to catalog and a horn to study and add to my book."

Tarquin smiled back. "Indeed, a great treasure for Clor."

Eldahir called out, "Hority, come quickly. Morganna has been sorely injured."

Hority stuffed the horn into his pouch, and ran to Morganna. When he arrived, the wood elf lay on her side holding her ribs. Blood trickled down her chin from her mouth. The dwarf knelt down and fished through his satchel. He brought out a vial of black ooze. "Here. Take this. It will stop the bleeding and ease the pain."

She looked at it curiously and drank it down in one gulp. The taste was vile, and she nearly threw it back up, but the pain subsided.

"What in the nine hells was that?" she demanded.

Hority looked at her seriously and answered, "It is the blood of the hard-shelled river slug. It may taste foul, but it is a serious healing draught."

He then placed his hands on the elf's side and began praying to Clor. A dark brown aura formed around his hands, and Morganna could swear she felt her ribs move back into place.

Hority brushed off his dirty hands. "Ye should be better in a few days. Ye must wrap yer ribs tightly to help them set." He then turned and wandered away, finally sitting with his back to the dead horse, where he busily scribbled away in his book.

It took a little time to locate the mules. Once they did, Celedant ordered, "Up in the saddle. We don't want any more surprises."

He looked to Hority and called out, "Young monk, you'll have to finish your examination come this night. You may keep the horn until then."

The others followed orders. Lacking a horse, Azimuth was about to climb up behind Tarquin.

"Wait, Azimuth," Eldahir called. "Take Morganna's horse for now. We can ride together on mine, where I can keep an eye on her."

"That's very kind of you, Eldahir," Azimuth said.

Eldahir helped his wife Morganna to mount up, then came up after, settling in behind her. She did not feel any pain, but she did feel like her ribs were moving. Settling against her husband, caused the sensation to go away. As they moved out of the ambush site, the heat soaked into their skin. They rode on, but the deep canopy of the trees did not allow fresh air or even a breeze to reach them.

They rode hard through the next couple of miles in hopes of getting clear of the minotaur's territory. When they reached the point where two roads intercepted, Celedant stopped to consult his map. There was no mention on the map of a road crossing their current position. "This road must have been cut after the Clorian map was drawn."

Tarquin motioned to the others. "Come, we must continue west."

After the crossroad, they slowed and began walking their horses along what was slowly becoming a path instead of a road. The air grew even more stifling on the narrow path. As the light decreased indicating nightfall, they quickly hacked a clearing out of the forest. After a cold dinner, they got what sleep they could, despite the biting bugs, while Azimuth stood watch.

They traveled several days until the sun began to shine through the jungle canopy, and a hot wind came from the west.

Celedant reined in his horse and turned to the others. "We have reached the edge of the desert. We must continue to conserve our water, especially for the horses. The crossing may take days or weeks. It's hard to tell as the map was not drawn to scale. Come, we must begin. We'll rest during the day and travel at night when it will be cooler."

They continued following the path and soon, the trees ended. They stared out at a vast desert with weathered rock outcroppings and withered trees that looked like bony hands reaching out of the desert sand.

Tarquin, heeding Celedant's advice, called out. "We'll camp here and venture forth in the night."

Celedant and Tarquin conferred with each other and both agreed it was worth the risk to send Azimuth on a scouting trip over the desert in dragon form. The heat would not bother the dragon in the least, especially with the cooler winds aloft. Celedant meandered over to his friend and in a hushed tone said, "I don't think it's time to reveal yourself to Zeffan just yet. We will wait until it is absolutely necessary. However, Tarquin and I think it would be a good idea for you to scout ahead and get a feeling for how far we'll have to travel in this desert."

Azimuth nodded his head. "No problem. I will slip from camp and go north to transform."

Chapter Twenty-Two

ater that day as the sun dropped lower in the west, Azimuth walked quietly from camp making sure Zeffan did not see him. The dwarf, however, saw a shadow pass and caught a glimpse of the wood elf as he ducked around a tree. Curiosity got the better of the dwarf. Besides, it would be foolish to wander into the wild alone, so he decided to follow.

For the dwarf, who was born and raised to follow tracks, it was surprisingly easy to spot Azimuth's trail. He had heard that elves left little or no footprints as they walked. Had that been a myth?

Then suddenly a voice rang in his head. *Fear not. This is Azimuth. I see you have followed my trail into the scrub.*

The dwarf spun around expecting to find the elf playing tricks on him with some magical spell. But there was no sign of Azimuth.

The elf laughed. *Do not be afraid. This is no spell. But rather one of my particular skills. You see, I am a dragon from Dragon Isle and Celedant's bonded companion. We have known each other since childhood many millennia ago. Come to the clearing, and I will show you myself in my true form.*

Zeffan advanced with his axe ready, wary of a trap of some sort. He called out, "Azimuth? Where are ye?"

Just ten more yards my friend, the dragon answered.

The dwarf came to the edge of the brush and saw Azimuth leaning against a boulder. He looked around the area to see if it was a trap. Afterall, he had known the people he was traveling with for less than a month. He saw no other footprints and stepped out of the brush, his axe at the ready.

Azimuth held his hands up and said aloud, "Easy Zeffan, there is nothing to be afraid of here. I am your friend."

Planting his axe in the sandy soil he answered, "I see no dragon. As a matter of fact, I see no fire drake either."

"Ah," Azimuth said. "True dragons stay in the shadows, living on the Dragon Isle and only venturing forth on dire mission or in elf form. We allow fire drakes lay claim to the name of dragons as it helps protect our true identity."

Zeffan nodded. "I have fought them on more than one occasion, and they are creatures of instinct and rather dull in the head. I always dreamed there were more to dragons then those creatures."

The elf nodded. "Come, let me show you a true dragon. I will change shape here in the clearing. I am over a hundred and fifty paces long, so I need a lot of space to transform. Afterwards, I will only be able to communicate through telepathy, just like we did a moment ago. All you need to do is think about what you want to say, and I'll be able to read your mind so to speak."

The dwarf looked long and hard at Azimuth, thinking through what he had been told. "I'm as ready as I'll ever be, I guess."

The elf climbed onto the boulder, scanned the area, and began chanting in a language Zeffan had never heard. A swirling rainbow mist formed, obscuring Azimuth. It grew larger and larger before disappearing. In its place was a pure golden dragon that stretched out his neck, giving a gentle puff of smoke from his nostrils. He then extended his wings, giving them several flaps. Sand flew around the clearing, blinding the dwarf momentarily.

Zeffan heard in his head. *I'm so sorry. I have been confined in elvan form for so long, I couldn't help spreading my wings.*

The dwarf thought back. *Magnificent! I thought I had seen most of the glory of this world, but this surpasses all.*

Azimuth surprised the dwarf by saying, *Come, I will take you on a ride. I'm going to scout the desert ahead. You need not fear. I won't drop you. I can summon a perfectly good saddle with attaching straps to keep you securely on my shoulders, just like I do for Celedant.*

Zeffan could count on his hand the number of times he had been frightened. This made number one on that list. He hesitantly walked towards the dragon, mesmerized by his size.

He thought to Azimuth. *Well, call me crazy, but I canna pass up such an opportunity. I'll accompany ye.*

Azimuth summoned a saddle and harness which attached just in front of his shoulders. Then levitated Zeffan up in the air. It caught the dwarf by surprise, and he looked foolish as he flailed his arms to steady himself.

He heard in his mind, *Don't hurt yourself. I've got you.*

Once settled into the saddle, Zeffan attached the harness and tightened the straps thinking, *So what can ye do. Breath fire, spit acid, or some other unearthly things?*

Azimuth turned his huge head back to stare at the dwarf. Zeffan's eyes bulged as he caught sight of the long-pointed teeth that filled the dragon's mouth. He felt the scales and envisioned his axe merely slipping off them in a fight.

Azimuth spoke to Zeffan, *I breath fire as do others of my kind. Usually, the color of the dragon dictates what it can do as far as that is concerned. However, we can all use magic as you saw with the levitation spell. But come now, the sun is setting, and we must be off. Let's see how long this accursed desert goes.*

He gave two mighty downward strokes of his wings and leapt off the boulder. With each downward stroke of his wings, the ground fell further away. He turned and swooped low over the camp. Everyone was awake by now, and they all pointed to the manically laughing dwarf riding Azimuth.

The golden dragon soared westward, the air washing over the two was cool compared to the hot humid temperatures they had been traveling in. As they went, Azimuth spoke to Zeffan, *The Clorians picked the longest path across the desert. It's never ending. They are indeed a strange lot.*

The dwarf wildly enjoying the ride replied, *At least a week across. I'll wager. But wait. Look there a city!*

You are right and it's a big one, Azimuth agreed. *Look the buildings stretch away from the city center at least a mile or more. But as we draw closer, they look more like ruins. I don't see anyone on the streets.*

They could be inside because of the heat. But surely some people would be up and about, the dwarf said.

Yes, Azimuth replied. *We shall have to warn the others. I don't like the looks of this place at all. Come, we must head further west before sundown.*

They continued west and an hour later, saw the first sign of life as the beginning of a forest appeared with mountain tops showing in the distance.

The dragon laughed in Zeffan's mind. *I would have won the bet with you. It will only take six days and that includes keeping a safe distance from that abandoned city.*

Azimuth banked suddenly, turning back east, nearly causing Zeffan to fall but for the harness. He winged it east, and the leagues flew past. Soon, they approached the camp. Azimuth backed his wings and came to a smooth landing, stirring up sand and dirt into a vast cloud. In the swirling sand, he levitated Zeffan from his back.

The dwarf had to cover his eyes to keep the grains of sand out. Then he felt a hand on his shoulder that led him out of the cloud and into camp.

The others gathered around them, and Tarquin clapped the dwarf on the back. "Welcome officially to our group. Even I have not flown yet. You are extremely fortunate. What was it like?"

Zeffan shook his head. "I canna begin to describe it. The freedom and cool air rushing past ye. Incredible. This easily jumps to the top of my list of favorite things I have seen or done."

They had a laugh, and Celedant handed the dwarf a wet handkerchief to wipe the dust from his face and eyes. "Just remember one thing. Azimuth's secret is to be kept within this group. Except for a few, only wizards, sorceresses, and elves know of their existence, and fewer still know about the dragons' powers of transformation."

"You have me given word. I am so privileged to be one of those few that I willna tell a soul. I swear on me honor."

"Excellent. Now, what did the two of you find out?" Celedant asked.

"It's about six days across the desert," Azimuth explained. "We have to avoid a ruined city that reeks of evil, which will take half a day to navigate around. Then it's a straight shot for about three days to a green forest and the mountains beyond."

"Not ideal. We don't have enough water to last six days," Tarquin said. "Only if we are extremely careful can we ration the water, but I fear for the horses. It will be hardest on them. Our barrels will only last so far. Then the horses will weaken, lengthening the crossing, and eventually dying, perhaps before we reach the far side."

"You saw no one in the city?" the wizard asked.

Azimuth and Zeffan both nodded the affirmative.

"Then I propose a scouting mission," Celedant suggested. "We will fly into the city during the day. Two of us will search for a well. If we're attacked, we'll be more than able to withstand it and simply fly away. If we find water in the city, we can enter it during the day, fill our barrels, and be on our way."

The others nodded in agreement and went about getting ready for their first night of travel in the desert.

CHAPTER TWENTY-THREE

As the sun set, they began their endless trek across the desert, where they found the temperature surprisingly cool at night. Yet, the hooves of their horses created a plume of dust as they tread on the hard, dry soil of the trail. Wrapping cloth coverings over most of their faces kept out the irritating dust. The dead trees were stunted, and their ends scratched at the riders and horses like the sharpened nails of the undead. This forced them to go slowly across the terrain to avoid the limbs and any holes that might have eroded in the desert floor.

Tarquin turned in his saddle and called back to Celedant. "This pace is maddening. We can't go any faster than a slow walk. It's going to take extra days. I fear the search for a well in the city has now become crucial."

The wizard nodded in the starlight. "The best laid plans often fall short. I fear we must travel in the daylight. We don't know who the warlocks might have sent to follow our trail. If indeed they have. Still, we need to remain ahead of them."

They walked and led their horses, conserving their strength for the day's sun, camping a little before dawn to give the horses a short respite. At midmorning, they mounted up and set a good pace across the desert. In the daylight, they could easily avoid the dead trees and see any obstacles in their way. Their mood was heavy. The usual chatter that often accompanied their travels dropped off. They rode in silence as the heat of the sun beat down upon them, and dust covered them all. On the third day in the desert, they came upon an adobe building. It looked like it might once have been a farm. There was a well, but it was dry and filled to the top with sand.

Azimuth dismounted and went to the well. He shook his head saying, "I cannot smell any water here, perhaps in the city." He pointed beyond them to a gentle rise of the land as it led up towards the abandoned city.

Morganna turned her horse around and stared back the way they had come, calling out to them, "Look on the horizon. It's a dust cloud. We are indeed being followed."

Tarquin circled his horse. "That's it. Now that the chase is on, we must hurry and find water. Else we'll ride our poor horses to death."

The group took off at a gallop towards the city. Hours later, they entered the ruins of the outer city. Buildings made from mud bricks stood empty on either side of them as the desert turned into a crumbled road. Riding point with Zeffan, Eldahir called back to the others, "I can see tracks in the sand. We aren't alone. The city center offers a chance at having a fountain or well near one of the businesses."

They quickly worked their way through the streets and halted in the main plaza. There had indeed been a fountain, and several wells fronted the larger buildings.

Azimuth went to each well and took a deep breath smelling the clogged wells. "I smell water in this one, not too deep under the soil."

"Any volunteers to go down the shaft?" Tarquin asked.

There was no telling how old the city was, and the walls probably would not be stable.

Zeffan dismounted and approached. "I'll go if I can be levitated down. We won't have to test the strength of the walls. Get one of them empty water casks. Fix a rope to it, and we can haul the dirt away in it."

Accustomed to tight spaces, the dwarf was teleported down the shaft by Celedant. Once on the bottom, he found it to be made of soft sandy dirt and quickly began digging out cask after cask, which were raised up and dumped beside the well. Soon he called up, "The temperature is changing, and I think I smell water. It won't be long now."

Night had already fallen. Working with a torch sticking out of the mud wall, Zeffan saw the first trickle of water ooze from the wall. "Water! We found water," he called up. "Throw me a rope in case the floor gives way under me. I donna want to plunge into an underground stream."

He soon had several feet of water in the bottom of the well, but Tarquin called down to him. "We need to get you out. There are signs that we are not the only souls in this city out this evening."

Celedant levitated the wet dwarf up and out of the well, settling him to the side of the huge pile of dirt he had sent up the shaft.

As he dusted himself off, the wizard informed him, "There is movement all around us. The others have retreated to that building to make it as defensible as possible. Grab your axe and hurry."

Celedant and Zeffan headed to the building where the others had taken cover, stacking mud bricks chest high, shutting off the doorway. They left one window open for their friends to scamper through. Botreg, Tarquin, and Morganna then built up the windows height with bricks. The horses were tethered at the rear of the room. Azimuth and Hority attempted to calm them down.

From outside the building, they heard the first signs of an enemy, and they quickly gathered at the windows and door. They waited and waited as out in the night a great number of shuffling sounds could be heard. Then a horrid face looked in through the window. It had once been a human but white pustules peppered its face. Apparently, the town was populated by lepers. Before it could call a warning, Botreg thrust his sword through the monster's mouth killing it. The group remained hidden, not making a sound as two of the deformed creatures fell upon the dead body. The disgusting sounds of their feeding churned their stomachs. The creatures continued to mill about the town throughout the night. As morning came, one of the horses let out a nicker. One of the lepers heard the noise. It shuffled on deformed feet towards the door of the building. As it reached the entrance way, Tarquin and Eldahir reached over the brick wall they had constructed, pulling the leper into the building. Zeffan quickly swung his axe decapitating it.

Luck, however, was not with them. Several lepers saw their comrade pulled in the building, and they smelled fresh blood. As they advanced, others caught whiff of the blood and a crowd formed, advancing on the group's hiding place.

"Botreg, you and the dwarves stand back and kill whatever gets through," Tarquin commanded. "Be prepared to take one of our places should we fall."

As the first creature reached the wall, Morganna neatly struck its head from the body. Two of the lepers fell on the body but more followed.

Then the familiar war cry of, "Foes!" echoed in the building as the wild-eyed monk dove through the window and rolled to a stop. Upon standing, he struck out with his branch. Lepers fell with each touch.

"He's leading them away from us. I'll not let him die alone," Tarquin said in utter astonishment.

He leapt over the wall and followed the monk. After he went over the wall, the others followed. The lepers were so busy concentrating on the little monk, they did not see his friends approach from the rear. With all their attention focused on chasing Hority, the others began cutting down the enemy. Ahead of them, they could hear the Clorian's war cry, and they followed closely behind. The lepers never realized they were being dispatched from the rear.

Once the sun crested the eastern horizon, the lepers covered their eyes and ran down the main street. Some even grabbed up their dead without even noticing their attackers, too busy making sure they dragged their potential meals with them.

After the sunlight drove the lepers away, Celedant walked back to the house where the horses were stabled. He kicked something, bent down, and brought up Hority's staff.

"Has anyone seen Hority?" he called out. "I found his staff, but I don't see him anywhere."

"I saw him dodging in and out of the creatures, but that was the last time I saw him," Morganna said.

"He was protecting our rear, beating off the lepers with his staff and magic," Eldahir said.

"Come we must track them to their lair and retrieve our dirty monk," Tarquin called out urgently.

Zeffan pointed to two drag marks. "Look he was either unconscious, or he purposely left us a way to follow."

They ran, following the drag marks until they ended at the mud bricks of a broad stairway some forty paces wide that led up to a gaping maw of a doorway. The wooden doors had long since rotted away.

Tarquin nodded to Celedant. "They like the darkness. This is the perfect place to hide. Light up your staff, and let's get our missing comrade."

With Celedant's staff casting a brilliant light, he led them into the hallway, where they were attacked. The lepers were huddled in rags along the walls of the hall, and smelling blood coursing through the party's veins, they shuffled forward. The group had an easy time cutting them down.

Many came from the doorways in the front hall, and Celedant cast a fireball spell that rolled outward, engulfing most of the attackers. Their rags on fire, many shuffled and patted their clothes, trying to put out the flames. The spell's light also affected the lepers. Its bright flame drove all the remaining ones into hiding. Celedant and the others rushed to the two corridors at the front of the hall, each going in different directions.

Tarquin called out, "Celedant, can you tell which way he went."

Azimuth answered before the wizard could. "I can smell him. He's down the right-hand passage."

"I'm sorry ye have such an acute sense of smell," Botreg said.

They rushed down the hallway. Every now and again lepers would come at them, but Tarquin and Eldahir, who were at the front, quickly cut them down. It was like scything through wheat. The lepers threw themselves at them without any weapons and were instantly slashed down. Then the corridor opened up to a room of tremendous proportions, lit by sputtering torches. Hority was tied spread eagle to an altar. There was a leper without a shirt on, pustules and putrid dead flesh hanging off him, who stood behind the altar with a knife to the monk's throat.

Eldahir wasted no time and grabbed his bow and an arrow, aiming at the priest. Just as the leper was about to make a sacrifice of the dirty dwarf, an arrow appeared in his forehead, and he toppled over backward.

The whole of the room gasped aloud, and Celedant cast a lightning bolt spell that cut through the assembled creatures. Then he held his staff aloft and sent a sheet of flame sliding across the floor, incinerating the lepers as it touched them.

Tarquin and the others rushed across the hall, avoiding the dead and burning bodies. The stench of charred flesh was nauseating. They reached the altar to find Hority struggling with his bindings.

Tarquin was first to get to him. "Easy, friend. I've got you," he said as he used his dagger to free the monk.

Then from the back of the party Azimuth called out, "They're back and in greater numbers!"

Celedant tossed Hoity his staff and the monk angerly said, "Let me deal with these abominations to Clor!" He lowered his staff and cast spell after spell like a man possessed. First columns of fire fell from the roof to engulf dozens of creatures where they struck. He then raised his staff calling, "Everyone close yer eyes!"

Then from the pumice stone of the head of the staff a bright light issued forth that lit up the whole room like it was full sunlight. The lepers remaining with their light sensitive eyes were driven blind. They fell holding their hands over their faces.

Hority called over the moans of the lepers, "The spells over! It's time to go!"

The others opened their eyes and were shocked at what the little monk had been able to do. Celedant was a little worried at how powerful the spell had been. He would have to discuss that with Hority at a later time.

They made their escape from the leper's den, charging through the cavernous room and avoiding the writhing lepers and massive charred places where the flame had fallen. The burned bodies made them hold their breath, but they finally reached the doorway out of the huge chamber. There waiting for them were more lepers, attracted to what had occurred in the great hall.

Tarquin and Morganna, who were in the lead, quickly cut a path through the creatures. But they seemed more interested in the enticing smell of charred flesh than in fighting. Even so, it was necessary to hack through them in order to get out. Once through the first hall, they emerged into the bright desert sunlight. They had to shade their eyes, but Tarquin chivvied them onward. "We must hurry to escape our pursuers."

Once they reached the horses, Eldahir climbed the tallest building and scanned for the riders following them. He descended to tell them, "They must have ridden through the night. They are but a day and a half, possibly less, behind us."

Celedant took command. "Lower the cask down into the well. I can purify the water, then let's get the horses and mules drinking before we fill our water flasks and casks, and ride away from this accursed place."

Having watered the horses, filled their canteens and barrels, and drunk their fill, Celedant leaned into the well and cast a simple energy spell. It bounced off the walls of the well to the bottom. After a slight tremor, the well fell in upon itself. "We'll not be leaving any water for our pursuers."

They mounted up, but Hority was missing.

Botreg went to find him and found the monk sitting in a shady spot furiously writing in his journal. "What's all this about?"

Hority did not look up. "I'm writing about the strange pustules on those creatures from last night, and I intend to study one of the mud bricks, too."

Botreg was taken aback. Usually, he would have to had to search for hours before turning up the filth covered dwarf. Yet, here was Hority, studiously working away.

"All right, Hority," the ex-assassin said. "Time to mount up and go, me friend. Our pursuers are hot on our trail."

The smelly dwarf stood up. Sand cascaded off him like he had taken a bath in it. "Praise Clor. This place is cursed with a cleanliness spell. Nothing here but regular sand. Discreetly he placed a mud brick in his satchel for later study."

Once they joined the others, they set off at a brisk pace, all too eager to be rid of the ancient city and its inhabitants. Whoever had been following them had ridden through the night and probably would stop to rest in the ruins to get away from the sun's bright light.

For days they continued westward with the cloud of dust always following until they ascended from the desert to a rocky landscape. To their relief, the sand turned to dirt where they encountered the first trees. They were stunted but green. After days of nothing but sand and dead trees, it was a huge relief to see life.

Eldahir rode back from his point position and called out with a smile on his face. "I see a forest!"

That declaration rose everyone's mood, and the horses seemed to have a spring in their step as they followed a game trail. With the trees growing in size, Celedant took one last look over the desert. There in the distance was the ever-present cloud of dust.

He called to the others above the sound of the horses' pounding feet. "Don't forget those that follow us. We'll need to camp well off the trail come nightfall."

That seemed to spur the riders onward at an even faster pace. As night slowly came to the heavily forested land, they began looking for a game trail that might lead to a good place to camp. Zeffan finally spotted a small trail that the animals of the forest had been using regularly. Once everyone was off the trail and heading deeper into the forest, Celedant cast a spell, and a wind came up that erased all signs of their passing. He turned off the trail and stopped on the game path.

He went to the entrance and whispered a spell to the bushes that surrounded the opening to the small trail. The undergrowth began growing at a rapid pace, with the branches becoming entangled, completely obscuring their passage. Tarquin led them well into the dense undergrowth before calling for a camp to be cleared. Then with their weapons, they cut away the brush, opening an area where all of them could sleep.

After eating a cold meal of jerked beef and water, the friends spent a sleepless night. When it was morning Eldahir went back the way they had come and waited for a turn of the clock, watching the path. As he was about to leave, his acute hearing picked up the sounds of horses on the move. He watched as a warlock with one arm flashed by, followed by twenty of the giant white orcs. He stayed in his position for thirty ticks of the clock before turning and following the trail back to camp.

The others had their horses and mules saddled and gear stowed, awaiting his arrival. As he entered the camp, Eldahir told Celedant, "I saw a one-armed warlock leading twenty of the great white orcs. Do you know this magic user?"

Celedant thought for a while. "Tarquin, do you recall a warlock matching that description in the tower of Dormin when Taza, with the aid of the staff of Adois, flew it to Dragon Isle?"

The vampire warlock had used the endless power of his staff and dark magic to lift the very castle of the city of Dormin up out of the ground and fly its tower to Edain to assault the Dragon's Tear.

"Yes, I remember a one-armed warlock clinging to his staff where it was lodged between two stones," Tarquin replied. "Despite what was going on, he reminded me of Melgor, the warlock that saved me from death at Zeiglon."

The wizard got a far-off look in his eyes and said silently, "I knew Melgor many years ago. I'm afraid he's been trying to kill me ever since. We must watch him carefully. I would not put any trust in him." Celedant asked one last question. "How did their horses look?"

"They look to be on their last legs," Eldahir sadly answered.

Chapter Twenty-Four

Hearing this, the others tethered their horses while Tarquin spoke. "We can't allow them to get ahead of us. Sooner or later, we will have to fight them, and I think we should use the cover of the forest to even the numbers. Morganna and Eldahir can take a few out once they slow down. Their horses cannot take much more. The weight of the white orcs is double that of a full-grown man. What say you? Morganna? Eldahir?"

"This undergrowth is thinning out the deeper we go into the forest, Morganna and I could keep up with them and pick two off at a time. Then we could retreat into the forest where you would be awaiting," Eldahir said after a moment's thought. "Or Botreg, would you be able to sneak into their camp and take care of the guards? Then we could ride over them, or Celedant could get close enough to cast a spell."

Tarquin nodded his head throughout the discussion. "I'd like to attack in the dark. Let's kill the guards. Then Celedant can roll a fireball spell through the camp and roast the remaining orcs and the warlock."

"I agree with Tarquin. The spell will greatly reduce their numbers and make it easier on us," Celedant replied.

Leading the horses back to the trail. Celedant removed the undergrowth barrier he had created and led them toward the orcs. Morganna and Eldahir were afoot well ahead of the others. Morganna's ribs were healed completely, thanks to the Clorian monk.

The two elves soon caught the smell of fires burning and slowed their pace. Ahead, they saw a widening of the trail and several campfires. Eldahir touched his wife's shoulder and pointed to the line of horses. Most had their heads down almost touching the ground, while one lay on its side dead. The orcs were using its meat for food. Eldahir sent Morganna back for the others and within moments, Celedant and Tarquin were beside the elf.

"There are two guards here and two on the other side of the camp," Eldahir said, pointing. "We'll kill these two. Then Celedant, it will be your turn. Tarquin then can ride down what's left of them." The two men nodded, and Tarquin retreated back to the others, who were mounted with their weapons drawn.

The two guards were facing each other and talking when the two elves let fly their arrows. An arrow struck through the throat of one guard. The other orc was hit in the temple both fell as Celedant rushed forward to cast his spell.

Meanwhile, Melgor was half asleep when he felt the magic of a powerful wizard. He threw off his blanket and rolled into the forest behind a massive tree.

Celedant's staff glowed white hot as a gigantic fireball rolled forth across the ground and into the camp of his enemies. The first of the orcs were incinerated, while still asleep. The remaining orcs ran about on fire.

Tarquin's horse ran over one of the burning orcs, and he neatly decapitated another that had stood up without any weapons. Eldahir and Morganna started firing arrows into the camp, while Tarquin led the charge. While in the saddle, Zeffan was almost as tall as the orcs. He leaned out, splitting one's head open with his axe. Azimuth was among several survivors of Celedant's spell, fending off swords and dealing death to the orcs that had him surrounded. Hority was struck from his saddle by a mace wielding orc. He fell, landing a few feet from the white monster, gasping for breath. He doubted anything was broken and began crawling towards his enemy. As he inched his way forward, the orc reared back with his mace ready to crush the dwarf's skull. But the monk reached out with his branch lightly touching the monster's foot. It died instantly and fell on top of Hority.

The remainder of the white orcs panicked as the horsemen surrounded them and slowly forced their way closer. While arrows kept pouring in, striking them down. Zeffan suddenly saw movement out of the corner of his eye and whirled around his horse. He dismounted quickly and ran to find the one-armed warlock with his back against the tree, hoping to stay out of the fight. When Melgor saw the dwarf, he calculated whether or not to attack. But he knew the orcs were being slaughtered, so he rolled his staff away and held up his one good arm.

"Stay there, or I'll kill ye," Zeffan gruffly commanded.

"Not a problem," Melgor said. "I have no intention of involving myself in that fight."

Finally, Tarquin turned his horse and rode into the orcan circle, splitting it in two. He fended off the blade of one orc as the other riders headed into the tightly packed creatures. Suddenly fist sized blue balls of electric flame roared in, striking the bloodied orcs. When a ball of energy struck an enemy, electricity ran up and down its body dropping it to the ground. Finally, there was one orc left, tirelessly striking and parrying swords with Azimuth. Then suddenly, two arrows appeared in the creature's chest and the last orc collapsed.

The companions looked around at each other making sure no one had been seriously injured.

"Where is Hority!" Botreg called out.

They heard the muffled sounds of yelling and Azimuth quickly stepped over to a dead orc, hefting it off the monk. Hority had been pinned under the considerable weight of the monster.

Hority sat up holding his chest. "I have taken a mighty blow. How went the battle? Once again, I have been left out of the scuffle. But I can write about this in me journal. The odor of this special orc was quite exhilarating." The others turned away from the monk as he got out his journal to record the nights events.

Tarquin called to Botreg. "See that the orcs are all dead." Swinging his sword in the air he nodded and stalked off to check if any of their enemies were still alive.

Then from the edge of the woods Zeffan called out. "Celedant, I caught the warlock for ye."

Melgor was huddled against a tree with Zeffan's axe pressed to his throat as Tarquin and Celedant advanced.

"We had an agreement that I got to kill you the next time we met," Tarquin reminded the warlock. "You seem to have lost an arm since then."

"What have we here? The warlock that has dogged my trail off and on my entire life?" Celedant asked sarcastically. "Why have you followed me here?"

"Cyra the sorcerous is responsible for both my arm and my being here." He replied, "She is pure evil, and I ended up being her lieutenant through no act of my own."

Botreg finished with his grisly task spoke up, "I remember. Ye fought with us on Dragon Isle."

"There was a woman that ended up in the Dragon's Tear when we were destroying the staffs," Celedant added. "She was expelled by the crystalline entity before Taza was killed."

"It was none of my doing," Melgor pleaded. "I saved Tarquin's life and fought with you. It was Cyra that teleported me to the northern mainland from the island. We hid there for almost a year."

Azimuth laughed. "A tall tale. No one is capable of a teleportation spell that strong."

"Yet, she did it," Melgor answered. "After several teleports, we were outside of Trudoc. She rode to gather orcs. I imagine it was you that caused the light show in the tower?"

"How did you follow us?" Celedant asked.

Melgor shrugged. "Cyra gave me a map and deduced that you would be following it, too."

Botreg butted into the conversation, "I say we kill him now and rid this world of his evil actions."

"What say you, Tarquin?" the Warlock asked. "I saved your life and offered up myself at a future date."

Tarquin looked at Celedant. "Can we trust him?"

The wizard looked deeply into Melgor's eyes, "I sense great fear in him and not of us. I tend to believe what he says. Though he withholds secrets. I say he is trustworthy to a point. He cannot run away in this inhospitable land and will stay with us for as long as he minds his manners and does what he is told. Just remember, Melgor, all our eyes will be upon you. Give us even the slightest reason, and we will kill you without a second thought."

The warlock grasped his staff, which he used to get up. "I will not run. There is nowhere safe from Cyra. I found that out with the loss of my arm. She will kill me for this failure to be sure."

CHAPTER TWENTY-FIVE

Mounting up, the friends and their questionable companion rode away from the massacre. They had a few cuts and bruises, but nothing deep. Poor Hority, however, was in such pain that he could not mount his horse. Celedant handed him a healing draught, and Morganna made him take off his frock, leaving him in nothing but a little washed loin cloth. He blushed as she wrapped a linen cloth around his chest and ribs. Being so close to the barely clothed odiferous dwarf made her sick to her stomach, and she longed to toss him into a tub and vigorously scrub him with a bar of strong soap.

Celedant took out his map to determine where they were, when Melgor said, "That's an exact replica of the map I was given."

The wizard nodded. "This Cyra is most adept at obtaining rare objects."

"What do you suppose is at the end of this trail?" the Warlock asked.

Celedant shrugged. "It was important to the Clorians and the Warlock Guild. So, who knows? Treasure I would think. One does not go to the trouble of drawing a map for no reason at all."

They continued west at a fast pace through the forest and several days later they entered the foothills. The ground began to rise and soon thereafter, what they had been waiting to find was right in front of them – the north and south path. Eldahir and Zeffan had dismounted and were waiting for the others to reach them.

Once Celedant and Tarquin were alongside them, Zeffan told them, "The path is well traveled. There are hoof marks, boot, and strange claw marks like I have never seen."

"Melgor did Cyra mention anything about something that might be make this type of tracks?" Celedant asked.

"No. I was told nothing," he replied.

"It could be anything," Azimuth said. "Guards from a distant kingdom, a caravan, highway men, or creatures of various sorts."

"Well," Celedant said, "we have several weeks of travel on this road before finding the path up into the mountains. Sooner or later, we most likely will find out."

As the wizard uttered those words, Tarquin got squeamish. Would he miss his child's birth? If so, Ress would never forgive him. These thoughts continued in his mind as they turned onto the road. Yes, he had wanted to get away for a while. But truth be told, he really did want to be there for the birth of his first child.

The track followed the contours of the foothills up one ridge and down another never ending. After traveling for a week, Eldahir stopped the column of riders.

He held up his hand. "Listen. There isn't a sound to be heard."

"This is an interesting development," Celedant said. "Something has hunted this area out of all available food sources."

They had been following the road for some time when they found Eldahir and Zeffan stopped off the side of the road. They reined their horses in around them, and the elf pointed to a spot halfway up a tree about thirty cubits.

"See the long spear stuck in the tree? It had to be thrown at a downward angle. So, whatever is hunting here either uses the trees as transportation or can fly."

Suddenly a spear came down from the treetops and struck Zeffan in the right thigh throwing him off his horse. He landed on his back in extreme pain, holding his leg with both hands. Morganna aimed and shot an arrow up into the tree. There was a yell of pain and a figure toppled from the tree. No one had seen such a winged creature before, but they had no time to examine it.

"Dismount and take cover behind those trees," Tarquin commanded." He pointed to a line of trees behind them. He then dismounted and in a hail of spears and arrows, he got to Zeffan. Grabbing the dwarf under each arm pit, he dragged the tracker to safety.

Unbeknownst to the company, five of the creatures landed behind them, advancing rapidly. Zeffan holding tightly to his leg saw them coming and shouted, "Look to the rear!"

The monsters could not walk very well on their feet, which were made for sitting in the tree branches and had to use their wings to skim along the ground. Tarquin and Eldahir darted out to meet them before they could get to the others. Tarquin ducked one blow but was caught by the creature's wing, which threw him backward. It came after him, but the Prince stabbed upward, catching it in the stomach. As it fell, Tarquin jumped up only to face another monster. Wary of the wings, he got in close to the creature, bashing it in the throat and crushing its windpipe. The winged beast fell away from him.

Meanwhile, Eldahir was surrounded by the creatures desperately trying to fend off their swords. He used his elvan quickness to stab one of the creatures and instantly parry a blow from another. The he heard Tarquin charged forward into the battle. Eldahir fended off one and stabbed the other through the shoulder. Then Tarquin was there, attacking the second one from the rear. He chopped down cutting though the creature's wing. This caused the monster to lose its balance and settle to its feet. It stood for a moment, its good wing beating furiously to keep it standing. But no matter how hard it flapped its wing, the creature fell sideways. Tarquin struck, slicing halfway through its neck. The elvan general dueled with the last one, blood seeping from its shoulder wound and as the creature saw it compatriots fall, it attempted to fly away. Eldahir struck out with his sword, cutting through its exposed leg. The monster flew away trailing blood behind it. The two warriors quickly ran to take cover behind the trees.

Morganna and the others sent arrows up into the foliage of the tree. Several of the winged creatures were struck and fell to the ground. Celedant and Melgor cast spell after spell.

Some of the spells set the treetops alight, and the monsters took off and flew down towards them. These were quickly shot out of the air by well-placed arrows. By this time, each tree they were hiding behind had several spears and arrows embedded in them.

Celedant called to Azimuth, "This could go on until night, and we'll be slowly slaughtered. Can you do anything?"

"Cover me while I retreat backwards," he replied. "It's time for me to show these cowards my true form."

Celedant called to the others. "Fire as many arrows as possible. Azimuth is about to transform. They complied and both magic users sent bright flames arching up into the trees.

Azimuth had run about a hundred feet when he felt a stinging in his calf. An arrow had struck him, and he rolled forward thinking all the while, "Its time."

In an instant, the swirling mist of colors began around him, and as they disappeared, his real form, that of a golden dragon, sat on the ground. He let out a mighty roar, his size crushing trees all around his body. The arrow disappeared. Standing up, he walked up behind his friends, pushing aside age-old trees as he went. Reaching their position, Azimuth extended his neck beyond their position, took a deep breath, and exhaled white-hot flame. It incinerated the treetops well beyond fifty paces. They heard screams, but that was all.

They waited ten clicks of the clock before venturing forth. There was a burned-out arch of the trees where nothing could have survived. Hority saw to Zeffan as the others gathered around the dead bodies of their attackers, who were man-sized, but there the resemblance ended.

They had clawed feet shaped to allow them to easily grasp tree branches, and bat like heads with huge ears to hear at night. Their skin was a mottled color to blend in with the foliage of the trees, and tough leathery wings sprouted from their shoulder blades.

Tarquin asked what was on everyone's mind. "What is it?"

Celedant shook his head and looked to Melgor who said, "I have never seen nor read about one of these."

Everyone offered guesses, but they did not ring true to any of the others.

Finally, Celedant said, "We can argue this point until dawn. Let's just chalk it up to a new breed from the west."

Hority was at the foot of the creature quickly sketching it, when Botreg asked, "Where is Zeffan?"

Without looking up from his book he answered pointing behind him. "He's recuperating against a tree over yonder. I have healed him and wrapped the wound with clean linen. He will be fine in a day or two."

"Hority, time is wasting," Tarquin commanded. "We must gather the horses and mules and get back on the road, out of these monsters' territory."

Chapter Twenty-Six

With Tarquin in the lead, they continued riding north through the foothills ever alert for an attack. The trees kept them sheltered from the sun, and there was a cool breeze coming off the mountains. The idyllic nature of the area put them at ease, as they recovered from their recent hair-raising adventure.

One day as they ate dinner, Eldahir and Morgana stood up quickly, calling out, "To arms! There is a tremor in the ground. Something comes this way!"

Some ways down the path coming from the direction of the mountain, they heard screeches. The smell of the campfire had given away their presence, and whatever was out in the night was coming quickly.

The company gathered with their backs to the fire and waited. Zeffan faced the path heading westward directly toward their camp. Using his natural dwarvan ability of night vision, he called out, "They are here!"

Eldahir and Morganna loosed their arrows, hearing the thumps as their targets fell. Then their unknown enemies were upon them. These creatures were scaled from head to foot, man-sized, with long, sharp, razor-like claws. With the fire silhouetting him, Zeffan blocked one's swipe from its long claws. The dwarf struck out, landing a blow deep into the side of the beast.

Fearing the worse, Hority ran towards the horses calling to Botreg, "We must protect the horses." Botreg followed, fearing for the Clorian's life.

But that was unnecessary as the dwarf swung his branch back and forth killing the monsters whilst yelling, "Foes!"

By now, everyone was fighting for their lives as the monsters pushed them back towards the fire. Tarquin fought off two creatures, his sword flaring brightly in the darkness each time he blocked and counterattacked. Celedant fended off one of the attackers, meanwhile casting spells into the massed attackers whenever he could with a variety of spells that brought down an enemy or drove them back. But the sharp clawed creatures continued the attack, and as one died another took its place.

This was taking a toll on everyone. They were tiring and started taking wounds. Botreg, who had followed Hority out to protect the horses, had one of the attackers pop up in front of him using a beak full of sharp teeth leaving a huge bite mark in his arm. If not for Botreg's quick counterattack, which penetrated the heart of his enemy, he might have lost his arm.

Melgor had followed Botreg to the horses as well. He mounted one of the horses and started casting spells of his own. Riding to the front of the trail, he sent a fireball rolling from his staff down the trail, illuminating the night and showing just how many creatures they were facing. There were dozens crowding the path waiting for a chance to join the battle.

Azimuth used his superior skill with the sword to kept the enemies at bay, sending one after another reeling away with grievous wounds. Then suddenly, five claws ballooned out the front of his shirt. Blood spurted in the air as he struck blindly backwards and felt his sword impact into something. He fell into a sitting position to compress the wounds and stop the blood flow. Then with a blood-soaked hand, he drew forth a vial with a healing potion in it and swallowed it down. The pain eased, but blood still trickled from the wounds.

Feeling the pain of his bonded dragon, Celedant called out into the darkness. "Hority. You are needed. Azimuth has taken a grievous wound!"

Out of the night came the Clorian monk, quietly dispatching several of the attackers with his branch. He slid to a stop before Azimuth and said, "Donna worry, me dragon friend. I'm here to help ye."

He immediately placed his hands on the wounds calling forth Clor's name, beseeching his help to heal his friend. Slowly a brown dusty cloud formed over the wounds, and they stopped bleeding. Hority turned Azimuth on his stomach to look at his back. Blood still oozed from the wounds. The arm of his attacker had been cut off at the elbow by Azimuth's backward slash. The dwarvan healer quickly pulled the clawed hand out of the dragon's back in a wash of blood, once again calling for the aid of Clor when he heard an attacker come up behind him.

He picked up his staff and with just a mild touch, the creature fell dead. Hority finished another healing spell, and Azimuth felt much better, but he could not protect himself and lay still on the ground.

"Donna worry friend. I will stand guard over ye," Hority assured his friend.

The dirty dwarf stood at the feet of the wounded wood elf, fending off the creatures. Soon there were a pile of dead bodies surrounding the two of them. The rest of their troop fought on through the night as more and more creatures came at them. Then as the sun came up the monsters began backing away, throwing their dead over their shoulders. Botreg exited the forest where their horses had been kept. "Grim news. Three of the horses are gone."

Still astride his horse, Melgor rode around the camp and reported, "They have taken all their dead and wounded. A strange attack as ever I have seen."

Tarquin sat next to the burnt-out fire on the blood strewn ground and called to his friend and mentor, Celedant. "What say you? These were strange creatures the likes of which I have never seen."

The wizard sat with his head back against a tree. "In my studies on Dragon Isle, I came across a reference that matched these beasts in description. Their name translated into the modern language is dragonettes. They serve evil dragons who keep them as a hive for getting food and treasure. I know you are wounded, but what do you think Azimuth?"

The wounded elf hoarsely said, "An evil black dragon has never been recorded on Muiria. But if one is hidden on this side of the world, we are in trouble. We have been told tales from the oldest of my kind about these types of dragons. The stories may have been embellished, but they portray a very power foe. I will have to be wary and ready to do battle at a moment's notice. In my wounded state, however, I could not face such a creature.

"We'll go further down this path and pick a good defensible position to let our wounds heal. Then when we are ready, we can move onward."

CHAPTER TWENTY-SEVEN

They traveled the road north east before finding a small trail alongside a stream. Zeffan rode back to report that they had discovered a promising trail. The companions fairly galloped up over a ridge and down, catching glimpses of running water through the trees.

Eldahir dismounted and examined the land beside the stream. He looked up at Celedant. "This is the most promising trail we have come across. It is well used and appears to have been cut through the undergrowth and lower tree limbs. There are also strange with clawed prints along it. I have never seen the like. It reminds me of the dragonettes."

While the wizard pondered the situation, Tarquin spoke up. "We can follow it to its source. There's water readily available, and I tire of this road."

"The map does not point out where the trail is," Celedant agreed. "But this seems right to me. What worries me are the strange tracks. This is a wild countryside, and we'll have to keep close watch. Azimuth, could you follow the trail in dragon form seeing what might await us?"

"I think if I fly low enough to the stream, I'll have no problem," the dragon replied.

The wizard laughed suddenly. "Do you mind a passenger?"

"Not at all," replied the dragon. "It has been a while since we've ridden together. It will be most welcome."

Hority, armed with his journal, dismounted and headed to where Azimuth stood. "It won't take a minute, and I'll be ready to go."

Azimuth smiled. "No, little one. I fear that those ahead might remember your odor as we fly. Remember, tis Clorians that found this place. They might have left an impact on the denizens that live here."

The filthy dwarf was disheartened but agreed. "I will have to wait until a better time to fly. To think I would be the first brother to have climbed into the heavens."

Before Hority could continue with his sermon Botreg stepped in. "Tis okay, Hority. I'm sure Azimuth will allow ye to fly later."

"Certainly," replied the elf. "I will gladly take you for a flight. But this time we need the map reader to accompany me." Though the thought of having the unwashed dwarf upon his back sent shivers down his spine. His acute sense of smell made being near the dwarf even harder on him. *Maybe I could 'accidently' drop him in a river,* he told Celedant mentally.

The wizard laughed.

Azimuth waded out into the stream that was knee deep and about twenty paces wide before casting the spell to turn him back to his natural form. A swirling multi color mist suddenly covered the stream and as it wafted away, there sat the giant golden dragon. Azimuth quickly summoned a saddle and harness then levitated Celedant to his back where the wizard, with sure hands, strapped on the harness.

With wings wider than the stream, the dragon launched himself upward with four powerful legs and with one flap of his wings. Those left behind were splashed with water from the mighty wings.

The companions enjoyed the shower of water, all except Hority, who danced around in an effort to shed his wet frock. "Tis unholy to be splashed by the clean water of the stream." Once he was down to his filthy loin cloth, he calmed down and went about carefully wringing out his frock trying not to get the dirt and grime off.

"I think you did that on purpose, my friend," Celedant said with a laugh, once they were out of hearing distance.

You bet I did, the dragon admitted. *Not quite as good as dumping him in the river, but it might help.*

Azimuth spread his wings, soaring high into the sky, telepathically speaking to Celedant. *It feels so good to get out of that confined body and be able to fly. I haven't been able to do that much lately, and it sorely pains me.*

"I can feel your joy," Celedant responded aloud. "And I'm sorry we've had to be in such confined spaces, but we need to get on with our mission."

You could spoil a fresh baked pie if you wanted to, the dragon said wryly.

Azimuth brought his wings in to his sides diving towards the stream, causing Celedant's stomach to feel like it had jumped into his chest ready to explode. Just as they reached the stream, Azimuth pulled up and soon they were gliding alongside the creek above the trees. He flew the winding course of the river, giving them a good view of the pathway.

As the dragon slowly flapped his wings, they went further and further into the foothills. And before long, they approached the beginning of the mountains where the path ran right beside the stream. Then suddenly, Azimuth banked right, heading back the way they had come.

He sped eastward calling to Celedant, who until the sudden change in the flight had almost dozed off.

"What is wrong my friend?" the wizard inquired.

Azimuth shook his head like he was clearing cobwebs from his mind. *I sensed a greater evil then I have ever faced before. I was afraid that without a spell to cover my magic and true form I would be revealed to this evil entity. Up here and this close, I feared my spell might act like a beacon and draw this evil to me.*

Azimuth curved and stayed as low as he could to the stream as he escaped eastward, finally coming upon their companions preparing to make camp. Celedant was teleported to land and Azimuth cast a spell that blanketed him in the rainbow fog and suddenly he was an elf again. He hurried through that frigid water to the camp site where the others had gathered to hear what had happened.

Celedant stood among of the group and relayed what they had learned during the hair-raising flight. "The path continues to follow the stream straight up the foothills and into the mountains. As we neared the mountains, however, Azimuth felt an evil presence. We turned around."

Reality set in as everyone realized that a presence of something evil enough to stop a golden dragon bode ill for their mission.

Azimuth took up the narrative where the wizard left off. "As I flew west into the mountains, I could feel the oddest tingling in every fiber of my body. Never have I known such evil to exist on Muiria. I don't know what resides in the far mountains, but we must be extra careful as we advance. I will reassume this form for the rest of the journey and cast a spell to shield most of my power, which should protect me from unseeing eyes."

Hority broke loose from Botreg and hastily said, "We must put our hands into the care of Clor. Me brothers once ventured here and survived. May we can do the same."

"Might I suggest two guards at night?" Morganna suggested. "Just to be on the safe side."

Prince Tarquin nodded. "I agree. We must take extra caution now that we're near our goal."

"We still have six turns of the clock before sunset. I suggest we continue onward," Eldahir stated.

Everyone agreed, and they broke camp, doubling up on the horses because of the loss of three. They followed the trail once more.

CHAPTER TWENTY-EIGHT

Back in New Partha, Princess Ress restlessly walked around her and Tarquin's suite of rooms. After their marriage, Queen Alicia had insisted they trade her son's bachelor suite for a larger one, more suited to a married couple. The suite contained a large luxurious bedroom done in peach and earth tones with a huge bed, comfortable ornate furnishings, and wall hangings, as well as a sitting room, smaller bedroom for when the Princess wasn't feeling well, a private bathing chamber, and a nursery.

Ress and Tarquin had begun decorating the nursery before her husband had gone to the Clorians conclave. But with the Prince gone, Ress and the Queen had to finish it. Not knowing when he would return, the women decided they could not risk the baby being born without his or her room ready.

"Darn your son," Ress said for what seemed like the 100th time. "I understand these things are important, but so is the birth of our child." Her long red hair was done in a thick braid that hung down her back, leaving a few shorter, wispy strands to frame her beautiful face. Had the King and Queen seen it before the monks and their god had healed the scars there, they would not have been quite so happy.

"His father and I aren't happy about it either. Timmons has yet to produce an heir, which makes your children even more important, should Tarquin have to assume the throne after his brother." She hesitated and her eyes misted up.

Seeing this, Ress walked over and hugged the Queen. "I understand."

"I'm sorry. I have not gotten over the loss of my eldest son. I don't think I ever will. Before Partha was destroyed and the terrible war with Zeiglon began, we thought three sons would cover it. Now, I'm not so sure. Timmons does not seem to be in a hurry to marry, even though the King has all but ordered him to do so," Alicia said.

Ress led her mother-in-law over to a chair and went to her favorite overstuffed lounge chair across from her. "You know it's not that easy, Mother. It is better to marry for love. It makes for a much happier life together," Ress said gently as she eased her pregnant body down and propped her feet up.

"I know, my dear, but a royal doesn't always have that choice. Sometimes, we must marry to secure an alliance. It's what King Benton and I did. Lucky for us, we fell madly in love, although not right away. But within a year, we knew that the two of us were meant for each other. With Tarquin the third in line, we didn't need to worry about an arrangement for him," Alicia said.

"Thank heavens for that," Ress said. "Otherwise, he and I could not have married."

The Queen smiled. "Although you are not of royal blood, you were born to be a princess. You have taken to royalty and your duties like you were born to it."

"Thank you, mother. And thank you and father for taking me into your hearts. With my own parents gone, it is comforting to have family about me." She stopped speaking and began rubbing the left side of her swollen belly.

"Is the baby kicking?" the Queen asked anxiously.

"Yes! Come feel."

Alicia jumped up and allowed Ress to guide her hand to the right spot. Her face lit up with a huge smile. "Yes, I feel it. He's a strong one, just like his father was."

As she went back to her chair, Ress said, "Or she."

"I'm sorry. What did you say, dear?"

"Or she. It could be a girl," Ress told her.

The Queen's eyes grew dreamy. "Oh, I know. The men always want the first one to be a boy. But a little princess would be so wonderful. During all three of my pregnancies, I used to dream about what it would be like to have a little girl. Maybe I'll get my wish through you and Tarquin. She would grow up to be such a beautiful princess with just the right amount of sass," she said with a wink.

"Just between you and me, I, too, have been wishing for a little girl. And Tarquin would be thrilled, as well. He would spoil her rotten."

"Not too rotten," the Queen admonished. "She would need to have the proper decorum, manners, sophistication, and…just a bit of tom boy in her," she finished with a twinkle in her eye. She sighed. "If only Tarquin had gone off to train with the elven ambassador, we had set up for him. He would not be in much danger so often."

"That's true," Ress agreed. "But then, he and I would never have met. And you must admit. He has formed some very strong bonds with the Wood Elves and their royal family."

"You're right, the Queen agreed. "And that would have been a mistake. I understand that now. But when he ran off to join the Borderers, his father and I were furious."

"However, thanks to Celedant sending him to the Borderers, he definitely knows how to take care of himself in a fight."

"Agreed."

"I wonder where they are now, and what they're doing. I hope they hurry up and find what they need for the Clorians. And I hope they aren't in too much danger from enemies."

Fortunately, Ress and the Queen had no idea just how bad it had been or was about to get.

Chapter Twenty-Nine

With three horses having to double up their riders, the friends decided to take turns walking and riding on the road deeper into the mountains. They traveled for five turns of the clock before deciding to make camp, but they found very little dirt to drive their stakes into the ground.

"We are drawing close to the rocky slopes of the mountain," Celedant mused.

It was a relatively new mountain chain. The forest ended where the slopes were made up of stones and shale that had been washed down from above. The road turned back into a path, but it was obviously well maintained with the rocks and loose shale moved to the side of the road and stacked up in mounds.

Zeffan gave a shout to stop them and pointed out what he had spotted. "Blood trails from the retreating dragonettes, so we know we're on the correct course. There must have been a short cut from where we were attacked back up into the mountains."

The horses had trouble finding their footing, so everyone dismounted and walked alongside their mounts. At each step, they ran the risk of sliding backwards into the following horse. So, they had to put as much distance between them as they could allow. Luckily, it had not rained lately, and they finally reached the top of the slippery stone slope. There, they found a proper path that hugged the mountain side and was free of debris. They still walked their horses, while Eldahir and Zeffan went ahead, scouting the path they were on.

A wise move as they soon stumbled across the opening of a cave where the blood trail disappeared inside. The two scouts edged up to the opening, a slash in the mountain five cubits wide and twelve high. Both peered into the gloom but saw no guards. They ventured forth into the darkness, but the passage ran straight ahead.

They returned to the entrance and waited for the others to catch up, always keeping an eye on the cave entrance. Once the others reached them, Celedant and Melgor took out their maps. The warlock and wizard compared the two for what seemed like the hundredth time.

Shaking his head Celedant said, "Neither map mentions any caves. They have the path ending at a large glade or crater. Perhaps an ancient volcano that helped form these mountains. What say you Azimuth do you sense anything?"

The elf shrugged. "I can't with this blocking spell I have cast. It works both ways. My powers can't be ferreted out, and I can't do the same. It is harrowing, but I am blocked from the magical world."

Following the conversation, Tarquin said, "Well its best we follow the map. I don't fancy running into those dragonettes in the confines of a cave. Let's move on to the glade or crater."

They made it another mile up the path before the light started giving way to darkness. They fed the horses and two mules and lay down in their blankets to sleep. It was a cool breezy night, and for the first time, their blankets were a necessity. Most slept against the mountain side of the path, knowing that there was a steep drop off on the other side.

The next day dawned with a chill wind from the west off the top of the mountains. Breaking camp, they ate a cold breakfast before continuing the westward heading. They had not traveled far when the mountains opened up, revealing a grassy area and in the distance, a huge crater.

The path led straight down the mountain onto the flat verdant land. The horses and mules ate the grass voraciously as the friends gathered together in the knee-high growth.

Celedant pointed out to the crater. "We are here. Or I should say, we have reached an impasse. The crater seems to block all the ways around and out of it. The trail ends here as the map shows. We will need to discover the answer to this mystery. But for now, I suggest we all get a good night's sleep. Tomorrow might be the fight of our lives, or we may have to go below ground into the confines of a cave system or indeed the crater itself."

The normally quiet Melgor spoke up. "I see no sign of lava here. That crater is from no volcano. It was made by something falling from the sky."

The others nodded and Tarquin added. "We must be ready for anything. However peaceful this feels, I sense danger all about us. Celedant, what say you to a ride to the crater. There is plenty of daylight left."

"I don't see why not," the Wizard agreed. "We need to scout it out today or tomorrow anyway. The rest of you set up camp. We'll be back soon."

The two friends mounted their horses and rode toward the crater. The grass lasted five hundred paces, then turned back into the black rock they had grown accustomed to. Slowing their horses, the two dismounted, staked them out in the grass, and ventured forth on foot. The crater was as Melgor had surmised. There was no sign of an explosion or cooled lava that would be associated with a volcano.

"I have to agree with Melgor. This is no volcano," Tarquin agreed. "Something crashed here…something very large and heavy."

Celedant agreed. "Melgor was right. We'll have to descend into it and see what we find. I don't relish having to go back to the tunnel and enter the mountain that way. It could take weeks to find our way underground to this point."

CHAPTER THIRTY

The black dragon was awake. Its children, the simple minded dragonettes, had brought word of a great battle fought on his doorstep. The horses they had brought him smelled of outsiders. Like the dark elf Martish, who had recently visited him on a mission for the vampire lord, Tibersu. Time was nothing to a dragon. He could not remember how long ago the evil Goddess Adois had visited him. She had promised him a new wing and a tail should he help the dark elf.

The goddess had been true to her word. She had stood on the balcony overlooking his cave and cast evil spells of healing upon him. Suddenly he had a new wing and tail, which had been severed off as numerous good dragons had flown through a portal from the nothingness that lay between the planets onto this barren rock. He had attempted to sneak through, but the portal had closed on him severing his wing and tail. Flightless, he had fallen through the sky and crashed through into this cavern. Countless eons had passed while he slept. Then the dragonettes had discovered him and revered the sleeping behemoth.

They saw him as a god, and they worshipped him, bringing treasure and piling it up in front of him. Awaking from his endless sleep, he discovered thousands of the small creatures all lined up and chanting in their guttural tone. He quickly struck and ate several dozen as the creatures pushed forward for the honor to serve their god. Sated, he searched for and quickly found the mind of the high priest. Entering it, he said, "Your worship pleases me. Go find me food and treasure and your flock can still stay here and do my bidding."

Yet now something was on its way to his domain. He had felt the power for a split second several days ago after his minions had attacked a party of adventurers. The dragonettes that returned had been soundly beaten in the encounter, but the power he had felt had not been used. The attackers had described a mere group of adventurers that had stood toe to toe with his children and slaughtered them. The only thing the battle had accomplished was to fill his belly and leave a mystery.

As Celedant and Tarquin stood on the edge of the crater, the Wizard spoke slowly with slight tremor of fear in his voice. "I feel great evil in this place, somewhere deep beneath us. I'm afraid Azimuth will be needed. But the minute he transforms, the evil will rise from this hole to the nine hells."

Tarquin had never seen Celedant quite so afraid. If anything, the wizard had a calming effect on him whenever there seemed no way out of a situation. He touched Celedant's sleeve. "Let's leave this place. It reeks of danger."

They mounted their horses and galloped back to camp where they reported what they had found. The companions stared at the ground deep in thought until Zeffan spoke up. "I will stand along with ye. I have never had friends, and ye come close enough to a family as I have ever had. It would be cowardly to leave ye here."

Eldahir and Morganna looked at each other. Husband and wife made up their minds without saying a word. "We will stay. Such evil as this must be destroyed."

Hority hopped up and down, causing a little dust cloud each time he landed with his arm raised. "Me god would be mightily disappointed in me if I did not stand with ye."

Botreg shrugged his shoulders. "I have to stay and watch over Hority." He shot Tarquin a glance that said it all. "As if I would every leave me best friend in a lurch."

Azimuth nodded. "I fear what awaits us and don't think you would last long if I was not there in dragon form."

Celedant looked at the warlock. "What say you, Melgor?"

The man looked directly into Celedant's eyes. "I have tried to kill you off and on for centuries, yet still, you saved me. I will fight beside you all and pledge on my honor to defend you with every breath of my life."

"So, it has been decided," Tarquin said, "In the morning we go to war."

"Are you sure, Tarquin?" Celedant asked. "I know you are eager return home before your wife delivers your first child. No one here would blame you if you wanted to leave."

"I appreciate your consideration, Celedant. And while what you say is true, I could not in good conscious leave you to battle this alone. I think every one of us will be needed to defeat this evil," Tarquin said.

He looked at each member of the company. They nodded and smiled at him.

"Besides," Tarquin said with a laugh, "I doubt I could make it back alone through this dangerous territory."

They cooked a hot meal, possibly their last for a while, then they lay in their blankets, wondering what was to come in the morning. Tarquin tossed and turned, remembering all the fun times he and Ress had shared both at home and during the war. Her laughter was infectious, and her red hair a beacon of normalcy in a world turned upside down. He had to survive the coming battle to return to her and their child. Once again, he wished nothing had occurred at the Clorian valley. Then he would not be out here in the middle of nowhere worrying that he would never see his child born.

As the sun crested the eastern horizon, they awoke one-by-one and retrieved pieces of armor that they had not yet worn: helmets, breast plates, and scaled gloves. Donning their armor, they tightened straps, and sharpened their weapons. Once they were ready, the friends left camp after staking out their horses and mules to graze on the thick grass. Everyone was on high alert, and they scanned not just the ground but the sky as well. Their arrows were notched, and each had their favorite weapon drawn, as ready for the upcoming as possible.

Once they reached the crater, Azimuth excused himself and went several hundred yards away to await the right time to transform into a dragon. Deep down under the collapsed rocks of the mountain, the black dragon waited. Through his draconic senses, he felt the footsteps of the group as they approached his lair. He called forth his flying dragonettes, ordering them to attack. There were two kinds of dragonettes: the foot soldiers that attacked Celedant and the others on the trail, and the winged ones that the black dragon kept in reserve. These he now released on the world. They flew a crooked way up through tunnels to the cool air of the outside world. Just like thousands of bats from a cave.

The companions waited, not knowing exactly what to do at the moment. When suddenly, they heard the flapping of wings and before them flew out the dragonettes, darkening the sky in a great black cloud. They screeched and dove at their awaiting prey.

Hority let loose his war cry of, "Foes!" readying himself for battle.

Both Melgor and Celedant let loose fireball spells that shrieked upward into the massed enemies. The fire incinerated the first of their attackers and as the spell lost energy, the fires still burned the outside of the dragonettes, including their wings. They plummeted down onto the jagged rocks of the crater.

Though the spells killed nearly fifty of the dragon-like enemies, the mass that dove toward them was still huge. Eldahir and Morganna fired arrow after arrow into the densely packed creatures, bringing down a dragonette with each shot. Tarquin and Botreg, along with Zeffan, fired into the mass, too, bringing down many more of their enemies. Though it seemed that for each one that died, more quickly took its place. The dragonettes were almost upon them when Hority the filthy monk cast a spell. Great columns of fire fell from the sky killing all beneath it.

Then the dragon-like creatures were upon them, viciously sharp claws extended ready to impale the interlopers. That's when the sword and axe work began. Bows were dropped and the companions were ready to receive the flying charge. Swords swung upward, cutting into the attackers and bringing them down to the ground, where they were quickly dispatched. Even with only one arm, Melgor wielded his staff with expert ease bringing down dragonette after dragonette. It has been many years since the loss of his arm, and he had learned to make good use of the one remaining.

Then the non-flying creatures emerged from various caves in the crater floor. Azimuth could wait no longer, he cast the spell that changed him from elvan form to that of his real form of a golden dragon. Launching into the air, he dove down on the emerging dragonettes. As he reached the mass of enemies all climbing up the jagged rock formation, he let out a blast of dragon fire. After two passes the remaining dragonettes raced back toward the holes from which they had emerged.

Deep down in the dragon's lair, the black dragon felt the power surge above him. It screamed that a dragon was present and was attacking his children. Using his wickedly sharp claws, the black dragon tore at the rocky roof of its lair. Ever closer to the top of the crater he came, while rocks crashed below on the cavern floor. Then he came across the dragonettes escaping the dragon above. The black dragon howled in rage, killing hundreds in the confined crater with a blast of liquid fire.

In midflight to aid his friends, Azimuth heard the howl coming from the crater and knew at once a dragon was about to appear. He swung around in midair and flew towards the bottom of the crater where the black dragon's head appeared. It used its front legs to pull itself free into the sunlight. At first, Azimuth thought that a feral dragon had come to live here, but then he saw something out of legend as the black dragon appeared. Stories of their battle and magical prowess came flooding back to him. One of the most powerful dragons in all of dragon kind had lay hidden in the very world that was his home.

The black dragon saw the streaking golden dragon and was afraid for just a moment. A golden dragon was more than a match for a black dragon, or at least the legends foretold. Before it could launch itself into the air, Azimuth was upon its back, his claws sinking deep into the black dragon's sides. The golden dragon reared back and breathed red hot flame at the head of the black dragon. But nothing happened. The heat did not penetrate the armor-like scales, although the other dragon felt the heat, no damage was done. Vapor rose from the head of the dragon into the cold air of the mountains.

The black dragon got its feet underneath it and pushed upward. Unbalanced on the black dragon's back, Azimuth was thrown, his claws dragging deep gouges through the scales. As the golden dragon lay momentarily on its back, the black dragon breathed its own fire, hoping that the other was not as powerful as he. Azimuth tucked his wings and rolled from the fire that barely missed him. Then he was up and launched himself into the air, hoping he could out fly the black dragon.

On the edge of the crater, the companions fought on. The flying dragonettes swooped down, claws extended and striking out at the defenders. Tarquin's helm had been knocked off, and Zeffan had taken a vicious cut on the top of his head. Blood streamed down his face, but he still plied his axe to dangerous effect. Hority was busy jumping up at the diving creatures, killing them with a touch of his branch. Already there was a pile of bodies two feet deep. Eldahir and his wife Morganna once again fought back-to-back, bringing down the dragonettes easily. Botreg had used up all his daggers and was now swinging his sword to good effect. The wizard and warlock continued to cast spells between fighting off the monsters. Great flashes of lightning shot forth from the magic users, its electricity frying many of the attackers. Small balls of energy sought out the flying beasts, burning through their thick hide and dropping them to the ground.

In the air, Azimuth rolled and dodged left and right, in an effort to throw off the black dragon's pursuit. Then a huge rod of ice flew past him, freezing his wing to the bone and momentarily causing him to lose control of his flight. Azimuth knew at once it had been a spell cast by his enemy. As Azimuth fought for control, the black dragon dove, wings flat against his body and slammed into the golden one. Claws pinned the golden dragon's wings to its body. Azimuth howled in rage and pain as the black dragon flapped its mighty wings going straight up.

The golden dragon had one good chance to stop the black. Twisting his neck, Azimuth shot twin beams of energy from his eyes at the head of the black. This was a trait of a golden dragon that he had kept hidden even from Celedant. The black dragon saw the energy beams and knew them for what they were. This dragon he fought was stronger than the usual goldens ought to be. He turned his head, to avoid the beams but one struck true. It hit the black in the snout burning completely through it. He could feel the energy explode out the other side of his mouth, spraying skin, scales, and teeth into the air. The black dragon had not felt such pain in eons, and he screamed, spraying bloody froth through the air.

On the ground, Melgor lay writhing in pain from a deep penetrating wound to his left shoulder. Hority knelt beside him, to hold him down and cast a healing spell at the same time. Tarquin held off the dragonettes, as the Clorian worked his magic. In another fight, both Eldahir and Morganna had taken wounds. Eldahir was kneeling, wiping blood out of his eyes where a dragonette's claws had cut across his face and nose leaving three deep cuts. Morganna's right arm was broken when a dead dragonette had slammed into her, fighting on using her sword in her left hand. Seeing so many of his friends hurt,

Hority ran to where Eldahir was kneeling, leaving Morganna's back exposed. There he let Eldahir lean on him as he fought off the flying creatures.

Celedant had felt Azimuth's pain sear right through him. He battled to shake off the pain and fear for his dearest friend to cast spell after spell, bringing down dragonettes in droves. Already their master, the black dragon, and Azimuth were mere dots in the sky above the mountains. The dragonettes were getting less aggressive the further away their master flew. After the wizard shot ten more of the monsters from the sky, he called out to his wounded band of warriors. "The further their master flies from here, the more the creatures lose their will to fight! It's only a matter of time now!"

Azimuth and the black dragon had flown many leagues away in their combat, each using magic, claws, and teeth in this battle to the death. They had reached the upper mountains, the highest in the area, as the black dragon smashed heavily into Azimuth. The two dragons were propelled forward at breakneck speed slamming into the side of a mountain. They both were unable to use their wings to stop their fall as they tumbled down the jutting side of the peak, stopped suddenly by a ledge when they hit it with the full weight of their bodies. Weary from the battle, they lay gasping for breath. But Azimuth reacted first. The back dragon was nearest the edge, and with a powerful swoosh of his tail, the golden dragon pushed his enemy off the ledge.

Azimuth crawled to the edge of the mountain and looked over. The black dragon was slowly winging back up the mountain. But the golden dragon could see that its right wing was beating slower. The dragon had to keep adjusting its left wing's speed to maintain a straight flight. Yet Azimuth was injured, too. He had broken several ribs in the fall, and blood misted from his nose every time he took a breath.

The golden dragon gathered himself and bided his time. As the black dragon drew close to the edge Azimuth leaped. Taking a deep breath white hot flame exited his mouth and covered the black dragon. The flame ate into all the places its scales had been lost in the battle.

The black dragon screamed and tried to counter the attack but was in so much pain, its spell failed. It fell backwards to gain balance taking huge flaps of its wings. Azimuth was not far behind. He launched himself down at his enemy like a lance, plummeting faster and faster until he drew close enough. Then he put on a burst of speed and slammed into the back of the evil dragon. He backed his wings, slowing in midair as the black dragon hit the boulders at the foot of the mountain.

The black dragon did not stir, so Azimuth alighted on a huge boulder some fifty paces from his enemy. Then in his head he finally heard the voice of the evil dragon.

"That was a fight worthy of the old ones. You are young and have fought well. You have brought me to my knees." As he said that the dragon coughed, and bright blood sprayed forth.

"I did not know a black dragon lived on this world," Azimuth said in a deep voice. "But I could not allow you to live. You reek of evil."

"My name is Junagle, and yes, I reek of evil, just as you reek of goodness." The dark dragon said as it coughed up more blood.

"Why do you give me your name? That is not a custom of your kind," the golden dragon asked.

Junagle bared his bloody teeth, the closet thing a dragon could do to imitate a smile. "I want my destroyer to know who he has killed. That way my name will live on in a way. Surely you will pass along this battle for all to hear and admire."

Azimuth launched himself into the sky and as he passed over the dying dragon he let loose with a blast of fire.

This time, the black dragon simply said, "Fare thee well." As it was overtaken by dragon fire and continued to burn, while Azimuth flew back to his friends. He took one look back and saw a smoke trail snaking skyward.

Back at the crater, Celedant had gathered everyone together, many lay wounded with Hority casting healing spells and bandaging them up.

Tarquin stood next to Celedant. "We should know which one survived the combat before long."

The wizard nodded. "I cannot contact Azimuth. I fear death is coming to claim us."

It was then that Tarquin spotted a dark object soaring towards them. Celedant was sorrowful as he said, "Death it is."

But much to their amazement, the dragonettes began withdrawing from the battle, giving them a respite from fighting.

Eldahir, the blood from the wound on his forehead held back by a spell and bandage, yelled out, "I see gold sparkling in the sun! It is Azimuth!"

A shout of joy went up from everyone.

The dragon winged his way to the edge of the crater and flew over his companions. He tried to back his wings but was so tired, they could not stop him, and he collapsed to the ground. Azimuth's great golden body tumbled to the earth into an eventual roll. His friends that could ran towards him. They could only manage a slow loping run as they were worn out from the battle. The others walked as fast as their wounds would allow.

Celedant was beside his oldest friend, and he could barely hear him, "Our battle is over. The black dragon is dead." Then his head drooped and collapsed to the ground great bubbles of blood popping out of his nose and running from his mouth.

Hority was beside the dragon and looked up to Celedant. "I must heal his worst wounds while he is in dragon form. If he changes into an elf, he will die."

Celedant relayed the message to Azimuth and Hority got to work. He called to the others, "All the healing potions we have. It probably won't help that much but it can't hurt."

Hority knelt down next to listen to the dragon's lungs and nodded, "I am right. A rib has punctured a lung, and he has other broken bones. But it's the lung that will kill him." He reached down and grabbed two handfuls of dirt and began rubbing it into his hair and frock.

He looked at Celedant and Melgor. "Can either of you put him to sleep. It would help ease the pain and make things go faster."

Celedant went to his friend's head "My friend, you must sleep. I will cast a spell, but you must not fight it. Just sleep while Hority does his job."

The wizard placed a hand on his friend's scaled head and whispered a spell. Within a moment, Azimuth's breathing grew slow and steady. Celedant called to Hority, "He is asleep now."

The monk took dirt and threw it on the dragon "This will help me connect with me god, Clor."

He then lay against the dragon his arms splayed out and fervently praying. Slowly a dusty brown cloud began to form, and he called out, "Clor, aid me!"

The cloud became dense, and the others could hardly see the monk. Then behind Hority there appeared a vague figure of a dwarf.

Eldahir called out over the wind and swirling dirt of the spell, "Tis Clor himself come to aide his most devout monk!"

The deity laid a hand on Hority's shoulder and suddenly they were obscured by the dust. Azimuth raised his long neck and gave a deep blow of breath. Instead of blood, air flowed forth from the dragon's lungs. The dirt began to subside leaving the monk still flat against the side of the dragon. Clor had disappeared. Hority then collapsed to the ground, exhausted from his spell. Tarquin and Botreg hurried to the unconscious dwarf, grabbing his arms and dragging him away. It would have been disastrous if Azimuth had rolled over on his savior.

Celedant came to stand over Hority saying, "He will sleep, while his body heals the minor wounds. What of our smelly dwarf?"

"He sleeps, too," Tarquin answered. "The healing took a lot out of him."

"Botreg pour some water on his face and wake him," the Wizard commanded. "We need to find out the status of his patient."

With a smile, Botreg took a leather water flask and poured it over Hority's face. The dwarf awoke squirming on the ground wiping his face. The dirt left runnels and his attempts at wiping it clean left dirty smudges across his face. "What in the nine hells is this," Hority shouted. "Clean water poured on me face. Clearly an affront to Clor."

Celedant joined the others, smiling at their eccentric dwarf before explaining. "My friend, you have healed Azimuth. While you cast your holy spell, we witnessed a figure behind you, offering support."

Hority then started rolling in the dirt throwing it all about, "It was Clor, his dirtiness, helping me. I called on his aid, and he came. This is truly a miracle. All praise his glorious presence. Without his help, I would not have been able to heal our friend."

Botreg attempted to stop the dwarf's exclamations. "Please, me friend, ye have praised yer lord enough. We would like to know Azimuth's condition."

"The dragon is healed to the best of me abilities and with Clor's help, he will live for many, many long years." Hority stopped and sat up with wonder on his face, "Do ye think the mighty Azimuth will allow me the pleasure to ride on his back as he soars through the air? It would make a wonderous addition to my journal."

Celedant smiled. "I'm sure he will be most pleased to do so. After all, you saved his life."

Chapter Thirty-One

Gathering their horses and supplies, they camped near Azimuth. Celedant stood watch over his bonded dragon throughout the night. The next morning as breakfast was being cooked, the wizard felt Azimuth stirring.

"Do not move," he said silently. "You were sorely wounded in your fight against the black dragon."

The golden dragon let out a loud puff of air that sprayed dried blood out of his nostrils and mouth. "Ah, I can breathe easily now. I suppose Hority had a hand in healing me. Quite the powerful little monk he is."

"I believe he had help," Celedant said. "We saw a figure resting his hand Hority's shoulder during your healing. We all reckon it was Clor helping his most devoted monk."

"I suppose I will owe Hority a ride through the skies." Azimuth said.

The wizard laughed. "That was one of the first things he brought up after throwing dirt around and offering great praise to his god."

"I would expect no more," Azimuth said. "I think I will rest some more first. The wounds in my sides where I was grabbed still pain me."

Celedant made his way to camp, and all looked at him expectantly.

"Azimuth has been healed of his most grievous wounds, thanks to Hority," the Wizard reported. "But he still has a number of smaller wounds that pain him. He will sleep and recover."

The next few days were spent relaxing in the cool mountain air, letting their wounds heal and keeping Hority busy. But Azimuth remained asleep, letting his body heal itself. Then on the third day they heard the dragon let forth a roar that sent the horses and mules running. Celedant received a message from his friend, "I will change back. It is best that Hority be nearby."

"I'm sure everyone will want to be with you when you change," Celedant replied.

The wizard called the others together, and they made the short walk to stand by the golden dragon. Celedant heard in his mind the spell Azimuth spoke to change into elvan form.

There was the swirling colorful mist and suddenly where once a dragon lay, was now a wood elf shakily trying to stand.

Hority rushed forward. "Daft dragon. Remain sitting for me to examine ye!" The monk cast several spells on the claw marks that still remained on the elf's side before he declared him fit to stand. The monk gave Azimuth a hand up and a shoulder to steady him as everyone walked back to camp.

The newly transformed wood elf said, "Do I smell breakfast. I'm so hungry, I could eat a horse. Give me a huge helping, please."

After breaking their fast, everyone went back to the crater. The hole that the dragon had crawled out of was completely plugged with rocks and boulders.

They stood around looking at it. Then Zeffan said what everyone was thinking.

"We canna get down and find out what was hidden for so long. We donna have ropes long enough, and it's too unstable to climb by hand."

"You are right master dwarf," Azimuth agreed. "We could go through the tunnel we found but we are fought out and have too many wounds

"Then I suppose we must settle for ridding the world of a most dangerous dragon of all," Celedant said. "If it had won the battle with you and decided to come out, there is no telling what damage it could have wrought."

"We must rest and journey through the tunnels," Melgor interrupted. "Cyra wanted something secreted there. I don't believe she knew anything about the black dragon. Also, why would the Clorians venture to such a clean place if not to find or destroy something powerful. Undoubtably evil."

Tarquin considered what the warlock said, and he hated to admit it, but it made complete sense. "I agree with Melgor. If there is something evil and powerful down there, we need to seek it out and destroy it."

With everyone in agreement, they set up a more permanent camp on the grassy plain and rested. They kept two guards in case the dragonettes reappeared. The friends spent a week resting and regaining much needed strength before they ventured into the caves. They left the horses and mules tethered to a long rope and gathered their belongings for the unknown conditions of the tunnels into the mountain. Once more everyone strapped on their armor for the coming dangers that might lurk in the caves.

Eldahir, his face newly scared, and Zeffan led them back down the narrow path until the jagged slash opened up on the trail. Both Celedant and Melgor cast spells bringing powerful, much needed light to the tops of their staffs.

The Traveler said, "A good old venture underground. I have not done this in years. Its best I take the lead with Eldahir."

Tarquin patted the dwarf on the back and stepped up to the elf's side saying, "Here we go."

They entered the tunnel system and noticed that the floor was flat. Someone had chiseled the floor to a smooth, even texture.

"Enterprising little folk these Dragonettes are," Celedant said, somewhat amazed.

There was an easy blood trail to follow where their enemies had carried their dead back from the fight in the foothills. Eldahir stopped their advance down the tunnel and took out two arrows. As quick as could be, he sent the two arrows streaking down the tunnel. They heard two thumps and hurried forward, where they found two dragonettes dead at a curve in the corridor. Tarquin patted the elf on the back and the friends continued.

The passage declined deeper in a circular way. This time the whole corridor was carved. Eventually, they came to a room that was forty paces by forty paces. Tarquin took a tentative step into the room and his boots crunched on something.

"Hold. It seems that more light maybe needed," Celedant said. He held his staff above his head and with a single word the light flared up."

The floor was littered with bones. Hority rushed forward before Botreg could stop him and started going through the remains. There were tears in his eyes when he held up a skull and said, "Dwarves and dragonettes. "A battle was fought here. I wonder if these are the remains of some of me brothers."

Botreg caught up with the dirty monk as he put a dragonette skull in his satchel and sagely said, "It's best we leave the dead where they have fallen. Nothing but bad luck can befall us if the bones are removed."

Hority agreed and dropped the skull. "I will remember what we saw here and enter it in me journal later."

Eventually the corridor headed west towards the crater. They had long since lost the blood trail.

"The long distance the dragonettes had to travel with their dead must have caused them to lose all their blood," Celedant observed.

Suddenly the passage split in two, bringing them to a halt.

"We need to rest. We've been on the march too long to continue now," Tarquin suggested.

The others agreed, and they settled down to a cold sleep in the deep underground tunnel. Five turns of the clock had passed when Azimuth silently woke everyone up. They could hear a song being sung off in the distance down the right-hand passage. The group silently gathered their belongings. Then Eldahir and Zeffan led the way towards the singing. The corridor gradually began to expand. The ceiling receded into darkness. The chamber opened up to wide proportions. There in the middle sat a group of huge humanoid creatures sitting and singing a song. They were all drunk as they passed around a huge barrel of liquid to drink.

"A clan of giants," Celedant whispered to the others. "None exist in the east. They were driven away long ago."

Eldahir pointed directly across from them. "Look. A man-sized door across the way."

Tarquin made a decision. "We must check out the doorway. We can't leave anything to chance."

"Some giants were good and easy to deal with," Celedant said. "Let's negotiate with these. It's better than bursting in on them and having a fight on our hands."

Tarquin shrugged, "You can give it a try. But everyone be ready for a fight."

The wizard stepped into the room and called out, "Tall ones I would parlay."

There was a genuine panic amongst the giants having been disturbed. They jumped to their feet and drew weapons. Celedant held his hand behind his back, motioning for the others to stay calm.

Seeing the little ones, a huge giant with a grey beard that hung to his chest nearly three times the height of Celedant stepped forward.

He wore a chain mail shirt that jingled when he took two steps towards the wizard. "Why do you disturb us? Are you looking for a fight? If so, we are ready."

The wizard held his hands out from his sides. Forestae his staff leaned against his body. "We do not look for a fight. We seek the small, scaled ones that look like miniature dragons."

The giant laughed. "Those things with sharp little claws. We have plenty of them living around us. They breed like men. No mean intentions. You would say rats. Why do you search them out?"

"They attacked us, and we seek revenge," the Wizard replied. "We followed a blood trail into these caves but lost them."

The giant nodded. "They are bothersome. I know not where they live but that they come from that passage you now stand in."

Celedant dared a question. "Does that door lead to more of the warrens?"

There was a change in the giant's demeanor as he answered, "No. That door is ours. If you attempt to get into it, there will be a battle."

Holding his arms out further Celedant answered, "Do not worry. We just seek the warrens of the small dragons and will return from where we came."

The giant sheathed his sword over his shoulder and said, "I wish you well on your quest. I hope you kill as many of the buggers as you can. Now you can go."

Chapter Thirty-Two

Celedant and the rest backed out of the room.

"We best hurry back to where the tunnel splits." Tarquin slapped Celedant on the back and added, "I did not want to fight those behemoths. It's a good thing we have a master negotiator with us."

They followed the corridor to where the split was and turned right. The tunnel continued onward with the occasional group of rooms. Then suddenly, the passage ended as the ceiling opened up soaring above them.

Eldahir held his hand up to stop the others and whispered, "I hear movement in the chamber ahead."

In a low voice Celedant answered, "Let's add some light to the situation."

He whispered a few words and a bright light coalesced in his hand and with a flick of his wrist it flew into the chamber. There was a scuttling sound and the light exposed hundreds of dragonettes milling about a semicircular room that opened up to their right into a massive cave. The roof had collapsed, and loose boulders and huge blocks of stone had fallen to the depths of the cave. It would seem they had reached their destination.

"I smell dragon," Azimuth declared. This is the bottom of the crater. The dragonettes mourn their fallen leader here."

In fact, the light and the appearance of the group drove many of the creatures away. But a few of the braver ones stood their ground growling and clicking their claws.

The transformed wood elf motioned to the others, "I can handle this. Clear me a way through those nuisances."

Celedant chanted and sent a fire ball rolling out into the dragonettes. That was all that was needed against these battle-weary monsters. They turned and ran. Once the way was cleared Azimuth ran the long distance to the edge of the drop off and morphed back into his true form that of a golden dragon. The dragonettes all prostrated themselves on the floor. Azimuth telepathically entered into the brains of the simple creatures. Things of habit were these monsters used to years of following their god the black dragon.

The golden dragon told them, "Go from here. I rule now and want you to leave me in peace."

All the dragonettes turned and sadly departed the chamber, leaving only Azimuth in dragon form. He cast the spell that morphed him back to a wood elf. Then waved the party over and looked down towards the bottom of the cavern.

As his friends arrived the wood elf said, "I think we'll need another of your light spells Celedant. Because even I can't see the bottom. There are stairs at the middle of the drop off so there must be something down there."

The wizard cast another light spell and sent it over the side of the semi-circular cavern deep into its depths it fell and fell then something glittered as it finally reached the floor of the cavern.

Every member of the group stood in awe.

"Gold!" Botreg whispered reverently.

They could tell that most of the black dragon's hoard lay concealed beneath the boulders and slabs of rock from the ceiling.

"This must be why me brothers came here. There must be something powerful down yonder. All that glitter stinks of cleanliness. Clor does not walk here," Hority added.

Botreg patted him on the back, despite the dust that rose up, "Do not worry. Clor is with ye wherever ye walk."

Tarquin looked at his friend and grinned. "Assassin, soldier, and now philosopher?"

"Come," Celedant called, "this is where we need to go. Down the steps. Let's start searching."

They carefully made their way down the narrow stairs that were carved into the side of the drop off. There were several switch backs as they descended towards the bottom of the cavern. At one place as they neared their goal, a boulder had struck the stairs, forcing them to make a harrowing jump over the missing steps. They tied each other together. The elves jumped first, neatly landing on the other side of the crushed stairs.

Horlty prayed aloud. "Me lord don't let me die here." He jumped and his feet caught the edge of the intact steps. Eldahir quickly reached out, grabbing his frock and pulling him over to safety. When they reached the bottom of the stairs, they stepped off onto a floor covered in coins, copper, silver, and gold. The treasure spread before them partially covered by the rock fall.

Tarquin was baffled. "What do we do now Celedant?"

"Hump," the Wizard said. "Azimuth, Melgor, and I will use our magic to search for the treasure. The rest of you must look for anything that is not coins and bring it to our attention."

Hority had sat down amid the treasure staring at a hand full of jewels and muttering to himself.

"What's the problem, me friend?" Botreg asked.

"I have never seen such pure baubles," the Monk said. "I find myself wanting to take them, but they are so pure and clean. I am being lustful against the teachings of Clor."

Botreg smiled. "Do not worry. Ye are no failure to yer god. It's the dwarf in ye. We all lust after such treasures. I me self plan on freeing some of these gems from this dragon cave."

Zeffan called out to them. "We need to search, but that won't stop ye all from lining yer pockets."

Thus, began the treasure hunt through piles and piles of coins. Celedant and Melgor wandered around casting spell after spell that would detect powerful magical items. Azimuth used his dragon senses to feel for the power the object might put off. But it was Morganna who stumbled upon a golden box trapped under a boulder.

"I think I have found something," she called out.

Slipping and sliding on the coins, Celedant and Melgor made their way over to the elf.

"What have you found?" Melgor asked.

Morganna pointed to the gold box. "It's partially buried in these boulders, but this end of the box looks in good shape."

Melgor cast a spell, and the box burned bright with white light.

Celedant who had joined him smiled. "I think we've found the treasure everyone was looking for."

Celedant and Melgor joined the wood elf, digging into the coins until they uncovered the end of the golden box. But it was firmly lodged in the boulders.

Morganna looked closely at it and said, "It looks partially crushed by the boulders but still intact. How do we get all this weight off of it?"

Azimuth drawn to the activity mildly answered, "I'll do it. In my dragon form I can pry up the boulders enough to slip the box out. But all of you will need to be at the top of the overhang incase these boulders fall. Worst of all, one of you needs to be here to pull out the box."

The wizard knee deep in coins said, "I will stay. You are my bonded dragon. It can only be me. I will not risk the lives of any others."

Azimuth smiled. "I would have it no other way. I will lift it ever so slowly, and you can pull it out. Then I'll grab you and fly up to the ledge. Simple."

"Simple," Celedant replied in a mimicking voice.

CHAPTER THIRTY-THREE

The others headed towards the stairs, looking back at the mound of boulders and rocks that Azimuth was about to shift. Botreg, absently mindedly reached down and picked up another hand full of gold, tucking it into an already bulging pocket. So did several others, including Hority who was having a full-blown dilemma between his want of the near perfect jewels and following his god's order on the evils of cleanliness.

Botreg went to hurry him along and seeing the deep battle going on inside the soul of his friend he said, "Take the jewels to be cataloged. I doubt any Clorian will ever be inside a dragon den again. These objects need to be written about. Showing that black dragons are unholy in the eyes of Clor and reek of cleanliness. Besides, you can roll them around the dirt to make them sufficiently acceptable to your god."

He helped the smelly dwarf up and headed to the stairs. The rest of the group were ascending, so Botreg nudged the filthy monk along.

Celedant waited calmly as the others reached the top of the cliff. On the outside, he showed no fear. Inside, his heart pounded fiercely, fearful of what was about to happen.

"Don't worry, old friend, you and I are not intended to die in some far-flung country," Azimuth assured him. "Especially in a cave that reeks of evil."

"I wish I shared your optimism," Celedant said. "But right now, those boulders looming over us suggest another outcome."

"Head over near the stairs and prepare to run. I'm going to morph here and hope my weight doesn't shift the boulders."

As Celedant retreated, he mumbled in his mind for Azimuth to hear. "Complete trust? You tell me it's safe one minute and that the boulders could shift a moment later."

The dragon did not even reply. Instead, he backed away from the pile of boulders, dug his feet firmly into the coins, and morphed into his dragon form. Celedant watched as the misty swirling haze surrounded his friend, leaving the golden dragon standing amid all the gold.

Azimuth with a hint of awe said, "I've always wondered what it would feel like being in my own cave amidst a lifetime of treasure."

"Tempting?" Celedant asked with a smile in his voice.

A little, but then, I'm not that kind of dragon. Those dragons think only of their treasure. I prefer the company of my fellow dragons, friends, and especially my bond mate. Come, Celedant, let's get to work.

The wizard waded back through the coins, taking up position near the box.

Stay under my chest to shield you from any falling stones, the Dragon said.

Celedant was mere feet from the box trapped among the boulders as Azimuth's giant claws gently hooked the stone entrapping the golden box. Using only as much force as he dared, the dragon attempted to move the boulder. For minutes, the stone stayed in place and small rocks tumbled and slid down the giant pile of stone that had sealed the crater. Adding a bit more pressure, the stone shifted and before Azimuth had a chance to speak, Celedant was on his knees pulling at the entrapped box. At first it did not move, but then it began to wiggle back and forth. But the wizard could tell the stone needed to be lifted further.

Celedant telepathically called out, *Just a little more.*

Azimuth lifted it as easily as he could, his claw scraping on the stone showering Celedant in dust. This time the golden box shifted more, and he could pull it out further. Moving it back and forth and using what force he deemed fit, he began to unwedge it. Then there was a scrapping sound above them and Azimuth let out a grunt of pain.

Celedant stopped for a moment but the dragon said, *Keep going that was a small boulder that caught me by surprise.*

The wizard strained and grunted, "Just a little more."

The dragon strained harder, the muscles of his forelegs flexing and shaking. The wizard gave one last pull, and the box came loose, sending Celedant sliding backwards down the piles of coins. Azimuth immediately teleported the wizard onto his back and gently let down the boulder. There was a rumbling in the stone pile and Azimuth's massive wings beat twice, propelling them both up toward the ledge. Just then the boulders collapsed, triggering the remaining precariously balanced rock. As Celedant looked back, he saw the boulders fall, sealing the treasure in. Dust blinded him and the rest of the group waiting at the top of the ledge. Azimuth cleared the pit and landed safely, coughing and letting the near blinded Celedant off his back. He then changed back into elvan form.

As the dust cleared, everyone saw the wizard holding a smashed, foot long golden box. He tried to get it open but failed. He called Botreg to come and help.

The dwarf looked it over and said, "The two locks are completely broken, and the rocks did so much damage, we'll not be able to open it from that side. I recommend we chisel out the hinges and open it from the back. It's made from gold, and we should be able to cut through it rather easily. This chest wasn't made to keep it safe. It's more of a display box."

He pulled out one of his daggers, which he had retrieved after their last battle, and placed it on one end of the hinge in hopes of cutting through the soft gold. He pushed the blade at first and then hammered it with the hilt of his sword. Then he called, "Zeffan, might I use yer axe for this?"

The traveler handed over his weapon, and Botreg got to work. He first used the axe handle to strike the dagger's blade down the hinge. More gold came off. He continued until both hinges were demolished, but the box would not open. He searched for a way into the box while the rest stared at him expectantly. He managed to drive his dagger under the lid of the box. With a smile he stood and before a nervous crowd, he took the axe over his shoulder and with a gigantic swing, struck the dagger's hilt. In the next instant, three things happened: the hilt of his dagger snapped in two, the box's lid flew into the air, and the box tipped over. The box contained a small unadorned silver rod that rolled out onto the floor. Fearing to move, the others stared at it, not knowing if it was safe to touch and wondering how such a powerful object could look so mundane.

Celedant quickly stooped down with a cloth and picked up the rod, wrapping it up before hiding it in the folds of his cloak.

"We'll take this to Dragon Isle and let the Masters of the Isles decide the best course of action."

Chapter Thirty-Four

Cyra had taken over the warlock's guild in a bloody coup, killing a third of the warlocks and sorceresses. She would have had it no other way. It had satisfied her blood lust and gained her the possibility of taking control of Trudoc. The remaining guras soldiers swore fealty to her, and now they and her white orcs patrolled the grounds. Cyra had taken over the largest room available until the tower could be rebuilt.

She wished that Talchic was present. Little did he know that Cyra trusted his advice on anything administrative. But he was in the West, tracking down Celedant and Tarquin and searching for the hidden treasure that the map had indicated. She would seize power of the ruling council in the near future, after letting the news spread that she had taken control of the guild.

Cyra would let her orcs out into the streets in a show of force. She ordered them to show no violence, just take up positions at key places like the Governor General's Offices and the Harbor Master's Castle.

Two long and harrowing days passed as the warlocks and sorceresses waited to hear from their new mistress. They feared for their lives and were ordered to stay in their rooms until summoned. Finally, the manor's bell ran five times, summoning them to the main hall, where they found Cyra seated in the high warlock's and now high sorceress' chair. They filed into the great hall and sat in the pews that had been arranged, facing the head of the hall. The normal tables where they ate were pushed against the walls. Cyra was dressed in a flowing red silk gown, which she smoothed out on her legs as the last of her minions found their seats.

Cyra looked them over and could sense their fear of her. She smiled. All was the way she wanted it to be. They were cowed and she had control. There would be no uprising to seize control of the manor. "Welcome, my friends. This is a new day. A day of power and control. Our first goal will be to take over running of the city of Trudoc from here in the manor. Everyone and everything will be under our control."

Seeing the smiles among the assembled throng, she continued. "In the following weeks, I will assemble the Governor General and his council of noblemen and take control. They will stay in place as figureheads to appease the population, but we will be the ones running things."

One warlock stood up and began clapping. It took no time at all for the whole audience to join him, shouting, clapping, and cheering.

"Long live Cyra!"

She had them all on her side. The beginning of her rule would start today.

Cyra procured the former leader of the Guild's scribe and met with him in her room. She did not bother learning his name. He was not a warlock but a human servant.

"Be seated. I need the name and addresses of all the council members. You will invite them to a feast in Trudoc's honor and to meet with me two weeks from now. It should contain a veiled threat that those who choose to come will be welcomed to our influence. If they refuse, however, I might look unfavorably upon them."

The scribe nodded. "Yes, milady. I'll have a rough copy in an hour. Once you approve it, the other scribes and I can have them ready to send out in the morning."

It took him less then and hour to finish, and he fearfully knocked on her door. The doors opened magically for she was sitting at her desk in the far corner.

"Do you have the invitation?" she asked.

"Yes, my lady," he answered nervously.

Cyra waved him over. "Do not fear me. I won't bite unless you turn against me. Now show me what you have written."

He went to her desk and placed a piece of parchment in front of her, "These are the addresses of the council members and the governor general."

She smiled. "These will be helpful should someone hesitate to come. A single orc stationed outside their house will chivy them along. Now what of the invitation?" She looked down at the parchment and read:

> *To the honorable and esteemed* ___________
>
> *I, Cyra grand mistress of the warlock and sorceress guild invite you to a reception in your honor. It will be held in the great hall of the manor in two weeks' time. Those who come will be treated to the best that Trudoc can offer along with intelligent and informative conversation. Now that I have taken the guild, we need to be amicable and do what is best for the great city of Trudoc. A strong and powerful guild can only benefit the city. Those members who do not attend can expect a swift visit from me to discuss their membership and station in the city. I look forward to discussing the future of the great city of Trudoc and our station as leaders in this community.*
>
> *Signed, Grand Mistress Cyra*

The scribe waited for Cyra to stop reading and look up. "I hope I did not take too many liberties?"

Cyra was happy with the invitation. She could never have written such a thing without direct threats of death and destruction.

The witch smiled. "Well written, my scribe. Have them finished. Once I have signed them, I will send a magic user and white orc to deliver them to each address."

CHAPTER THIRTY-FIVE

The friends retraced their steps. Eldahir and Zeffan remained vigilant, scouting ahead. There was no telling what might lurk around the corner or even dragonettes that had not heeded Azimuth's call to leave. Melgor was having a difficult time. Basically, evil to begin with, he found it more and more difficult to keep control as the object they had found called to him. He needed it to the point that he was seriously thinking about killing everyone to get the magical wand.

That night as they bedded down Melgor went to Celedant. "The wand is calling to me. It must be evil because I have to fight for control to keep myself from attacking you and taking it. The wand cries out to me." His words came out as a plea.

There was genuine concern in the wizard's eyes. "I had not considered this. It is good of you to have come forth with this new."

Celedant took out the wand from where it was hidden on his person and laid it, still wrapped in cloth, beside them. The wizard saw genuine lust and longing spring to Melgor's eyes.

Celedant gently began a spell, bringing Azimuth to his feet when he felt the use of magic. The wizard held his hand over the object and chanted. Slowly a green light emanated from his hand and covered the wand.

When he was finished, he asked, "What do you feel now, Melgor?"

Melgor smiled. "I know there is evil there. But I no longer desire it. The call in my head is gone. But how long will this spell last?"

It was Celedant's turn to smile. "It will last until I erase it."

"Good," he said with a sigh. "I doubt I could have withstood its call for much longer."

The wizard agreed. "It is good you came to me early enough to conceal the evilness of this magical item. I'm sorry I did not realize what affect it would have on you."

After two days in the tunnels, the scouts finally saw sunlight ahead. Eldahir went forward to see to the trail, while Zeffan returned to the others to report the news. As they came closer to the entrance, Eldahir met them.

"It will be turning dark soon," he reported. "We won't make it off the path before dark."

"Then, we'll camp here till morning and go for the horses," Tarquin ordered.

The journey back to Markdale was somewhat uneventful. The only set back came when a band of orcs came up the path and seeing them, prepared to defend themselves. Eldahir, Zeffan, and Tarquin charged. With the horses coming at them, the orcs ran off the road into the woods. They had not been looking for a fight. As soon as the riders rode by, the orcs filed back onto the road and continued north.

Reaching the desert and having learned from their previous crossing, they filled their water barrels to the top to make the crossing. The first time they had crossed the desert, they had drunk their water and not refilled the casks. They avoided the desert town and were soon in the hot, humid jungle. They passed the place where the minotaurs had attacked, but there was nothing but scattered bones. It was all they could do to keep Hority from jumping off his horse to gather some bones for further study. But since he was seated in the saddle in front of Botreg, the little monk never got the chance, as he felt the assassin's arms tighten around him. Eventually, the jungle ended, and the port of Markdale was insight.

Zeffan found a middle-priced inn and went to the harbor master to see about getting a ride on a ship going to Trudoc. There were none available, and he was told to check back every day.

They decided to use some of the time to eat a nice hot lunch. While they ate, Celedant and Melgor became locked in conversation.

"What of Trudoc and this witch Cyra?" the Wizard inquired.

Melgor was nervous about the subject. "By now, she will have set up her seat of power in the warlock tower. From there, she will be able to rule Trudoc. She is powerful enough that she will be able to detect us when we land. You and Azimuth are too magically charged to get past her sight."

Celedant grew concerned and chewed a bite of food thoughtfully. He did not want to battle all the warlocks in the tower. When they had gone into the tower in search of the map, the magic users had been a small group, and it was the middle of the night. They had been able to sneak in and out without rousing all the warlocks. But if Cyra indeed could sense them, she would have all the exits blocked and heavily guarded.

After mulling over the subject, he asked Melgor, "Do you know a way out of the city?"

"No, I wasn't there long enough to get a feel for the city," the Warlock answered. "I was assigned only to watch the tower."

Celedant put his face in his hands and rubbed his eyes. "To be honest, I don't know what to do. But what keeps coming to mind is that we will have to kill or drive away this Cyra to escape. After she is out of the equation, we can easily escape through one of the gates."

"I think your plan might be the only way to accomplish an escape," Melgor agreed reluctantly.

The wizard turned serious. "Can I count on you not to turn on us?"

"I don't want to be under her control anymore then you," Melgor said with a shudder. "She would kill me outright for not bringing the artifact to her. I also failed to ascertain that there was a black dragon and to persuade it to fight for Cyra. I have been thinking that I will seek asylum on Dragon Isle. I have had death knocking on my door for far too long. I am curious if they would hide a warlock amidst their land?"

"I will vouch for you if we survive this venture," Celedant assured him. "Killing Cyra will be no walk in the park."

Melgor nodded. "I vote to kill her for very personal reasons. If we leave her alive, she will be able to locate me, teleport to the Isles, kill me and be gone before the alarm could be raised. That is a testament as to how powerful she is."

Celedant realized he could trust Melgor to a point but had to remain leery of the man. "Come let's finish our meal and join the others in conversation."

CHAPTER THIRTY-SIX

The day of the party, the mansion staff worked extremely hard, not wanting to upset the new grand sorceress. The cooks had been up for hours baking and preparing to cook the appetizers, main meal, and deserts. Other staff workers cleaned the main hall so it would sparkle in the candlelight. The tables were set the long way with white linen tablecloths covering the top and a silk runner placed precisely down the center, adorned with vases of beautiful, exotic flowers. The pews had been replaced with soft cushioned seats up and down the tables.

Tapestries were hung on the walls, depicting warlocks and sorceresses doing battle against various monsters and armies. Another hint to the guest as to the types of power Cyra could call upon. Opposite that message and beside her chair sat two cages with pure white doves. Behind her chair were two palm trees that overhung her huge chair or as she thought of it, a throne.

That night, the staff wore white suits with tails that hung behind their knees. A man would announce the arrival of each guest, accompanied by a single blown note from a horn. The guest would receive a seat at the head of the tables, while the warlocks and sorceresses filled out the other ends, clearly outnumbering them.

Cyra walked the room and visited the kitchen, where she encouraged the workers. She made a show of good faith, commenting on how wonderful everything looked and smelled. Then she visited the great hall and smiled. The staff had out done themselves. It was exquisite. The witch then proceeded to her room to get ready for her guests' arrival. She dressed herself in immaculate green silk from the deep south of the western coast. A single strand of exquisite pearls was draped around her neck. She looked at herself in the mirror, disgusted at what she saw. Her youthful appearance was totally gone, thanks to the gift of more power from the vampire warlock Taza. She had returned to the West with a wizened body and face, no longer beautiful and young. But the power she had gained was well worth the sacrifice.

As the hour to the feast approached, the cooking staff sent platter after platter of venison, beef, and fowl out to be placed on the tables. There were plenty of potatoes and green vegetables. Afterward, there would be cakes and pastries for the guests' sweet tooth. Cyra had also made sure that the guests had bottles of the best wines from the Western nations, including after dinner drinks, and the best coffee money could buy. She had spent a small fortune of the Warlock Guild's treasury on this party and hoped the night would not end in any deaths. Cyra knew it would not be hers, but the guests were fair game.

At the appointed time, the manor's bell was rung, and the warlocks and sorceresses assembled in the great hall. They milled about drinking wine while waiting for their guests to arrive. Sometime after the bell, a portly nobleman dressed in the military uniform of the city guards, entered with his wife, who was wearing a high-necked flowing gown. The horn was blown and after their names were announced, Cyra was the first person to greet them. Then a steady stream of nobles began entering, and Cyra memorized each and everyone's names and faces.

Then entered the Governor General of Trudoc, dressed in full ceremonial attire. He was very charismatic, tall with flowing grey hair, an altogether haughty and aloof man. Cyra hated him at first glance and could sense that the hatred was returned by him. She was certain he would have to die tonight or at a later date in the near future. After he was announced, Cyra left the front doors of the hall and mingled with the guests. She had a wine glass that she never drank from, and much to her consternation, was forced to engage in small talk, which was something she thoroughly despised.

Much to her surprise, several noblemen and women came right out and stated that the city needed a strong force to keep the countryside free of bandits. These nobles she marked as potential allies. It was time to eat without the food getting cold and the manor's bell tolled once. Cyra made her way to the head of the main table and sat down, signaling that the rest should also sit. The Governor General sat to her right and began filling his plate. She had a servant place a plate full of fresh venison and greens before her.

Cyra stood and raising her glass said, "A toast for Trudoc and the future it holds."

All the others stood and echoed her sentiments. She looked the picture of regal nobility in her green silk and straight-backed posture. The Governor General turned out to be a dour conversationalist, but the man opposite him jabbered on throughout the meal, keeping Cyra's attention. After coffee was served to those not still drinking wine, the sorceress stood up.

She clinked her glass with a knife for some time until the guests reseated themselves. Then Cyra began an impromptu speech to either sway the crowd to her side or pick out the ones who would be her adversaries.

She started out simple enough. "I hoped you enjoyed the meal. I tried to gather dishes from around the many ports along the western sea as possible. I believe in the future that all of us can serve such dishes, and our populous can have the same available to them. I see a larger role for Trudoc in this world. A navy imposing its will upon the high seas having more power over our allies." There were claps of pleasure at this idea. Though the Governor General looked on disapprovingly. She warmed up to the task, and the members of the party eagerly looked on.

She sipped some wine and continued. "I see our farmlands spreading outward, not just under the protection of the city walls. I see an army capable of providing safety to these farmers. I see ships packed with soldiers taking on the other navies of the West and asserting our authority on the high seas. No longer will we just be a trading city. We will be a power!"

After her speech, most all of the nobility smiled and clapped. She noted that the Governor General left the party early. Cyra knew she would have to take care of him soon, making a subtle example of him. An action she herself would be able to deny, but still a hard truth to support her or die.

CHAPTER THIRTY-SEVEN

Several days later, Zeffan came back to the inn with good news. A ship had just come into the harbor. Its next destination was Trudoc. Celedant and Tarquin went to the docks, located the ship, and arranged passage for their group and their horses. The mules had been sold off to get more gold to buy three new horses to replace the ones lost on the journey west. Everyone had a fierce desire, unwilling to get rid of the dragon gold, not just the dwarves but the human and elves, too.

The Captain was a jovial fellow and soon had them laughing as they settled on a fair price. Once out to sea, he invited Celedant and Tarquin to dine with him and his senior staff. The meal was delicious with venison and thick, red, juicy beef, as well as whipped potatoes, and a thick chocolate pudding for dessert. There was plenty of wine to go around, and soon everyone was in a fine mood.

"We rarely get such a fine meal," the Captain explained with a grin. "And the cook has out done himself with this one. I did say we were having a wizard for dinner. That might have spurred him on to such grandeur."

Tarquin answered for both of them, "It has been quite a long time since we have had such a fine meal and good company."

"Well, you're lucky," the Captain said. "We rarely eat such a feast, except when we restock supplies in ports."

"Have there been any changes in Trudoc that you're aware of?" Celedant asked. "When we left, there was quite a shake up with in the Warlocks Guild."

The Captain was silent for a minute, weighing his words. "There have been rumors that a new power had arisen in Trudoc. Also, that the accursed white orcs roam the streets."

"I would like to avoid the orcs, if possible," the wizard said slowly.

"I have no love for orcs either," the Captain answered seriously. "We can unload your horses during the night and get you on your way quickly enough."

Tarquin stood up, his wine glass raised. The others followed. "To the Captain."

The sea cooperated, and the crossing was gentle. A day out from Trudoc, the passengers assembled together on the fore deck.

"We'll need to stable the horses until we find out the situation in the city," Celedant began. "Melgor explained to me that he believes that the witch, Cyra, has taken control of the guild and has designs on the city itself. The Captain confirmed that a new force had risen in Trudoc. During the time we have been gone, anything could have happened. If she is as powerful as Melgor tells me, and I see no reason for him to lie, I would guess that she is controlling the city, or is, at least, a puppet master of the nobility. According to Melgor, she is immensely powerful and will know when Melgor, Azimuth, and I set foot on shore, though not where exactly. We must get lost immediately in the warrens that run throughout the city. Zeffan, you and Azimuth stable the horses near the east gate, which is closest to the guild. Then I can telepathically guide you back to us."

"What of her?" Tarquin asked. "I don't like leaving an enemy behind me. Especially one that is so talented at teleportation. She and her warlocks could easily lay a trap for us in the wilds."

"She brought two hundred white orcs with her," Melgor said, speaking up. "The gates are sure to be guarded by them. As soon as they are breached, she will know."

There was an exhale of breath, and the former assassin, Botreg spoke up. "It may be me old profession breaking through, but we need to kill this witch."

"I'm afraid you are right," Celedant agreed. "We must storm the tower and deal with her."

Hority jumped up, his hand raised like a schoolboy. "We can go through the sewer and water drains like before."

Celedant nodded. "Yes. Tis the safest way in."

That night, Tarquin lay in a swaying hammock, thinking of his pregnant wife, Ress. He could not remember how long he had been gone. Time seemed to be accounted for by each encounter where they were attacked or reached a point on the map. If he lived through the following days, he thought he could easily make it home with the help of Azimuth. He would have to ask him first thing in the morning. With that thought, Tarquin dropped off to sleep.

Chapter Thirty-Eight

The Governor General would not cooperate with the guild. He ordered all the orcs from the gates and escorted the great white orcs from the nobility's enclave. Everywhere an orc went, it was followed by five guardsmen.

Cyra was furious. The new head of the Sorceress' Guild would not tolerate such treatment. Three weeks after the introductory party, Cyra finally decided to strike the Governor General's mansion. Irritated with how the vain man was responding to her actions, she chose three of the most powerful warlocks and three of her best sorceresses, along with ten white orcs to accompany her. At midnight, enclosed carriages picked them up for the short ride to their target.

They took a circuitous route to reach the Governor General's home. Cyra had the carriages stop one street over, and the party of assassins slipped out. With little traffic in this part of town, they made good time to their target. Once out of the carriages, they walked in single file along the darkened edge of the street, aided by hedges and cloudy skies.

Cyra walked up to the gate and found it locked. She also noted two small guard shacks just paces inside the fencing. She rattled the gate, and two guards approached the witch. She muttered one word and the men dropped to the ground in a peaceful sleep. Then one of the warlocks came forward and tapped the lock with his wand. The chain fell away, allowing Cyra to enter the compound. As they passed the sleeping guards, she motioned to one of the white orcs. Without a second thought, the creature bent down and neatly sliced their throats. The orc then hid the men behind one of the guard posts.

They reached the front doors to the mansion, where the Governor General lived and found two more guards. The intruders repeated what had happened at the front gate. Once inside, Cyra cast a spell, locating their target. She led the way to the man's sleeping quarters. The Governor General was asleep with his wife in a tremendous bed. She motioned for the magic users to station themselves outside the door with the orcs, then she motioned to two of the orcs to accompany her inside the room.

Moving quietly across the carpeted floor, she pointed one orc to the wife's side of the bed, while she and the other went to stand by the man's side. Cyra pointed to the wife and the orc reached down and quickly broke her neck in the silence of the night. She then cast a paralyzing spell on her target and shook him awake. Unable to move, the Governor General tried to shout out, but the orc slapped a giant hand over his mouth.

Cyra leaned down to his ear. "This is a warning to the nobility. Your death will propel this city to the forefront of power."

However, she was unaware of a ring he wore that protected him from minor spells. The man, as paranoid as anyone in power, drew a dagger from a sheath tied to his arm. He struck upward through the bedding into the orc's heart. Then quickly reached up to pull the cloth cord that hung above his bed. He gave it two tugs before throwing the dagger at Cyra. The witch easily deflected the weapon and called forth a mighty flame that engulfed the bed. The screams of the dying Governor General ripped through the silence of the night.

The fire spread quickly along the carpet, and she ran for the door followed by remaining the orc. The flames spread through the room, and Cyra called out, "Fire the mansion!"

Just then, an arrow hit one of the sorceresses, dropping her to the floor. Two of the orcs returned fire, and they heard shouts of pain from down the hall.

"Retreat!" Cyra commanded. Kill any resistance and burn the place to the ground."

They ran as the magic users cast fire ball spells into each open room. The orcs, who were out in front of Cyra, ran head long into the guards. There was a quick battle, but the orcs' size and strength quickly overcame the humans. Reaching the outside, they saw that a whole wing of the mansion was in flames. They quickly ran back to the carriages to find the drivers had disappeared. Cyra had planned on killing them, and they apparently had guessed as much.

She ordered the warlocks and sorceresses to drive the carriages, so that the white orcs were kept hidden. They did not know the exact route, and it took extra time to make it back to the manor house. Once there, Cyra ordered the carriages burned, and the gates shut with extra guards placed on the grounds. The sorceress retired to her room with two orc guards stationed outside her door. It could have gone better, but the nobility would get the message and be inclined to follow her orders from now on.

CHAPTER THIRTY-NINE

The ship reached Trudoc late in the afternoon. They waited for high tide and sailed into port as dusk fell.

Guided only by its top sails, the ship eased up to the dock and quickly tied off. The sailors went about their business as Tarquin and the rest debarked. Celedant stayed behind, giving the captain a bonus in hopes of garnering favor and keeping their secret.

They watched as the horses were lifted carefully with slings out of the hold and onto the dock, where they were quickly saddled. They rode off individually into town, mixing in with the crowd. They watched as two well-armed white orcs walked past, pushing through the flood of people. Once off the dock, the friends met in an alley where the horses were handed over to Azimuth and Zeffan, who went off in search of a stable closer to the east gate.

The others went into the side streets, wandering through the mazes of the less than savory portions of the city. Celedant finally decided on a rundown inn called The Bells. It was as bad on the inside as the outside hinted it would be. The common area was a mishmash of furniture, however the bar attended by the inn keeper was immaculate. There were plenty of rooms and they paid for their own rooms, not wanting a rumor that a whole group of foreigners were staying at the inn, thinking that it might draw too much attention to them.

Putting away their gear, they met in the common room, where Celedant mentally contacted Azimuth. *How goes the stabling of the horses?*

Azimuth's voice came into his head telepathically. *We have found a stable located at the east gate. It is a quick run from the witch's tower.*

Celedant turned to the others. "The horses are stabled and Azimuth and Zeffan are on their way here."

They sampled the inn's brew, which was good despite the rundown surroundings. Then their two friends entered and joined them.

Zeffan sat and exclaimed, "Tis a better inn to hide out in than any I could find."

Once they were all assembled, they ate a bland meal. Afterwards, they separated into small groups and walked to their target to scout out the witch's tower, which was being reconstructed to repair the previous damage. Squads of orcs stood guard at the entrances.

Hority, who was following Botreg like a little puppy said, "See I told ye that the sewers were the only way in."

The assassin nodded. "Yes, now we must find the service entrance that allows the sewer workers in to clean and unclog it."

Two streets over, they found a railing leading down below street level. At the bottom of a short flight of stairs was a wooden door with the smell of the sewer wafting up out of the hole.

Hority smiled at their discovery. "We found it. The others will be happy with us. Come we must go."

Botreg held him up musing, "This street is full of businesses that will be closed come dark, and few people are moving about. It will be the perfect place to enter the sewers."

They waited till nightfall the following day before venturing out, dressed in black except for Hority, his dirty frock fitting in perfectly in the darkness. It was a moonless night, and they made quick time to the sewer entrance. Once there, Botreg hurried down the steps and tried the door. As he suspected, it was open. He peered into the darkness and seeing no imminent danger, he motioned to the others to follow.

Once through, Botreg closed the door, plunging the tunnel into complete darkness. Celedant and Melgor each whispered a word of power, and the tops of their staffs glowed bright white. The light pushed back the darkness, and they discovered that they were standing on a three-foot ledge with the sewer running alongside it. Only a rusted railing kept them from falling in.

"This walkway is used by the sewer workers to monitor the flow and clear up any clogs," Botreg explained. "When I was an assassin, the sewers were a favorite place to dump bodies, and the sewer workers took care of them. The nicer assassins would leave coins in the pockets of the deceased's clothing for the sewer workers."

"We must head south if we are to reach the tower," Celedant informed the others. "This tunnel runs east and west. We can go west towards the harbor and hope we find a tunnel that leads to the tower. There is a chance that we will run into the very tunnel Hority found. A mansion that big is bound to have its own sewer system running underneath."

They continued until they came across an intersection, but it was lit with several torches. Celedant touched Botreg on the shoulder, questioning what was ahead. The dwarf shook his head. Celedant and Melgor dimmed the light on their staffs as they neared.

Botreg hugged the wall as he advanced with Hority close behind. Both of them well used to the darkness of the sewers. Up ahead, they saw three men holding a fourth's head under the flowing sewage.

Botreg drew two daggers and called out, "Hoy, what goes on here!"

The three men sprang into action, letting the body fall lifeless into the sewage as they charged them.

Hority called out his familiar battle cry, "Foes!"

Botreg let fly two daggers. They struck the first man, but did not slow him down. Before he knew it, the men were upon them. The assassin was knocked over the railing and if not for a last-ditch grab to take hold of the rail, he would have been swimming in sewage. Hority caught one of the men in passing with his branch, and he exploded into dust.

Recognizing this Hority called out, "Vampires!"

The other two vampires clawed, bit, and pummeled them before the others could react. Tarquin was shoved against the wall and his backhand swing easily blocked by the strong forearm of one vampire. Celedant used his staff to bash one in the head and as it stumbled against the railing, Azimuth sliced through the undead's neck. It, too, burst into ashes. After dealing with Tarquin, the third vampire clawed at Eldahir and Morganna's armor, hissing and baring his teeth. The elves fought back to no avail. Eldahir bashed the vampire in the face with the pommel of his sword, which only caused the creature to smile wider, its white fangs sparkling in the wizard light. Morganna struck with her sword, cutting through the monster's side. Knowing that this would do little but distract it from her husband. The vampire did not move but swatted her backwards to land on the walkway.

Tarquin came up behind the vampire, placing his sword over its head against the creature's neck. Then grabbing the sharp blade with his chain mail glove, he pulled back on his sword, cutting into the vampire's neck. The creature tried to claw Tarquin's hand away, but its fingers kept slipping off the mettle scales that incapsulated it. The prince gave one last hard pull on his sword and sliced through the neck. The vampire exploded into ash momentarily blinding both Tarquin and Eldahir.

Hority helped Botreg up and over the railing and accidentally touched the assassin with his magical branch. Botreg thought he was dead and scooted on his bottom to the wall.

The monk laughed. "Ye should do that more often friend. It puts a smile on me face."

Botreg's voice was filled with dread. "But I was touched by yer staff! I should be dead!"

Hority leaned over and gave the dark dwarf a hand up, "Donna worry, me friend. Clor knows friend from foe and would never allow the staff to hurt any of ye."

The monk got tears in his eyes at the thought that he had friends. To hide this fact, he turned and started walking to the torches from where the vampires had appeared. The others followed, and when they reached the torches, they found a heavily braced door.

Celedant pointed to it. "Probably leads to a den of the fiends. We must keep going but watch our backs for enemies."

Botreg and Hority took the lead again as they continued their search for a passageway south. They had gone about three hundred paces when they came upon a dark passage that opened to their left. It led in the direction of the warlock manor. Crossing the sewer on a narrow mettle grate, they continued south until they came upon a place where the pipes leaked sewage that was coming from the roof of the tunnel.

"I'll bet we're under the mansion right now," Celedant said. "We need to find a doorway that will lead up."

Before he could say more, a white orc charged out from the dark and into the wizard light. Tarquin pushed his way to the front, his sword blazing red fire. The orc stuck out, the clash of swords ringing in the tunnel. Using his innate elvan ability to balance on the thinnest of objects, Eldahir jumped up on the railing his bow up and arrow drawn to his cheek. He could see a white orc about to escape through a door, and he let fly his arrow. Just as the orc was about to enter the doorway, the projectile struck it in the temple.

Tarquin continued battling the white orc that had attacked him. They exchanged blows back and forth on the narrow walkway. Tarquin's blade, Dragon Bolt glowed as it struck the orc's sword from its hand. It flipped up into the air then dropped into the sewage below.

The orc never missed a beat as it drew a long dagger and slashed at the Prince of Parthia. Then suddenly, a dagger appeared in the orc's chest. It looked down in astonishment. Using the distraction, Tarquin lunged, plunging his sword deep into the belly of the creature.

He looked around and saw a smiling Botreg. "I thought ye needed help. Beside ye were taking too long, and the echoes were sure to attract attention."

Eldahir jumped down from the railing. "We need to hurry. I killed one orc trying to escape, but I can't be sure if any others made it up the stairs."

They ran down the grating, but the white orc Eldahir shot had fallen against the door, slamming it shut with the lock engaged.

"Search the bodies for the key. If we can't find it, we'll have to break it down," Tarquin commanded.

While the others searched the bodies, Botreg went to the door and peered at the lock. He got out his picks but after several tries, he declared, "It's too rusty. Me picks willna open it."

"We can't use magic," Melgor advised. "Cyra will feel it, know we're here, and raise the alarm."

Zeffan stepped forward. "Might I use with me axe. A few blows and the lock will break."

Celedant looked at Tarquin who nodded. "It's the only way. If there aren't any guards at the top of the stairs, we'll be all right. If not, we'll just start the fight earlier then we wanted to."

Zeffan approached the door as the party cleared away from the portal. He took two practice swings and then hit the lock as hard as he could. Sparks flew, but the door held. Although, there were signs that the wood around the lock was splintering. He reared back and gave it another mighty blow, and the wood of the door separated from the iron lock, which fell to the metal grate of the walkway with a clang.

Tarquin was first up the stairs and sliding to a stop when he reached the top. A tapestry hung over the exit and he waited for the others to gather behind him before moving it. Ever so gently, he reached for the tapestry's edge and opened it enough to peer out. The exit led to a hallway and so far, everything remained quiet.

He let the tapestry fall back and whispered, "Can any of you sense Cyra?"

"I feel great evil to our right," Azimuth replied. "I am certain it's her."

CHAPTER FORTY

Exiting the hidden doorway, they took the hallway to their right that was long with doors along both sides.

Celedant motioned to the rooms. "I believe these are sleeping quarters," he whispered. "We must be careful of them during a fight."

Suddenly, the huge double doors at the end of the hallway opened and out stepped Cyra. She laughed at them. "You thought you could sneak up on me? I sensed your presence the minute you entered the sewers. And you, Talchic? Somehow, I knew you would desert me when the time was right. I'm surprised you stayed with these ragamuffins as long as you did."

She began moving her arms to initiate a spell. Celedant stepped forward and started spinning his staff creating a vortex of varying colors. All around them, the doors opened, and the friends were faced with twenty-five warlocks and sorceresses. Surrounded and outnumbered, things did not look good. But then, that always seemed to be the case whenever they were in for a fight. Still, the group of friends had never faced so many magic users at once.

The door beside Tarquin opened, and he found himself face-to-face with a half-dressed warlock with a surprised look on his face. The prince quickly ran him through with his sword.

Cyra released her spell, sending a dark red energy bolt straight at Celedant, but the vortex he had created absorbed the magic and sent it back at the sorceress, surprising her. She had not realized how powerful the wizard was. She barely had time to cast a simple spell, allowing her to jump up and over the oncoming spell. The redirected spell impacted on the partially open double doors to Cyra's room and sprayed splinters of wood throughout the hallway. They never reached Tarquin or the others, but the witch caught a fair share in her back, causing her to collapse to the floor in pain and with blood leaking through the fabric of her robe.

The others had their hands full dealing with the warlocks and sorceresses, who had left their rooms. The explosion caused when the spell had hit Cyra's door, set off the alarm bell, and at the rear of the company, Melgor heard the stomp of boots as soldiers rushed forward to protect their mistress. A warlock with a dagger stepped out behind Melgor, but Eldahir was there with his bow, shooting him from three feet away.

Melgor saw a column of white orcs running at him, and he funneled all his hatred of them and Cyra into a fireball that shot forth from his staff rolling down the hallway like a blazing sun. The orcs tried to stop, but the spell was on them in an instant. The hallway channeled the fireball spell, adding to its effectiveness as it rolled into the orcs, completely engulfing row upon row of the creatures. Seeing their comrades charred to bone and feeling the heat, most of the remaining white orcs broke ranks and ran.

Meanwhile, Eldahir and Morganna used their bows with quiet efficiency, sending arrow after arrow down the hallway, slowly killing the warlocks and sorceresses that had exited their rooms. Having no one to physically attack, Hority was busy casting spells towards Cyra. Most were brushed aside, but he did call down a rain of fire that fell upon her. Once she saw what was coming, she put up a shield of power above her head. The flames beat upon her shield denting its energy in places but diverting most of it around her. But as she dropped the shield, her robe was smoldering.

Celedant called forth a lightning bolt that shrieked down the hallway. Cyra flattened herself against the wall as the lightning bolt missed her, but jagged arms of electricity shot out of the bolt as it flew past and these caught her. She withstood them, but the shock knocked the air from her lungs, and she dropped to a kneeling position on the floor.

She crouched and cast an offensive spell at Celedant. Blasts of energy flew out from her fingers the length of the corridor, impacting the front of the invaders. Hority was struck in the chest and bowled over to lay unconscious near his friends. Azimuth sent his own fiery spell at the witch and knelt down, using his hands to put out the fire burning a hole through the monk's habit and felt for a heartbeat, which he found. Standing back up, he sent another firebolt down the hallway. He was joined by the two wood elves, who sent a barrage of arrows down the hallway. Cyra sensed this and cast another shield spell, deflecting all the deadly projectiles. Standing at the front, Celedant took the most damage from her energy projectiles. He was struck by several and thrown backwards to land momentarily stunned.

Knowing that he could do little in the front, Tarquin ran to stand next to Melgor as more warlocks and sorceresses came running to the sound of the warning bell, joining the few white orcs that had remained. Melgor cast a spell and suddenly in the middle of the evil magic users, seven ogres appeared. The monsters attacked with determination, grabbing and throwing the warlocks and witches against the walls of the hallway.

Tarquin patted Melgor on the back and ran back down the hall into the melee followed closely by Melgor. By the time they reached the fight, the ogres had been delt with by the magic users and the two men barreled into the crowd. Tarquin's sword dragon bolt was soon bloodied to the hilt. Melgor used his staff like a mace, battering in the heads of their foes. Soon all but the most ardent of Cyra's supporters were left. The others seeing the massacre of their comrades left the battle to seek safety outside the building.

There were but three white orcs left from Melgor's fireball spell. These attacked Tarquin, while Melgor slid into one of the unoccupied rooms. The prince dodged and parried blows from the orcs. He struck one down with a blow to the thigh. It crawled away trailing blood. Then Melgor leaned around the corner of the doorway and sent small darts of energy at the white orcs, directing them around Tarquin to strike the orcs. Like regular arrows, these penetrated the armor they wore, bringing both orcs to their knees. Tarquin ran them through with Dragon Bolt.

With Celedant temporarily out of commission, Cyra stalked down the corridor towards the others. Botreg threw his daggers. One she swatted away, but the other struck her in the pit of her stomach. Reaching down, she withdrew the dagger, and tossed it back. It sped through the air back at Botreg, who saw it coming but could not get out of the way. The force of the dagger struck deep into his shoulder, slamming him backward where he tripped over the dead body of a warlock and fell.

With his head finally cleared, Celedant propped himself up on his elbows and leveled his staff, Forestae at her. He chanted a spell under his breath that lit the sigils of power in the staff, bringing forth its power. A bright green pulse of energy shot out of the end of his staff, catching Cyra in midstride and knocking her back to slide all the back into her room.

His clothes still smoldering, Celedant stood up and called out. "Follow me!" As he ran towards where Cyra had disappeared, only a few of his company were able to follow.

Azimuth, Morganna, and Zeffan charged after him. The rest lay wounded in the hallway or fighting at the rear of the column. Eldahir lay clutching his thigh, where a warlock, hidden in a room, had hit him from behind with the end of his staff. The elf had quickly struck him down but now sat against the wall in extreme pain from a broken leg. While Hority still lay stunned from the spell.

The small group charged into Cyra's bedroom to find her pulling herself up by the bed post, bleeding and singed by wizard fire. Morganna emptied her quiver at the sorceress, but her arrows all broke apart as they struck an invisible shield. So, she dropped her bow and drew her sword.

Azimuth was at Cyra's side first. He took a mighty swing with his sword. She caught the blade barehanded with her left hand, however, and punched with her right, sending Celedant's friend spinning to thump against the wall. Zeffan slid on the marble floor passing within feet of the witch. He swung out and his axe sliced through the top layer of her thigh. Screaming in pain and frustration, she spun around and used her magic to pick up the dwarf and slam him to the ground, where he bounced on the marble floor to lay unconscious. Morganna ran at the witch but with a simple brush of her arm, Cyra sent her crashing to the floor and sliding until she slammed against the wall.

At the other end of the hallway, the warlocks and sorceresses were gathering in the main hall to charge Tarquin and Melgor.

With the alarm now silent, Melgor called out to them. "Your mistress is dying, and the white orcs have fled. Leave us be. Go before you die, too."

Nearly half of their enemies ran from the main hall. Although they had liked the idea of increasing their power over the city and its ports, once they learned that she was dying, they had no intention of dying with her. Melgor lowered his staff and stepped into the open, where he cast a lightning spell that cut their crowded enemies in half killing as it went, throwing burned warlocks and sorceresses aside. Tarquin took this respite in the attack to charge, his blade still bright with fire. Behind him, Melgor threw balls of bright yellow energy at their enemies. As Tarquin reached the mass of magic users, dealing death with his sword, the balls of energy cast by Melgor struck. For each strike, their enemy was pulverized and fell in a heap on the floor. Tarquin was in amongst his enemies striking left and right hardly able to miss the tightly packed men and women, who were unable to fight back with magic in such close quarters. Melgor joined him plying his staff with expertise.

In Cyra's room, Celedant continued forward and when the witch turned to deal with Zeffan, the wizard brought Forestae up and over her head, pulling it tight against her throat. She grasped the staff, pushing with all her might so she could breathe. Then she called forth a spell and her hands glowed red hot in an effort to burn through Celedant's weapon. But the magical staff used its innate ability, drawn from the forest and earth, and fought off the attack. Though the fire left burn marks on the staff, Cyra was unable to push it away. Letting go of the staff, she drew her dagger and plunged it into Celedant's side. He let up on trying to strangle her but then used his pain to put even more force on her neck.

Cyra was dying slowly, and she knew all that she had obtained was for naught. But she had been through too much, and she twisted and turned the dagger in Celedant's side. Fighting through the pain, he used it to add more pressure, but he did not know how much longer he could hang on as his blood seeped from him. Then Tarquin and Melgor ran into the room.

"Your minions are dead or have run away," Tarquin cried out. "Give up Cyra!"

Seeing the dire straits that Celedant was in, Melgor called forth a narrow beam of energy, which he directed with his staff at the witch. It hit the arm, drawing a line down to the hand holding the dagger. Both arm and hand blew apart, rendering her incapable of fighting Celedant or her new attackers.

Azimuth opened his eyes, and realizing that the battle was not yet over, he quickly assessed the situation by probing his bond mate's mind. Jumping to his feet, he ran over to the bed. "Cyra! Look at me."

The deep growl to his voice compelled her to do as he asked.

"Of all the death and destruction, you have caused, there is one more I wish you to see." And because she was a sorceress, he entered her mind and showed her the black dragon, his death, and what he has said as his final words.

Cyra's eyes grew wide. "He...he should have been mine. We would have made a perfect bonding," she gasped.

"Yes. Instead, you will join him with the depths of the seven hells." His eyes changed from that of an elf to his dragon eyes.

"No!" she screamed. "Do not torment me golden dragon. Leave me!"

Azimuth stepped aside as Tarquin called out to Celedant. "Turn!"

The wizard whipped her around blood squirting from her arm and raising Dragon Bolt over his head, threw Dragon Bolt at her. It struck true. Unable to keep the barrier up, Cyra saw the blade spinning through the air and felt it strike her in the chest and plunge through her heart. The sword ballooned out the back of her robe, penetrating into Celedant's chest, and they both collapsed. Melgor and Tarquin ran to their fallen friend.

Tarquin left his sword sticking out of Cyra's chest and knelt beside his mentor and friend putting pressure on chest wound as Melgor chanted and holding his staff above the dire wounds in Celedant's side. A bright blue light emanated from his staff and a tight beam struck the downed wizard in the wound, cauterizing it. He continued to the penetrating chest wound and then pulled Celedant into a sitting position with his back against the bed.

The wizard grasped Melgor and whispered, "Poison. Look in my bag for a potion."

The wizard quickly retrieved Celedant's bag and rifled through it pulling out several vials of potions. Then he saw one labeled "anti-poison," uncorked it, and poured the contents down the wizard's throat.

Celedant smiled calmly. "Thank you, my friend. I'll live for now. See to the others."

His words stunned Melgor, who as he realized the implication of those words, smiled. And for the first time in his life, he felt pride and happiness swell inside him because of the good he had done.

Tarquin turned to Melgor. "See to Morganna and Zeffan. I'll get Hority up."

The Parthian Prince rushed from the room to where the party had made their first stand and found both Hority and Eldahir. The monk was stirring, He sat up, and the first thing out of his mouth was, "Foes!"

But Tarquin calmed him down, saying, "We need your healing prowess. There is wounded spread all across this hall and bedroom."

Hority looked to Eldahir and saw that the elf had broken his bow in half and fashioned a splint using the bow string to tighten the wood to his leg. Tarquin helped the monk up and put his arm around him to keep him upright. For once, the prince was glad of the dwarf's stench. It reminded him of healing.

He looked to Eldahir who picked up his sword saying, "I'll be all right. Get Hority to where he is needed most."

They entered the bedroom, and Hority looked around. It appeared that Celedant needed attended to immediately and with Tarquin's help, he reached the wizard.

"I was poisoned but took a potion for it," Celedant told the dwarf. "Melgor cauterized the wound, but I can tell I am bleeding internally."

Hority shook his head. "Once again, I missed the most epic of battles. Come now and lay down. I'll see what I can do."

The monk held his hands over the wizard's side and began chanting. A dirty brown haze formed, and Hority called forth on the mighty Clor to heal Celedant. He then moved to his chest and repeated the healing process. By then, Zeffan had awoken and sat blowing blood out of his broken nose. Using both hands, he reset his nose with a grunt of pain, and then retrieved his axe.

"Eldahir is in the hallway and needs help. Go to him," Tarquin ordered.

The dwarf sped off. Hority next went to examine Morganna, who was in a more serious state. She had slammed her head against the wall and lay in a pool of blood. Having regained his balance, Hority ran to her, grasped sides of her head and called on Clor for healing.

The same brown haze formed, but blood still ran from her head. The dirty monk fished through his bag and pulled forth several potions and for once, an amazingly clean bandage. Sitting her up with Tarquin's help, they gave her the healing potions. Hority then carefully wrapped the bandage around the elf's head.

Zeffan walked into the bedroom gently carrying Eldahir, who was in quite a lot of pain with his leg splinted.

The dwarf called to Tarquin. "The guardsmen are running rampant through the manor stealing everything they can. I frightened a few off but more came."

"Place Eldahir next to Morganna," Hority told Zeffan. "Their proximity might aid in the healing."

The monk then repeated his healing process on Eldahir, calling on Clor for aid. The wood elf felt the healing taking place, and his leg grew numb, killing the pain.

"Ye will heal slowly from such a major break," Hority informed him. "But ye'll be fine."

Zeffan, who had taken guard duty at the door called, "They are coming."

Melgor ran to the door and shot off a fireball spell that rolled down the hallway incinerating the guardsmen.

"We must go," Tarquin called out. "We can't hold off the guards for that long in the shape we're in."

Celedant hobbled up to the door using his staff as support. Azimuth followed, carrying Eldahir, and Zeffan gingerly picked up Morganna. The battered friends slowly walked down the hallway. Hority called to Azimuth, "Careful of her head. Wounds like that take a while to heal…. If ever," he muttered under his breath.

The guards once again began gathering, and one stepped forward, "We'll be taking what we need from you."

Then from behind the battered friends came the word that delighted them all. "Foes!"

Hority rushed past and attacked the wall of guardsmen, followed by Tarquin and Melgor. The monk danced through the men, dealing out death with his branch, while the prince entered the melee, swinging his sword back and forth, blood flying. Melgor followed, wielding his staff one handed, caving in skulls and breaking bones as he went.

Soon the guards retreated to the great hall and as the group entered, they parted and allowed them to exit the building. Word must have spread that the warlocks and sorceresses had run because there was rioting in the streets.

"We must reach our horses and escape this mess," Tarquin called to the others. "We need to rest not to battle through the streets."

"Come follow me," Zeffan replied. "The horses aren't far."

The traveler led them down the street to a quieter part of town where the riot had not reached. They eventually made it to a stable guarded by several armed men.

"Halt. What business do you have here?" the leader demanded.

Zeffan, still carrying Morganna, demanded, "We've wounded here, and our horses are in the stable.

"We were told no one in or out," the man insisted.

Celedant dug in his bag and tossed the man a pouch of coins.

The man grinned. "This," he said holding up the pouch, "speaks volumes."

They were let into the stables. As quickly as possible, Tarquin and Zeffan saddled up everyone's horses, and they began to mount up. Azimuth used his draconic strength to lift Eldahir up into the saddle, before getting on his own horse. Then Tarquin placed Morganna on the saddle in front of Azimuth. Trailing a horse and two mules, the battle-weary friends rode to the gate. It was manned and shut with the portcullis down.

A guardsman called down to them, "You can't pass through this gate. There's rioting in the city, and we've been ordered not to let anyone out."

Zeffan rode to the front of the group and called back, "It is I the traveler. I've got a wizard and warlock with me, both capable of turning this gate to dust and knocking down your gatehouse."

"I'm just following orders," the captain replied. "We'll let you through traveler." Instantly the portcullis slowly rose, and several guards came out of the shadows to remove the thick bar from the gate and push it open.

Zeffan called to the Gate Captain, "Where are the white orcs?"

"We were lucky they ran. A pox on all their kind," the human yelled back.

"Then you'll be happy to know that their mistress is dead, and your city is yours once more," Zeffan said as they rode through the gate and into the darkness to cheers, looking for a safe place to let them rest and heal.

CHAPTER FORTY-ONE

As the weary group of companions rode out of the eastern gate of Trudoc, Tarquin looked back at his friends. Eldahir held Morganna upright in front of him on the same horse. Her head leaned back against his shoulder to keep it as steady as possible. The Prince also saw the pained look on the elf's face as he fought the strain of the newly healed broken leg pressing against his horse's side. Celedant was slumped forward, his chest and side wrapped tightly from wounds that Cyra had inflicted upon him and from Tarquin's thrown sword that had eventually killed the witch. Melgor rode beside him to keep him in the saddle. Zeffan's eyes were almost swollen shut from his broken nose and the collision on the granite floor. Azimuth kept a constant watch on Celedant and Hority looked pale from the drain and strain required to heal his friends.

Tarquin shouted out the them. "We need shelter to rest! I see a wooded area ahead. We can make camp there."

The band followed their leader into the woods until Tarquin found a relatively cleared area. He called to Azimuth, "Help me get them off the horses, and we can assemble makeshift tents for the wounded."

Azimuth nodded, using his draconic strength to help the wounded dismount, while Tarquin and Zeffan got them bedded down under their tents. Despite his exhaustion, Hority made it clear that he was going to see to his patients. Once everyone was settled, Tarquin got a fire going and put on a cauldron to make hot beef soup for them all. He doubted anyone would follow them this quickly with the riots going on in Trudoc. The ones that could, took the soup gladly and soon most were asleep. We should both stand guard tonight while the others rest," Tarquin suggested.

"Agreed," Azimuth said.

The following morning dawned misting with rain, but everyone was feeling better. His leg on the mend, Eldahir gently held his wife Morganna, waiting for her to awake. Celedant leaned against a tree and swore to Hority that he was mending well. Tarquin rode his horse to the edge of the woods to see what was happening in Trudoc. He found that they had not traveled very far from the city during the night. He could still make out the warlock's tower over the low hills and saw that there was smoke rising from the city. He stayed there for an hour but saw no sign of pursuit.

While he waited, he thought about the situation and realized they might not need to worry about it. The city had too much to deal with the rioting. The warlocks and sorceresses might not pursue them after so many of their ilk had died fighting them. As for the orcs, one could not be certain. They would no longer be tolerated in the city and probably would return home. Yet if they ran into the wounded party, a fight would surely ensue.

Upon his return, Eldahir was smiling and called to Tarquin, "Morganna is stirring."

Tarquin smiled back, weary from standing guard overnight. "Good. I see our Hority has worked miracles again."

The dwarf looked up from where he was examining Celedant and replied, "I told ye, head wounds take time to heal. We can't move her until we know she's all right."

Tarquin told them what he had seen, ending with, "I believe they have their hands full quelling the riots and reestablishing control of their city. I doubt anyone will have time to worry about us, at least for now."

Exhausted, he went and lay inside his tent, instantly falling fast asleep. It seemed like only minutes had passed when Azimuth shook him awake. But darkness had fallen, and his friend was handing out the night's dinner. That night, Azimuth went to the forest's edge to keep a watch for anyone that might be following them, while Zeffan kept watch on the camp. In the middle of the night, Azimuth heard the jingle of horse tack and using his keen elvan eyesight saw a column of white orcs riding northeast. With their mistress dead, they were afraid to return to their original master without the heads of those who had killed the witch.

A week passed in the woods while they healed and rested. Finally, Morganna's eyes flickered open while Eldahir walked about gingerly on his leg. She raised her arm and called out weakly, "Eldahir where are you?"

The elvan general nearly ran to her side, and Hority hurried over, too.

"What happened and did everyone make it out alive?" she asked.

With tears in his eyes, Eldahir answered her. "Cyra is dead, and we all survived. Though without Hority, many of us would have died."

Hority blushed and said, "Come now, let me look at the wound."

He gently unrolled the linen bandage and felt the wound through the blood matted hair. "The wound is healed," he declared. "But ye may still have a concussion. We must not hurry that along. Rest and good food are what ye need."

Azimuth came to Tarquin after a day of watching across the land from the edge of the tree line. He informed the Prince, "I just saw forty more white orcs riding northeast. We are lucky that our path here has been hidden by time and rain."

Tarquin thought a few seconds before replying, "So, it's not the magic users coming after us, unless they reformed under another leader and sent them. When we pull up camp, we'll head east to parallel their path. We will soon reach the grasslands, where it will be easier to see their passage. Besides, we are days behind them. That should account for something."

They stayed an extra week until everyone was feeling fine, even Morganna. She was up walking around thanks to extra healing spells cast upon her by Hority. Remarkably, she had even grown used to his smell and the moldy odor that came from his habit, due to the unholy rain that fell on them at times.

One night, Tarquin told the group about the white orcs ahead of them. This brought about much discussion.

"Hority are we ready to travel?" Celedant asked him.

"Yes, I believe so," he replied. "Ye all seem recovered from yer wounds."

Celedant looked to Tarquin and asked, "We leave tomorrow?"

Tarquin nodded. "We head east and hope we don't come across the orcs."

Zeffan spoke up. "One last good night's sleep, and its back on the road for us."

"So Zeffan, you intend to stay with us?" Eldahir asked.

"I've never been past the grass lands and the East seems to be interesting after what ye've told me," the Tracker replied. "Besides, I might have worn out me welcome in Trudoc for now. I need to give them some years to forget me."

The next day they broke camp, loaded their belongings onto the mules, filled their casts with water, and mounted up heading east.

Chapter Forty-Two

Their hearts were lighter as they headed east towards home, eventually exiting the forest lands and entering the great grasslands.

"Eldahir, ride a mile in front of us," Tarquin ordered. "Zeffan be a rear guard so no one sneaks up behind us. Also keep an eye out for any sign of the orcs passage."

The two scouts searched but found no sign of trampled grass in either direction. So, the party continued heading east. The swaying grass reached up to the rider's knees, and a gentle wind made for perfect riding. At one-point, Tarquin nearly dozed off in his saddle. He awoke and instantly thought of Ress and their unborn child. The thought that he may have missed the birth of his first child broke his heart, but each mile brought him closer to her. He could ask Azimuth to fly him back, but that would leave the group one man and one dragon short, and he could not do that to his friends.

Three days later they spotted smoke coming from a campfire up ahead. Eldahir slipped off his horse and continued on foot.

Thirty clicks of the clock later, Eldahir returned with bad news. "There are five white orcs ahead. It appears that they have been camped there for some time."

"Then we can't slip past them," Celedant mused.

"There is a trail leading north and south. Most likely mounted patrols going from post to post," Eldahir added. "Even if we dismount, the orcs will see our horses or their trails. I suggest we wait for darkness and sneak by the guard post."

"Even if we get by, our horses will leave a plain track to follow," Tarquin said. "I don't know about you, but I don't fancy fighting white orcs on this open terrain. We can cross the path in single file and hide our numbers. They might not send many soldiers to check us out if they think there aren't many of us." He sighed. "Wishful thinking, I know."

"Maybe we can catch them in a trap," Eldahir suggested. "Surround and kill them all. It will give us more time to get as far away as possible."

Celedant considered the ideas and looked to Tarquin. "I say we pass by tonight in single file. Zeffan will lead the way, and Eldahir will bring up the rear."

Everyone nodded in agreement. They waited, trying to sleep until nightfall and awoke as the sun was setting and ate a cold meal of beef jerky and water. Finally, the stars came out, and a quarter moon was high in the sky. They mounted up and in single file headed east. Zeffan went first. When he was about a hundred paces away, the others followed. Eldahir waited for the others to get ahead of him before nudging his horse forward to follow.

Upon arriving at the beaten path the white orcs were using, Zeffan looked both ways. He saw nothing, so he crossed still followed by the others. They rode in single file for two turns of the clock before finding Zeffan waiting for them where the grasslands left the hilly area and turned into flatlands. They let Eldahir catch up before breaking into a trot. Riding until morning, they ate breakfast in the saddle, then alternated between walking and riding their horses.

Two days later, Eldahir rode up from the rear yelling, "Their behind us. We must search out a place to make a stand. He rode onward at a gallop. The others followed until they found Eldahir and

Zeffan stopped. As they drew close, Eldahir pointed out a slight rise in the land.

Tarquin called out, "Hority take the horses behind this rise."

"I know," Botreg said dejectedly. "I'll make sure he does it right."

The companions dismounted and prepared to fight.

"We wait hidden until they get closer and let loose our arrows," Tarquin commanded. "That should bring down a good many. Then we fight."

They waited ten clicks of the clock before they saw the oncoming orcs riding at a gallop. When they were twenty paces away, Tarquin stood up and loosed an arrow. Three of the ten orcs toppled from their mounts. Eldahir and Morganna shot two more from their saddles as the five remaining orcs came up the slight slant and engaged them in battle. Then they heard the familiar cry of, "Foes," as Hority ran straight into the battle, followed by Botreg.

One orc came directly at Zeffan. The creature swung its sword countless times, but each time came up short of striking the dwarf. Then Zeffan struck. Swinging his axe, he caught the orc on the leg, cutting through its leather boot and going deep into the flesh. The orc instinctively grabbed at his leg, and the dwarf quickly brought his axe up, striking the orc under the chin and knocking it off its horse. Zeffan leaped forward where the orc lay dazed on the ground and buried his axe in its chest, splitting its armor.

Tarquin faced off against one of the remaining white orcs. The huge monster launched itself off the horse hitting the prince head on. Tarquin had the air knocked from his lungs and lay on the ground gasping for breath as the white orc straddled him sword raised. Tarquin had just enough time to bring up his sword, Dragon Bolt, to block the blow. But he barely had enough strength to withstand the attack. The white orc was bigger and stronger, and its sword started inching downward, until Celedant came to the rescue. Using his staff, Forestae, he caught the orc in the face, giving Tarquin time to run it through.

Seeing their comrades dying around them, the last two decided to make a run for it and galloped away.

Having had no one to fight, Hority shouted at their fleeing backs, "Cowards!"

But Eldahir wasn't about to let them go. With his bow drawn tight to his face, he let fly first one, and then two more. The first arrow struck the retreating orc in the back, and he fell off his horse dead. The second struck the white orc in the helmet, knocking the creature forward and off its horse.

Morganna left the group, running after the downed orc. As she ran, she called back, "You call yourself an archer?" As she drew near the downed creature at a full run, she drew back on her bow string and shot the orc in the heart.

Recovered from his near-death experience, Tarquin called out to the others, "Gather their horses. We can't risk one of them returning to their camp to alert the others that we're here."

Once the horses were rounded up, Celedant said with a smile, "Its high time to return to the Valley of Clor."

But he was interrupted by Azimuth's voice in his head. "Not quite yet."

The dragon had morphed back into his real shape and telepathically called to Tarquin, "It's high time you returned to your wife before she gives birth."

Hority seeing the dragon called out, "Do I get to ride ye? All hail Clor."

But Azimuth told the dwarf, "Not yet, my friend. First, I must take Tarquin home to his wife. You will receive your ride after I return."

The filthy monk stopped dead in his tracks and yelled out, "The dragon speaks to me in my head! A miracle of Clor!" He then dove to the ground and started pulling at the grass and throwing handfuls of dirt all over his body. As Tarquin flew away, he watched Botreg struggle to get the dwarf up off the ground until he lost sight of them. Azimuth went higher in the sky, winging towards New Partha.

Chapter Forty-Three

Leaving his friends in the grasslands was hard for Tarquin. He had been with them for so long and shared so many dangers that he felt like he was abandoning them. Tears of concern filled his eyes, and he hoped they would make it to their respected homes.

Azimuth flew as fast as he could to get Tarquin home in time for the birth of his first child. They talked along the way, each learning more about the other, stopping for a brief time for the dragon to catch a couple wild boars. He quickly roasted part of one for Tarquin and gobbled down the rest. After traveling for a day and a half, the valley of New Parthia came into to view.

The dragon's voice came into Tarquin's mind. *We need to find a place where I can land without being seen.*

"We can land near Dugan's Way Station and purchase horses, if they have any. If not, it's just three days across country to New Partha." Not used to speaking telepathically, Tarquin had spoken aloud.

Up and down the dwarvan roads were established way stations, safe havens for travelers in the sometimes dangerous mountains. They were small fortresses guarded by ten dwarvan warriors, along with the owners and his workers.

That sounds fine to me, Azimuth replied.

The dragon flew high above the valley, making sure no one saw him and approached Dugan's Way Station. *Get ready for a rough ride. I see a clearing near the mountains about a day from Dugan's. I'll dive in and make an abrupt landing.*

Azimuth picked up speed, tucked his wings against his body, and dove for the clearing. Tarquin thought he was going to vomit from the dive. It felt and looked like the crazed dragon was going to crash into the ground. Azimuth extended his wings, and in a few flaps, he settled down in the clearing. Tarquin was at once levitated off his back, and the dragon quickly cast the spell that changed him back into a wood elf. Tarquin bent over with his hands on his knees taking deep breaths of the cool mountain air as he tried to settle his stomach.

Azimuth approached him. "You survived. That was a difficult landing usually only the most experience riders can handle."

Tarquin held up his hand. "Just a minute. I'm still recovering."

The wood elf laughed. "Come we need to move. We have a day to travel and little food and water."

The two of them hiked south toward the way station. They had gone nearly halfway when Azimuth held up his hand and said, Wait! I hear something ahead."

They crept forward and saw a camp of orcs and a great ogre.

Tarquin touched Azimuth and whispered, "This bodes ill for Dugan's. We must reach the way station before these creatures do."

Azimuth nodded and the pair ran through the woods in an effort to out distance the orcs. Luckily, the forest had a thick layer of needles on the ground to cover the sound of their passage. After an hour's run, they burst onto the dwarvan road that led to the human city states to the east and the dwarvan capital Nars in the west.

It took Tarquin a few minutes to ascertain which direction Dugan's lay. "I'm fairly sure it this way," he said. "I've traveled this road enough time I should know. But with darkness falling I just can't tell for sure."

They ran east. Tarquin discovered that keeping up with a wood elf was almost impossible. He had seen Eldahir run, but he had never run with him. Now Azimuth was out pacing him."

Just as darkness fell, they sighted the torches of the way station ahead of them. Tarquin called out to the guard stationed above the gate. "There are orcs on our trail. Open the gates."

The gates were opened, and after the two slipped inside, a bar slid across to secure the thick iron bound gates. Tarquin bent double, practically gasping for breath. Azimuth was hardly breathing hard. The guards called for their sergeant and the inn's owner, Dugan. Tarquin readily accepted a flask of water from the guard while they waited.

His breath easing, he waited for the two dwarves to arrive. When they did, he addressed them. "Sergeant and Master Dugan. I am Prince Tarquin of Parthia. There are thirty or so orcs with an ogre coming this way."

"How do we know who you are?" Dugan asked suspiciously.

"I fought at Southgard during the war after the battle," the Sergeant said. "I saw him aplenty. He is who he says he is. Major Tarquin of the King's Borderers and Prince of New Partha."

Tarquin grimaced. "That was a sad battle. Too many dwarves were lost. I was sorry I was not there for the siege. But it looks like we'll fight together here."

"Tis and honor, me lord," the dwarf said.

Tarquin took over the defense of the way station, ordering the dwarvan soldiers to man the walls with their crossbows and bows, while Dugan and his workers reinforced the gate. A dozen dwarves in the inn also took up weapons to fight their age-old enemies. In the middle of the night, the orcs approached the station. The defenders could hear the noise of the orcs' armor made as they approached.

Tarquin and the others on the wall crouched behind the crenellations of the fort holding torches ready to be lit. When he thought the orcs were close enough, the Prince of Parthia lit up a torch and threw it outward. The orcs were back lit by the fire, and the dwarves began raining arrows down upon them. There were screams in the dark, and the ogre lumbered up to the gate.

It threw its massive weight against the door, causing a mighty blast of sound. The wood creaked but held. Azimuth jumped off the ledge and took up position behind the gate. The ogre hit it again and several of the thick planks broke inward. Azimuth drew back an arrow and shot through the hole, bringing a roar of pain from the ogre.

The orcs fired a volley of arrows but in the darkness, most missed their intended targets. Several of the dwarves pitched backward into the yard wounded or dead. But Tarquin kept firing out into the darkness. Several more torches had been thrown out at the orcs, giving the dwarves clear targets. Then the ogre struck again, and the reinforced gate fell inward. But Azimuth was there waiting and released his missile. The arrow flew straight at the ogre, striking it in the eye. It teetered in the gateway and collapsed half in and half out of the gate.

Tarquin jumped down, and he and Azimuth stood in the gateway with the ogre's body in between them. Both had their swords out as the orcs charged. Many of the orcs were brought down by arrows from the battlements, but it wasn't long before they were upon Tarquin and Azimuth. They had watched the orcs running toward them and suddenly, they were engaged. Tarquin blocked and parried blows, stabbing back penetrating orcan defenses, but the mass of bodies were too much, and the orcs fell wounded only to be trampled by their comrades.

Several of the orcs climbed upon the dead body of the ogre to attack the defenders, but suddenly from behind them, bows strings twanged and arrows appeared, piercing the attacking orcs. They fell and slowly slid down the dead ogre to the mass of attackers. Two of the dwarvan warriors with crossbows stood behind Tarquin and Azimuth, shooting into the attackers. Azimuth used his massive years of sword training to efficiently kill the orcs that faced him, until an orc jumped at him with a dagger drawn. It hit him in the chest, knocking him onto his back amidst the dead orcs. His sword flew from his hand, and they both grappled for control of the dagger. But before it went on for very long, Dugan himself was there, caving in the orc's skull with a giant wooden maul.

On the horizon, the sun began coloring the eastern sky, and the remaining orcs broke and ran away. The dwarves on the walls continued firing arrows, bringing many down.

Dugan helped Azimuth up and smiled. "I thought ye was dead there, me elf."

The wood elf replied with a laugh. "You weren't the only one."

Chapter Forty-Four

As the sun rose in the east, the dwarves of Dugan's Way Station cleared away the bodies of the orcs. In all, twenty-seven orcs had been killed, and two of the dwarves had died.

The dwarves had to use four horses to drag the ogre to where the soldiers were burning the bodies of the orcs. Dugan gave Tarquin and Azimuth two horses for their warning of the pending attack and their part in the defense of the way station. They ate a meager meal for lunch before leaving, and all the dwarves gave them a rousing send off.

They rode south, eventually reaching the turn off to New Partha, where they met a patrol of Borderers.

The Captain in command recognized Tarquin and hailed him, "Me Lord, what are ye doing on the road alone? There have been orc raids recently."

"I am on my way home," Tarquin replied. "You should head to Dugan's. The orcs attacked the way station last night. We beat them off but some escaped."

"Thank ye, me Lord," the Dwarf replied. "We'll track them down." That said, the company of dwarves rode hard for Dugan's.

Tarquin and Azimuth picked up the pace to reach New Partha before nightfall. They passed the outlaying farms and as night fell in the valley, the city appeared. Tall battlements surrounding an industrious city with a huge castle built in its center. Upon seeing Tarquin, the guards at the gate stood aside and came to attention. The two riders seeing how close Tarquin's home was, picked up speed, riding hard for the castle.

The guards at the castle gate also stood aside for the horsemen, and as they dismounted, two stablemen came up to take the horses. Tarquin explained they were Dugan's and should be returned as soon as possible. The two friends rushed up the steps to the main doors leading into the great hall. Both were worried that Ress had already had their child. They burst into the hall as his father, King Benton was breaking bread with some of the nobles of the city. Tarquin saw Ress's red hair sitting at the table, and when she saw him, she let out a shout of joy and struggled to get out of her seat. Tarquin had made it back before the baby was born.

Her stomach had grown considerably, since he had last seen her, and she walked uncomfortably to him. They hugged, and he kissed her. She was wearing a beautiful dark green silk dress with a white fur stole around her shoulders.

"I missed you so much," Tarquin told her. "I thought about you every night as I went to bed. I begged the gods that I would get home before the baby was born. I see that I barely made it."

Ress answered in tears. "Yes, you made it home. Though I doubted it many days. The Clorian monk brought word of what had happened and that you were going to avenge the massacre. I understood why you went, but I kept thinking that you would never return, that I would be a widow, and that our child would never see its father."

The dinner guests applauded at the home coming for Tarquin, while Azimuth quietly tried to slip away, not wanting to take away the enjoyment the husband and wife were having.

But he had no luck. Ress saw him and called out, "Azimuth! Come and give me a hug!"

He had no choice and could not miss out on a welcoming hug.

The red headed Ress playfully slapped his arm, "I hope you took care of my husband while you were away."

He smiled and answered, "You know I did. Although it was hard to do. You understand how hardheaded he is. He attracts danger like a magnet."

King Benton stood and called to his son, "Come Tarquin. You and Azimuth shall sit up here with the family. You shall regale us with your adventures that kept you away for so long."

"Come Ress, you must sit and rest," Queen Alicia said. "The baby is ready to come at any time now."

Holding hands, they approached the head of the table. His brother Timmons smiled hugely as Tarquin and Ress sat down.

Once seated, his elder brother said, "Welcome home, Tarquin. It is good to see you at the table again."

"You can't believe how great it feels to be home and eating in the hall," Tarquin responded.

The king must have been on a recent hunt, because there was venison and a whole hog at the end of the table. The servants sliced up the meat, heaping on fried baby potatoes and carrots. While they ate, Tarquin regaled them with stories of the West. When suddenly Ress grabbed his hand and placed it on her stomach. The baby was kicking like a marching soldier. Feeling it, he smiled, leaned over and kissed her cheek.

Later that night as they were getting ready for bed, Ress, who had been feeling minor labor pains without realizing it, was hit by a much sharper one that made her cry out and grab her stomach. She lurched for the bed and spoke through the pain. "Quick Tarquin! I need the midwife. I think the baby is coming."

Tarquin rushed from the room calling for the midwife. He turned the corner and ran into two guards, who were rushing to his call.

"Quick! Go fetch the midwife," he commanded. "My wife is having the baby."

As Tarquin turned away the guards ran past several rooms, stopping and beating on the door they wanted. An ancient dwarf dressed in a thick night shirt came to the door. He was a cleric of Dolgar, and he specialized in pregnancy. He had been sent to New Partha by the Abbot Baldo, who had fought in the wars with both Ress and Tarquin.

The guards both spoke at the same time. "Princess Ress is about to give birth."

The dwarf calmly answered, "I'll get my bag and be along in a second. Fetch Matilda, too."

Tarquin propped Ress up with pillows and was holding her hand when the doctor entered. "Prince Tarquin, I'm brother Unden and am here to help in the delivery of yer child and see to Princess Ress. Matilda the midwife will be along in a moment. I now must ask ye to leave the room."

At that moment, the midwife entered and shooed Tarquin out of the room. He was able to give Ress a final kiss and hug until he was dragged from the room by an astonishing strong Matilda.

When Tarquin exited the room, and the door was firmly shut, he saw Azimuth hurrying up the hallway. He stopped by Tarquin and asked, "How is she doing, and how about you?"

"She is in great pain but seems in good spirits," Tarquin said truthfully. "As far as I am concerned. I'm a nervous wreck."

They sat with their backs to the stone wall and listened to the noises coming through the closed the door. Soon all of Tarquin's family had joined them. Servants came, too, bringing chairs for everyone to sit in between pacing in the hallway.

Tarquin's mother was there to assure her son that everything was all right. "These things take time, my son, especially when it's a first born. We must be patient."

Her words proved true. Several hours passed, with loud moans coming from the other side of the door at regular intervals. Potions could not be given for pain in child birth, as they could affect the baby. As the labor grew more intense, the moans grew louder, turning to screams when it was time for Ress to push. Another scream, and the cries of a baby came through the door. Tarquin had been pacing, and when he heard the cry, he rushed to the door.

Several moments passed before the midwife finally opened the door and seeing all the people outside said, "Come, your Highness. The Princess is well, and your baby is healthy."

Tarquin entered and saw his wife holding a small bundle that was making an extraordinary amount of noise.

"It's a girl," Ress said beaming, but tired.

He hugged and kissed first her forehead, and then the baby's. "She's beautiful, my love. Looks just like you, he said, stroking the baby's cap of red hair.

"Ah, but I think she has your chin," Ress replied. "That means she'll most likely be as stubborn as her father."

Queen Alicia was thrilled. "Finally, a girl in the family. I had so wanted one, but all I got were boys," she said with a grin and a wink.

"Ah, she'll be spoiled, I can tell you that," King Benton said, beaming. "And why not?"

"Yes, why not?" Tarquin replied. "A princess for all time."

Chapter Forty-Five

With Celedant taking the lead, the remaining companions rode towards the desert in hopes of finding the canyon they had descended from the foothills. As they rode forward, the grass grew shorter, a sure sign they were close to the desert.

Then Eldahir galloped back to them and yelled, "The nomads are waiting for us. They are not grouped up but spread out in a semicircle across the hill in single file."

"They learned from our earlier clash," Celedant said. "Come, we ride north into the canyons, where we may be able to trap them."

They had been riding hard for an hour when they finally spotted the exposed crags that told them they were near the foothills.

Azimuth's voice sounded in Celedant head. *It's a girl and as heathy as can be.* His words came across as beaming, and the wizard knew that if he were facing the dragon, he would see a huge draconic smile.

"That's great news, my friend," the Wizard responded. "But we are in a wee bit of trouble ourselves. There are fifty or more nomads coming after us. We're heading into the canyons in hopes of springing a trap. Otherwise, it does not look good for us."

Do not worry, Azimuth replied. Hold out for a full day, and I'll be there to lend a hand. I wonder what they would do if they were attacked by the full force of dragon fury.

Celedant chuckled and relayed the information to the others. It raised their spirits.

They galloped onward until they reached the canyons, slowing because the floor was so uneven, and they were afraid one of their horses might break a leg. They continued upward but a defensible position never offered itself.

Zeffan rode up from the rear and reported, "They are not far behind. I fear they will catch us before nightfall."

The wizard whirled his horse around looking at the ground. "We dig in here and stack rocks for our protection. Riding single file in this space would not benefit them, so our spells will be of use.

The companions dug all night long, making pits they could stand in and fight from. As the sun came up, Celedant heard the mental call of Azimuth.

"Celedant I am here over the canyons. Where are you? I only see the tan dirt walls of the canyons."

"To tell you the truth," the Wizard answered, "I can't say which one we went up. But soon the nomads will be on the move and stir up the dirt, or you'll see flashes of our magic. We are dug in awaiting their appearance."

"I'll get to you as soon as possible," the Dragon replied.

They ate a bit of dried beef and drank some water, before they saw the dust churned up by countless horses. Readying their weapons, they were ready as the horsemen turned the corner and came into sight. The nomads were covered head to foot in long flowing garments to shield them from the sun. Many carried lances, some had bows readied, but most had their hands resting on their swords. Celedant gave the order to fire on the leaders and released his magic.

The arrows flew, bringing down the front riders, who fell from their horses. Then Melgor called upon his gods for a straight lightning bolt and let loose his power. The bolt shot down the valley right into the midst of the milling nomads, cutting through them like a scythe and impacting the canyon wall with such force, it sprayed rock and debris over the column of riders. Men and horses went down screaming, clogging the path momentarily.

"Hority, can you bring fire down behind that jutting trail?" Celedant called out. "There are sure to be nomads milling about, trapped for the moment."

Hority prayed to Clor and cast his spell. The fire was blocked from sight by the turn in the trail, but they saw the flashes and heard the men screaming.

Eldahir sent arrow after arrow into the packed and confused nomads. "I feel bad for their horses. But to escape alive, I can't argue with the gods."

Just then, the front of the nomad's column that had made it into the open, charged. The nomads, not quite sure of where the spells and arrows were coming rode blindly up the trail. Celedant and Melgor sent magical spikes of energy at the column of charging nomads, who were screaming their war cries. Wherever the spikes struck, the rider was thrown back into the horses behind him. It completely broke the charge and as they milled about, arrows were still being shot into them, although their supply was running low.

Then, to Celedant's relief, he heard Azimuth.

"I see smoke in the valley and can hear the battle. Be ready to duck."

The wizard, much to everyone's delight, called out, "Down in your holes! Azimuth is going to make a pass!"

They heard the giant flap of his wings as the massive golden dragon soared into the valley. Sighting the lead nomads, he let loose his fiery breath. The front of the column ceased to exist, and the followers were set ablaze. Then he turned the corner, and smoke rose into the air, followed by more screams. Having blasted most of the column, Azimuth made a wide turn in the air and dove down into the valley once more.

Hority sat on the edge of his pit fascinated as he watched Azimuth swirl towards the defenses and let loose one more blast of dragon fire.

This caught Hority just as the flame went out. The monk was thrown backwards, his robe and hair giving off smoke. Botreg jumped to the aid of the stinking dwarf, patting out the small smoldering pieces of his robe and strands of hair that were burning. As Botreg rescued Hority, the dwarf continued scribbling in his journal.

"Ye could have gotten yerself killed pulling a stunt like that!" Botreg said harshly.

"I was in Clor's hands," Hority replied serenely. "And besides, I had ye to help, too. Such wonderful things I have witnessed with me friends on this adventure. We must all praise Clor in his infinite wisdom and protection." He then rolled in the dirt and rubbed great clumps into his hair.

Azimuth walked up behind them and said, "Why are you still hiding. What's left of the nomads are racing across the desert by now."

The others climbed out of their holes and embraced their savior.

Celedant asked what was on everyone's minds, "What of Ress and Tarquin?"

The dragon in his elf shape replied with a grin. "They are both doing fine. Ress delivered a healthy baby girl they named Macara. It means one who brings joy."

There were smiles all around and Botreg said, "Time for a toast. I have a wine flask that I secreted away from the manor."

They all cheered and passed the flask around.

Hority began jumping up and down, causing a small sandstorm, his hand held high. "May I fly now? Ye promised."

Azimuth sighed. "I suppose this is as good a place as any."

The little monk slowly stood up and asked in amazement, "I'm I really going to fly?"

"Yes. Let me change forms." Azimuth went about fifty paces away from them and began the morphing process. Slowly the air churned around him in the colors of the rainbow. It grew and grew until it dissipated, leaving Azimuth in all his golden splendor. Hority dropped his journal, pen, and ink as he stood motionless in front of the dragon. He had watched as Azimuth had battled in fights but never the change from elf to dragon.

"*Come, little one,*" Azimuth's voice echoed in Hority's head.

The dwarf ran towards the dragon and in midstride, Azimuth cast a spell, lifting the dwarf up to maneuver him into the saddle. Hority kept moving his legs as he was lifted off the ground. Running in midair, the dwarf was lifted into the saddle that had magically appeared on Azimuth's back.

Stop running, Hority, or you might fall off, the dragon said. *Come settle into your seat and buckle up.*

Much to everyone's enjoyment, Hority was soon tangled helplessly in the straps. Celedant levitated up to help untangle the monk. The dwarf had the biggest smile on his face, not worried about a thing in the world as he was strapped in by the wizard.

The dragon entered the dwarf's mind again. *You might want to hold on to the handhole in the front of the saddle. Are you ready?*

But he did not hear any reply, so he curved his long neck around to face Hority. The monk was examining the saddle and the few scales he could reach. Azimuth blasted a breath of clean air into his rider's face and said, *Little one, you must think or speak what you want to say. Then we can converse.*

Hority nodded, his head breathlessly thinking. "Blow in my face again. It was invigorating."

Azimuth tried to reason with the curious dwarf, *If I keep doing that, you will not get to fly, and that would be a shame to deprive the almighty Clor of this experience when you write it down in your journal.*

The dwarf nodded. "Clor has offered me a miraculous chance today, and I must not delay it."

Azimuth bunched his legs up underneath him and with two huge flaps of his wings, he launched himself off the ground. The dragon soared through the air, and all he could hear of Hority were whispered prayers.

What say you Hority? Is it like you imagined?

The dwarf responded for the first time while in the air. "It's a miracle of Clor. I am lifted closer to the gods then ever I was. I am truly blessed."

Would you like to fly higher? Azimuth asked.

"Glory be to Clor. Can you?" he asked.

The dragon banked, going ever higher until Hority was shivering in the thin cold air. Then he dove, folding his wings as he plummeted towards the ground. He pulled up backing his wings to slow and looked back at Hority, who sat in the saddle with a serine smile on his face. The dragon then flapped his wings to settle softly to the ground of the canyon, making quite a dust cloud.

In his head Azimuth heard, *Clor is so incredibly pleased. A holy dust fills the air and washes about me.*

Hority went to get off but forgot about the straps and as he kicked his leg over the back of the saddle to dismount, he became hopelessly entangled. He hung his head down and wiggled to get away from the straps.

I think we need your help again, Azimuth told Celedant.

The wizard cast a spell and rose to be next to Hority, thinking to the dragon, *You might want to lower him to the ground, so he doesn't fall on his head.*

Celedant also called on the aid of Botreg. "Come stand beneath this worrisome dwarf and see that he does not break his neck when I release him."

Sure enough, despite Celedant's pleas, Hority kept fighting the straps until he was held by only one. And as the wizard undid it, the monk fell straight into Botreg's arms, creating a small dust cloud.

CHAPTER FORTY-SIX

Eldahir was sent up the valley to see if it continued up and into the southern hill lands. Meanwhile, the others rode down the valley to see the destruction wrought by their spells and dragon fire. The first men they encountered were the ones brought down by arrows. Morganna and Zeffan retrieved what arrows they could.

Then they came across the nomads that their spells had killed. Again, there were some wounded but far fewer and those too gravely injured, Botreg quietly took care of. Only Celedant had seen what true dragon fire could do before. The others were stunned. Burned bodies were everywhere. Some caught in the initial blast were imprinted into the stone. Others had crumbled to dust as the wind blew through the canyon.

"It's a shame all these men had to die, but a necessity in the end," Azimuth said sadly to Celedant.

"Yes, you were protecting us," the Wizard replied. "If you had not come, however, we would be the dead in this accursed valley. There are over a hundred bodies strewn about. We could have never lasted against those odds."

He then turned to the others. Several had ashen faces. "Come, we must follow Eldahir up the valley and leave these men in peace."

Botreg looked at Azimuth. "Remind me to never make ye mad. I never knew how hot dragon fire could be."

"Don't worry, my friend," the dragon replied. "I would never visit such death upon a friend, for any reason."

They followed the canyon upwards and an hour later, the wood elf returned. "This canyon does indeed lead up into the hills. There is a steep climb. But it's better than the one leading to the dragon's crater. Come follow me."

They rode through the dry, dusty, and barren canyon, until they reached the end and the trail that Eldahir had spoken to them about. There, they dismounted and began the tenuous trek upward.

"I thought ye said this was better than the dragon trail," Zeffan called out.

Eldahir laughed. "If I had told you it was worse, would you have come?"

The dwarf thought a minute. "I'd probably trusted ye and followed anyway."

They continued in silence, concentrating on their horses and the path with the mules plodding along behind them. Reaching the top, they looked down over the rocky slope. And in the distance, they saw the start of the forest.

"Let's get out of this god forsaken sun and under the trees and find a stream," Celedant called to the others. "We could all do with a bath." He glanced at the Clorian monk. "I know what you'll say Hority. You are the exception."

They skirted several villages and finally came across the ogre city that the guras mercenaries had attacked.

Celedant cast a protection spell and rode slowly up to the open gate. The ogres rushed out with weapons drawn to see the wizard sitting calmly on his horse.

He called out across the distance. "We are the ones who came to your aid after the men sacked your city."

One ogre stepped forward. "We remember. It has been sometime since you came here. What is it you want?"

"We seek food and drink if you have any to spare, and we'll pay for it."

The ogre shook his head. "No, we owe you enough. I will gladly supply you with what you want. But not the long beards. We have had enough of them at their accursed fortress."

The wizard called forth Morganna and Eldahir to bring up a mule as Celedant went on talking to ogre chief. "We need a haunch of venison and a small barrel of ale. We just came from the south through the desert and tire of water."

The ogre barked orders to his villagers, and they brought forth the food and ale. Morganna and Eldahir quickly tied the food and drink to the mule and led it back to the others.

Celedant bowed to the ogre and thanked him. He then turned his horse away and joined the rest of the party. They continued east just inside the tree line, and Celedant sent Zeffan and Eldahir ahead to find the passage south that the guras had used. It took several weeks of looking back and forth for the path. Then Zeffan spotted a shiny object at the top of one of the valley entrances. Upon further examination, he realized that it was a buckle off a guras' armor.

Zeffan called the others and passed the buckle around. They all agreed that this was from a guras and that the terrain looked the same as the one they had come upon out of the valley. Eldahir and Zeffan proceeded down into the valley with the others following. They found the orcan ambush site, nothing but orc bones now, and knew they were on the right track.

Emerging onto the sandy soil of the desert, they knew that they were within reach of the Valley of Clor. Eldahir and Zeffan led them east to the valley. They reined in their horses and looked over where the adventure had begun. The valley was as barren as always but at the library, a small fortress was being built. Flying from the wall was a light blue banner of Thierry. Next to it was the brown banner of Clor. Hority was beside himself and dove from his horse and started praying, while rubbing the dirt and grass of the ledge in his hair, face, and habit.

CHAPTER FORTY-SEVEN

The evil goddess Adois had mourned the deaths of both the black dragon and Cyra. Each had had the potential to continue the goddess' plan to wreak damage to the wholesome planet. Sure, there were dangers on Muiria, but they were only small skirmishes between mortals that did not inflict damage of prodigious progress for evil. She had watched what had happened to her precious Cyra and the black dragon, and who had done it. In her madness, she was determined to destroy the wizard, Celedant and his pet dragon, Azimuth.

Following in Cyra's footsteps, she went to the white orc city. Her plan was to gather as many warriors as possible, find Celedant, and kill him. She was irate and manifested before the self-proclaimed Bloody Claw. The orc was cowed by her sudden appearance in his great hall and called for guards. Adois simply waved a hand, and all the guards fell to the ground dead.

Using her mind, she shut the doors to the great hall and addressed the ruler. "You will lead your army forth and do my bidding or die here and now in a most painful way."

Bloody Claw was terrified, for he had seen what had happened to his guards after but a wave of her hand. And that was far beyond what his witch could accomplish.

"What is it that you want?" he asked hesitantly.

She smiled. "I want your army. All of it and your leadership. I march on the ones that killed Cyra."

Little did the orc leader know that it had been Adois who had gifted the young Cyra with powers and killed her parents, driving her to the white orcs for protection.

"I can't leave my city defenseless," Bloody Claw protested. "I can take three thousand warriors and follow you."

Adois pointed a finger at him and a bright red light shot forth. The pain he felt was the worst he had ever experienced in his life. It engulfed him, stinging like a million wasp bites. Then she ended the spell.

"That is just a sampling of what I am capable of doing without killing you. Now how many warriors can I expect?"

He flopped to the floor and prostrated himself. "All five thousand of my soldiers. I can lead to battle."

She threw him a map and said, "Meet me there in three weeks' time. That is when I will strike. I have drawn where you shall assemble your soldiers. If you are seen by the enemy, you will be the first to die."

Celedant had been in the library helping the Theirrians go through the thousands of documents of the Clorians, when he suddenly clutched his heart and yelled out, "To arms! A great evil is upon us!"

They ran to the unfinished battlements and looked over the stone blocks out into the desert foothills. The wall at this point was just the base structure. It measured only a cubit high joining the two towers that had been finished. Azimuth joined him along with Hority, Zeffan, and Melgor. Eldahir and Morganna had been flown back by Azimuth to their homeland's weeks earlier.

They peered out into the desolate lands and saw a lightning storm coming. Celedant cast a spell allowing him to see what was approaching. He witnessed a single woman walking through the desert towards Clor's valley. Her face was beautiful with long dark tresses and dressed in simple leather armor. As she approached, lightning shot out from her hands into the sky. She flicked her wrists and sent the lightning shooting towards the unfinished fort.

"Everybody down!" Celedant yelled.

Just as the onlookers ducked, the lightning bolts struck the stone. There was a massive crash, and they felt the wall move, but the thick cubit deep stone held. Then there was a flash of light, and Celedant and the defenders raised their heads over the wall. There where the bright light originated was a man, wearing a golden toga and a scowl on his majestic face. He stepped forward. Celedant knew at once, who was approaching. It was the lady Adois and her brother Adaman. Both were polar opposites Adios as evil a god as there ever was. Adaman as good a god as could be found.

Adaman called to his sister. "Adois! I will have no more of your machinations on this world. The black dragon and the witch were the last straw."

Adois smiled evilly. "Dear brother, I don't understand your desperation to hold onto this piece of rock. These mortals are nothing to the gods."

At that moment, Celedant felt the rock the wall was built on quiver. He glanced back. The Theirrian monks were all down on their knees, their weapons across their chests. It was the dwarvan god, Thierry, and he walked over to stand next to Celedant.

"Stand up brothers there is a battle at hand," Thierry said.

He then turned to Celedant. "This world owes ye greatly. Ye have accomplished what none of us thought possible. When Azimuth killed the black dragon, it was a great deed. If the witch had gotten hold of it, there would have been more trouble, then ever before."

Out on the barren hills, brother and sister faced off. Adois issued a challenge. "You can't win here. My forces are gathered and ready to attack. Not to mention my allies."

Then she raised her hand and from out of the ground rose two demon lords, both holding flaming swords. One bore the semblance of a skeleton. The second, a muscular crocodile wearing a helmet with two curved horns on it. It had a tail with spikes riveted into the skin where pus and blood oozed out. They raced towards Adaman, who cast a spell causing a rock wall to separate them. But the demon lords broke through as if the spell were nothing.

Adois raised her arm and a thousand paces from the half-built fort a white orc army of five thousand rose from hiding and charged.

But the rock wall gave Adaman enough time to ready himself. The crocodile like creature attacked first, swinging his sword low, and aiming for the god's legs. Adaman blocked the attack with his shield driving the sword into the ground. The god of goodness brought his sword down on his opponent's weapon, shattering it. The god's blade was too well forged to succumb to the demon lord's evil blade. Then the skeleton demon was there, beating a regular tattoo of strikes upon the shield of Adaman. The god of goodness was fearful of his shield's integrity, because it started bending at the edges.

Hority was ready to jump over the wall as he yelled, "Foes."

Botreg was in New Partha with Tarquin, so there was no one to hold the monk back.

A deep voice called out, "Hold, mighty Hority. Ye will stay here and fight with yer friends."

Such a great stench drifted from behind them that Thierry exclaimed, "It has been many a year since I have seen ye, me brother."

"It is good to fight alongside of ye," Clor answered. "Let us send these foul things back to the hells from whence they came.

Hority turned around and fell to the ground prostrating himself. For before him was his god, the mighty Clor.

Azimuth tapped Celedant on the shoulder. "I can do more from the air. I hope to see you after this battle."

The dragon then jumped the wall and cast the spell that would change him back into a dragon. The whirling multicolor vortex formed and suddenly he had changed to dragon form. With two hard flaps of his wings, he took off. Azimuth swooped in and out of the orcan army, spewing forth dragon fire and leaving incinerated bodies behind.

Already the dwarves of Thierry were firing crossbow bolts and arrows at the on-rushing orcs. Celedant and Melgor added their spells to blunt the attack. Then Thierry and Clor stepped over the small wall and walked towards the approaching enemy.

Thierry wielded two plain looking war hammers and with each swing he sent dozens of orcs flying through the air.

Thierry called to his brother, "Keep the enemy at bay. I go to help Adaman."

Heeding his brother's advice, Clor stayed and fought the attacking force, casting spell after spell. He called down wide swaths of flame and sent forth a muddy brown colored haze that engulfed hundreds of the enemy, who fell dead from the noxious fumes. The gods continued cutting a bloody swath through the orcan army as the other gods fought.

Thierry was beside Adaman in a second and using both hammers, he pounded the skeleton, breaking the monster's bones with each strike. The crocodile demon lord swung his tail, catching Thierry on the back with its spikes that penetrated the god of goodness's skin with ease. The skeletal demon lord let go of Adaman and turned his attention towards Thierry. Its primordial evil mind turning to the one it had been hurt by.

Suddenly Thierry was faced by two demon lords. He struck out with his hammers. One blow struck the skeletal demon, crushing its shoulder.

Thierry yelled to Adaman. "Go take care of yer sister!"

The dwarvan god turned to the Crocodile hell spawn and battered it with his hammers, striking faster than was possible to see. It swung its spiked tail in a desperate attempt to keep Thierry at bay.

When the skeletal demon lord jumped on the dwarvan god's back. The creature tried to strike down with his sword, but Thierry caught it with his hammer, deflecting the blow. He then used his second hammer to strike the crocodile demon lord on the metal spikes of its tail, driving the spikes deep into the ground. The creature tried to pull its tail free but did not have enough time. Thierry backhanded his war hammer, crushing the demon lords' head. It struggled to stay upright, but Thierry struck again, driving the hammer deep into its chest destroying the hell spawn.

The skeletal demon lord kept trying to strike the dwarvan god until it drew back its sword and drove it into the back of the deity. Thierry roared in pain and flipped the hell spawn over his back. As the creature struggled to get up, Thierry struck it with both hammers on the chest. The bones turned to dust as the creature died. The dwarvan god laughed despite the wounds in his back. This was the best battle he had faced in many years. He then headed back to the battle before the walls of the half-built castle.

Adaman raced to his sister, Adois, who was casting spells against the castle. All aimed at destroying the small wall that separated her orcan allies and her hated enemies within the castle. The lightning and energy beams struck the wall, gouging great holes in the stone but never penetrating through them. The debris from the attacks spayed outward, killing many of the white orcs.

Upon Adaman's arrival, they continued their fight. Their spells did little damage to the two gods. Both yielded swords and bore shields. Lightning spells and other magical beams of destruction were deflected from their shields. Then Adaman conjured up a thick rope and bound up his sister. As she struggled, he cast multiple spells. Fire rolled from his fingertips to engulf her and lightning struck her.

Between her brother's spells, Adois cast one of her own and the thick ropes dissolved around her. From the smoke that surrounded her, she shot forth a spell summoning eight black dragons, whose one goal was to attack Adaman and give her a chance to recover from the bombardment of spells she had just endured. The immensely powerful dragons attacked Adaman, all breathing fire at him as he grew to enormous size to battle them. Then the creatures advanced. Two grappled with him, and he threw them off, but not before they had clawed off great patches of skin. He then dropped to a kneeling position and turned in a complete circle, severing the heads from the all the dragons, their blood drenching Adaman. He shrunk back to human size, and before their heads reached the ground, Adois struck.

Flying from midair, she swooped down upon her brother. Luckily, he spotted her out of the corner of his eye. Adaman held up his shield, but under the power of the blow, it cracked in twain, but he could still use it. They set about, dueling so fast that a mere mortal would have trouble following the movement. Adaman drew first blood as his sword cut through Adois shield and followed through, cutting downward into the evil goddess's thigh. She responded with a swing of her sword, cutting upward and catching Adaman's shield. Gigantic sparks flew as his broken shield went flying through the air, ripping at the skin of his arm.

He then took his sword in both hands and went on the offensive, striking downward and driving his sister to the ground. He cast a spell electrifying his sword in hopes of breaking his sisters' weapon. But the only thing that happened was that when their blades struck, great sparks soared through the sky. Adois grew desperate. She dropped her sword and with one hand, hit her brother in the chest, sending him flying a thousand paces to tumble across the barren ground.

Adaman was filled with rage now. His planet was in danger from his sister, and they both were equal in power. He ran at her and with electricity flowing up and down his blade, and struck down her shield, breaking her arm as she dropped it. She had taken up her sword again in her off hand and black flames surged around the blade as they fought. It was apparent that the fight was going to be a stalemate between the gods.

Then from out of nowhere a war hammer struck Adois on the side of the head crushing her skull. Without a second thought, she looked to the roaring battle with her one remaining eye and saw Thierry and Clor wreaking havoc amongst the orcs. She knew that the dwarvan god Thierry had thrown the war hammer.

Then, in front of the two gods as their battle continued, a red swirling mist appeared and suddenly, the guardian of the Dragon Tear, the red gem like faceted being was before them. He was tiny compared to the gods before him, but his voice carried around the plains. "I am the guardian of all that is good on this planet, and I cannot allow this to continue!"

He started swirling his right arm about in a circular motion forming a red vortex that encompassed Adois. Adaman saw his opening provided by the former wizard that had taken on the defense of Muiria at the beginning of the first mortals. The god paused. Could or should he kill his sister? He had been created with her. Twin gods – one that gravitated to good, and one that took on the power of evil. Though they were bitter rivals, he could not strike.

Then Adois flung her hand and the faceted man flew through the white orcs, tossing them about like rag dolls to slam through the wall of the half-finished fortress. Seeing this, Adaman struck, thrusting his sword into his sister and penetrating her black heart, ending her life.

She fell and in her dying voice said, "I love you brother, no matter what sides we picked. Take me from this accursed world."

Adaman cried openly as his twin sister died by his hand before him. He let his sword fall and gently picked her up. With a bright flash, they were gone from Muiria.

Meanwhile, as the dwarvan gods walked through the white orcs, killing as they went, a swirling white light appeared in the middle of the castle. From this light stepped a being in a sapphire blue robe with a long beard. It was Dolgar, the dwarvan god of healing, who was responsible for turning Morganna from an illanni or dark elf into an elf of light. He went to the faceted man and knelt beside him. The man was crushed against the inner wall of the castle, his crystal-like skin cracked and chipped. Dolgar bent down and said, "Ye are not meant to die here or at this time."

The Dwarvan god placed both hands on his chest and began chanting. This was something even a god would have trouble mending. The being before him was an integral part of the planet and tied to its pull to either good or evil. Dolgar lowered his head, sweat forming on his brow as he sealed the cracks in the gem like man. He had to go from flaw to flaw sealing the injuries. The strain of healing was taxing on him and several clerics of Thierry stood guard over their god so he could concentrate. Slowly the red light of the faceted man began to glow as the healing took hold.

As Dolgar was busy healing, the orcs swept around the castle, despite the stalwart defense the dwarves were putting up. Already some orcs were within the walls, fighting the dwarves of Thierry. More streamed over the rear walls of the castle and the hole in the battlement that was created when the facetted man had been thrown through it. Then suddenly mighty streams of fire started falling from the sky, splashing on the orcs coming around the castle and attacking the unfinished rear. Celedant heard the battle cries of the Clorians as the monks charged up the valley to the rescue of the tower. They were still enraged over the massacre of their brethren earlier in the year.

The orcs in the courtyard of the castle faced intense fighting. The warriors of Thierry fought like dwarves possessed, their countless days of weapons training in the monastery for just such a moment was paying off as they cut into the orcs.

Hority finally got to attack. He shouted his war cry, "Foes!" and was off into the melee.

Celedant stood away from the wall and cast spell after spell as small lit balls of energy shot forth from his hand, killing the orcs as they climbed on top of the wall. But the fifty dwarves of Thierry were quickly overcome by the greater number of orcs that had entered the courtyard. Then the monks of Clor came to the edge of the yard and started hand to hand combat, using their staves, sweeping orcs off their feet and smashing in their heads or breaking bones. Melgor appeared atop one of the towers, where he cast balls of energy at the orcs that were inside the castle grounds.

The attacking white orcs had retreated from the Clorian valley and joined the main force in front of the castle. There, they faced the enraged visage of Clor, who had summoned two tree trunks that he now swung about him like clubs, killing all that stood in his way. Unable to find Bloody Claw, the white orcs melted back to the hills from which they had started the attack. In fact, the orc chieftain and his most trusted generals were several miles from the battle. He had seen his patron Adois brought down and decided it was time to go.

Chapter Forty-Eight

After the battle, thousands of white orcs lay scattered in front of the half-built castle in the valley of the Clorians. If not for the gods bringing their own defenses to Muiria, the castle would have been overrun. Celedant watched the gods as Thierry and Clor met in the middle of the battlefield to have a deep discussion.

Azimuth joined him after changing back into a wood elf. He had changed into dragon form and spent the battle flying over the orcs, unleashing his breath of fire upon them. He said to the wizard, "That was exhilarating. Just what do you suppose they are discussing?"

"I don't know," Celedant replied. "The ways of the gods are beyond us mortals."

There was a great smell about the wall as Clor's faithful servants tried to see their god. Then the two gods began walking towards the castle. Celedant looked about at the Clorians, who all bore the look of awe. The Theirrians bore grim visages of the warriors they were. The gods stopped at the wall, fearing to injure one of their flock should they step over the barrier. Instead, they both shrunk down to normal size and vaulted the wall to stand amongst their differing flocks. The dwarves in all the yard knelt before their lords.

"All rise, yer patrons acknowledge yer platitudes," Thierry commanded them.

Clor saw Dolgar busily healing the wounded of the battle and rushed to his side, his odor preceding him. "Brother. Tis good to see ye. A great battle was fought, and me flock accounted for them mightily. I could not be prouder."

Dolgar still healing the wounded said, "Yes, brother. It seems yer flock holds ye in great esteem. For they fought well for ye. It says wonderful things for their worship."

"I shall go find the abbot and bless each and every one of them," Clor replied. "Again, it is good to see ye. We must meet and discuss our tenets soon."

"Go see to yer flock," Dolgar answered. "We will meet as soon as possible." Later, if possible, due to the rancid odor produced by Clor.

Clor walked over to where the new abbot had walled himself up in a cave. He was closely followed by all the Clorians, including the faithful Hority.

Surprisingly, Melgor joined them and said, "You know. Part of me never believed in the gods. In all my life, no one gave me a moment's notice. Yet today I have seen five of them and the power they yield, and even the death of one. Amazing!"

"Yes," Celedant said. "It seems only in the times of the greatest needs that the gods come forth to aid us mere mortals. You and I will die many, many years from now and know there is a place for us in the afterlife."

Zeffan came from the line of wounded in front of Dolgar and joined in on the conversation. "Ye know, I was never one to pray to the gods. But after today and what I have witnessed, I think I shall follow Dolgar. He is a gentle and caring god."

"You have come to a mighty crossroads from nonbeliever to believer," Azimuth said seriously. "May your path be forever clearer now."

Celedant sighed. "You'll never be a philosopher, my dear friend. Stick to being a dragon and all that it entails."

Then suddenly, the guardian of the Dragon Tear was before them. "It is time to stop talking of gods. I believe two of you need to fly to the Isles and face judgement. I must warn you Celedant, you are not the favorite of the council as of now."

The wizard agreed with the facetted man. "Yes. I have never been a favorable member of the council. Melgor and I need to return to the Isle and face judgment."

They bid the guardian farewell, shook Zeffan's hand, and started the long walk up towards the cliff top.

It was a slow flight back to Dragon Isle, flying leisurely all day and camping at night. Eventually they flew above the North Sea. Celedant pointed out the isle, when he finally spotted it, and Azimuth landed on the beach outside Edain. Celedant called to all the masters using telepathy that he was back and wanted to meet in the council chamber.

Celedant led Melgor deep beneath the ground down many flights of stairs to where the masters met. "I needn't tell you to let me do the talking. Do I?"

"I am in your hands now," Melgor responded. His trust in Celedant was solid. "What happens will happen."

The council was seated at a long table at the end of a dark hall, lit by torches spaced along the bedrock of the chamber. Celedant and Melgor advanced and the head of the council, Oristil spoke.

"You have been gone a long time, unaccounted to this council, Celedant. What have you to say for yourself?"

Celedant launched into a long tale of all that had happened, including Melgor's part in it.

After hearing of Celedant's adventures, the council talked amongst themselves. Some of the discussions turned into arguments as members picked sides. Celedant could hear them arguing whether or not to expel the wizard from the Ilse or not.

Finally, the head of the council spoke to the two wizards. "What you did was most extraordinary. But we must take into account that you did not warn us of what you were doing. Although some of us deem the need was too dire to hesitate and waste time with the council, and that you acted accordingly. You are exonerated of your actions by this council. However, bringing a warlock to our island is another matter. This is not the place for him. He must be expelled."

"Fellow members," Celedant interrupted. "May I speak on his behalf?"

Oristil, a high elf and the leader of the council nodded and said, "Yes."

Celedant was surprised that he had agreed so quickly. The two wizards did not have the best relationship concerning Celedant's tendences to travel afar without announcing it to the council.

Some of the council openly objected.

But Celedant continued over the objections. "Melgor stood beside us without any problems from the moment we took him in. He gave us his word and kept it. Melgor could have run at any time but did not. He was sent to recruit the black dragon for his mistress. Instead, he stood with us and battled the evil forces that inhabited the lair. I must tell you that it was Melgor who convinced us to go into the dragon's lair and seek out the evil that his mistress was so keen on possessing. Without his sage advice, I could not present you with this."

Celedant approached the table and pulled a wrapped item from his cloak, placing it on the table. He unfolded the cloth and great evil radiated from the small rod. The whole of the council gasped for breath as they felt the powerful darkness before them. Oristil quickly covered the rod with a cloth.

The wizard continued. "We found this item in the dragon's lair. If it were not for Melgor, it would have remained there to be found by anyone. Who knows who's hands it would have fallen into if that had happened? I do not know of its powers, because I was afraid to subject myself to them. But I must endorse sanctuary for my friend, Melgor.

Without him, I fear that much evil would have been wrought from this item."

The council's leader Oristil took a breath and nodded. "It must be locked and sealed off within the vaults of the city, never to be seen again. Such power cannot fall into the hands of evil." He continued. "In light of the evidence just shown, I believe that I can speak for the council that we owe a great debt to the warlock, Melgor. We shall offer him sanctuary as long as he follows our laws, and understands that he is forbidden from practicing the dark arts.

Celedant and Melgor smiled and shook hands. After years of practicing dark magic, it would seem that the warlock was finally on the right path. And Celedant was certain that if he worked at it, he would make a fine wizard.

About the Author

Steve Stephenson has a BA in History and a Master's degree in Library Science. He and his co-writer have published five epic fantasy books set in the world of Muiria.

K.M. Tedrick is a writer and ghostwriter in the fantasy, science fiction, adventure, Christian, and young adult genres with one book that was made into a movie, and over sixteen books that have been published.

Note from the Authors

Word-of-mouth is crucial for any author to succeed. If you enjoyed *Death of a Goddess*, please leave a review online—anywhere you are able. Even if it's just a sentence or two. It would make all the difference and would be very much appreciated.

Thanks!
Steve Stephenson & K.M. Tedrick

We hope you enjoyed reading this title from:

www.blackrosewriting.com

Subscribe to our mailing list – *The Rosevine* – and receive **FREE** books, daily
deals, and stay current with news about upcoming
releases and our hottest authors.
Scan the QR code below to sign up.

Already a subscriber? Please accept a sincere thank you for being a fan of
Black Rose Writing authors.

View other Black Rose Writing titles at
www.blackrosewriting.com/books and use promo code
PRINT to receive a **20% discount** when purchasing.